"A skillfull follow-up to their juggernaut *The Nanny Diaries, So Close* is a sharp cultural examination of ambition, politics, and the exhausting climb that can be chasing dreams. Amanda Beth is both a heart-breaking and refreshingly relatable protagonist. Female readers will enjoy smiling and crying with her, as we see Amanda battling the wrong attractions while trying to rise above her life's cruel station. Playfully barbed commentary makes this all the more fun."

— COLLEEN OAKES, best-selling author of the *Elly* series, *Queen of Hearts* series, and *Wendy Darling* series

"Emma McLaughlin and Nicola Kraus have created a fascinating world with relatable, ambitious protagonist you can't help but root for. *So Close* is a must-read if you've ever wondered what it takes for a politician to be elected."

— LISA HENTHORN, author of *25 Sense*, and television writer of *Swingtown, The Beautiful Life*, and *The Glades*

"Emma McLaughlin and Nicola Kraus have done it again. *So Close* is a page-turner about loyalty, love, ambition, family, and friendship. Amanda is a strong and vibrant character who stays with you long past the last page."

— SUSIE SCHNALL, author of *The Balance Project* and *On Grace*

"Emma McLaughlin and Nicola Kraus deliver an engaging story of a young woman determined to change her trajectory. *So Close* is about love, loss, and the choices one makes on the road to success. This is an endearing read that makes you want to root for the underdog."

— NICOLE MEIER, author of *The House of Bradbury*

Past Praise for
Emma McLaughlin and Nicola Kraus

On *The Nanny Diaries*

"A national phenomenon."

—*Newsweek*

"Impossible to put down."

—*Vogue*

"McLaughlin and Kraus . . . [have a] carefully calibrated sense of compassion and delicious sense of the absure."

—*Entertainment Weekly*

On *How to be a Grown Up*

"Such a cupcake of a book, it feels like you're doing something more self-indulgent than reading."

—*Kirkus Reviews*

"This humorous and rewarding look at one woman's second act is . . . smart and lively."

—*Booklist*

So
Close

So Close

A NOVEL

EMMA MCLAUGHLIN
& NICOLA KRAUS

SparkPress, a BookSparks imprint
A Division of SparkPoint Studio, LLC

This novel originally appeared as serialized fiction in *Cosmopolitan* magazine.

Published by SparkPress, a BookSparks imprint,
A division of SparkPoint Studio, LLC
Tempe, Arizona, USA, 85281
www.gosparkpress.com

Published 2016

Printed in the United States of America

ISBN: 978-1-940716-76-3 (pbk)
ISBN: 978-1-940716-77-0 (e-bk)
Library of Congress Control Number: 2015959517

Cover design © Julie Metz, Ltd./metzdesign.com
Author photo © Plain Picture
Formatting by Katherine Lloyd, The DESK

To

Our Loyal Readers

you have rocked our world

Part I

Chapter One

THE DAY I FINALLY PUT TALLYVILLE, Florida, in my rearview, my skin prickled from the anticipation of how different life was going to be. As Diego's car sped down the interstate in a hot tunnel of sunshine, I let my apron from Kath's Catfish Heaven fly out the window and thought, *This is it. This is what I've been waiting for.*

But South Beach, where cooling off was impossible and hydration fleeting, quickly conspired to make my twenty-first summer indistinguishable from those that came before. Counter to every hope, my days in Miami were mounting in a string of stifled yawns. Showing tourists to their tables for hours on end left me restless. And the overpopulated motel room where I was living offered little chance of sleep.

Or so I told myself night after night as I followed coworkers to the strip, where we made dinners of umbrella-speared garnishes from drinks so strong the edges of the club gradually softened. Tucked inside the velvet banquette of wherever we landed, the air conditioning evaporating the sweat from between my shoulder blades, I'd tip the waitress as much as I could afford. With blunted senses, I could tolerate the thought I swatted away all day—I had made a mistake. After all my efforts, I was in the wrong place. This city, this job, this life offered no more promise than Tallyville.

I had no idea that I was about to be proved wrong. That the people who would radically alter my life were on their way to me right were I was. They would both arrive, in fact, on the very same day.

By August I thought I was a seasoned hangover veteran, but the pain radiating behind my eyelids that Saturday morning shocked me. I was immediately aware from the thread count of the sheets that I was somewhere I shouldn't have been. I just prayed to God that I wasn't already late for my hostess shift.

Whipping upright on the king-sized bed, I braced my head with my fingers, my eyes focusing on the fading blue Sharpie blob next to my belly button—the vestiges of the tiger my ex, Diego, had been trying to convince me I should get tattooed. The marker he'd used had outlasted his devotion. I angrily scrubbed at it every morning in the motel shower while I tried to make sense of his abrupt departure. He'd left me with an apartment I couldn't afford, a security deposit I couldn't get back, and one wheezing Honda hatchback.

Forcing my eyes to stay open, I realized where I was and it wasn't good. Beside me, in the mess of deflated pillows, a tan frat guy with rooster boxers was splayed as if on a pool float. I stood, compelled to pause for a second until my balance returned.

Hunting for my dress, I took a squinting survey of the trashed penthouse suite. The Raleigh hostess and Fontainebleau waitress whom we'd met up with the night before were sprawled on the couches in the adjoining living room. Alicia, one of my room-mates from the motel I had moved into, was curled beside them. The recently reddened tips of her hair made it look like a wild fox had found its way inside. Alicia had been the one to convince me to leave the club for that new place where she knew the bouncer, and I had blindly followed her behind another velvet rope damp from the salty air.

A guy stirred from the flokati rug at the girls' feet just as I spotted my dress in a heap by the glass doors to the balcony. Swiping it up, I stepped outside through the billowing curtains and into the sun banking off the white tiles. A breeze as refreshing as a close-panting dog rippled the Jacuzzi. A flash of the evening came back to me while I retrieved my bra from where it'd been discarded with the other girls', as if my fifth-grade teacher's rainbow rubber band ball had exploded. Dropping my dress, I re-cinched the yellow lace.

I was bending to grab my dress when I spotted him on the far end of the vast terrace. He was leaning on his forearms, blowing out a stream of smoke that dissipated over the ocean thirty floors below, his khakis and caramel skin and hair giving the impression of camouflage. He looked bemused as I clutched my dress in front of me. Did we hook up? I would have remembered that. I darted my eyes for a changing spot that didn't involve dealing with the passed out revelers inside. You'd think a terrace that size would at least have had a potted palm.

"I'd offer you one," he called over.

"Sorry?"

"A cigarette. But I know how you feel about that."

"Do you?" Fuck it. I dropped my dress to step into. I wasn't about to shimmy-tug it on with an audience.

"Yeah." He hung his head, his hair sifting over his cheekbones, his muscular shoulders rolling leisurely forward. "I don't recall much from last night, but you made your opinion on smoking pretty clear in the limo."

I remembered. He'd rolled in behind a crowd of guys with appraising eyes and monogrammed money clips. I thought he was an asshole. All of them were. But that was my last clear memory before we accepted their bottle service. I nodded and slid my arms through the straps of my dress as if this was just another day. Flicking his cigarette over the edge, his finger and thumb made a ring around a pale stripe on his wrist.

"I lost my watch. My Dad's. Which kind of sucks."

"I'm sorry." I spotted my heels under a chaise and strode over to push them on.

"Thanks."

"You sound surprised." I glanced over my shoulder to see him staring at me.

He shrugged. "Didn't expect your sympathy."

"Just my opinions."

"Yes. Got a full tank of those last night, thanks."

Whatever. "Well, you don't really have it." Where the fuck was my clutch? "My sympathy." I stepped back and tried to nonchalantly search under the row of chaises.

"Looking for your bag?"

"Uh-huh."

"Snakeskin?"

"Target would like you to think so, yes." I finger combed my blond hair, the sun-bleached ends still damp.

"Powder room by the front door. You left it there when you, uh—" He averted his eyes. "Went in with Trevor."

Uck. Rooster boxers. Awesome. "Thanks." I nodded and clicked toward the rippling curtains.

"Now you sound surprised."

"Didn't expect your assistance in my departure," I said over my shoulder.

"Well." He grinned. "You don't really have it." We held eyes for a moment across the mess of white furniture. If my brain hadn't been screaming, it would have been a cologne ad. The wash of blue behind him, his tanned hip bones arching out from those sagging pants. The instinct to prowl my way across the chaises flickered.

But I couldn't be late to work.

And there was the unfortunate fact of Trevor.

I managed one more nonchalant step through the billowing drapes before I flat out ran past the sleeping partiers to the powder room, then the hall, where I tucked my head against the security cameras and remained tucked all the way down to the lobby's side entrance, then out to my car. Jamming my key in the ignition, I tugged my gas station sunglasses from the glove compartment and then slammed it a thousand times to get it to stay closed. I had exactly twenty-three minutes to get home, get changed, and get to work— at the exact hotel I'd just woken up in.

Minding my dragging muffler, I cleared the South Beach speed traps, drove past the hotel signs, and continued on toward the motel signs. I'd been staying at the inaptly named Majestic with its rickety railing and cemented fountain since Diego announced he was going back home to Columbia (the country) via text, which I received while standing inside our emptied apartment. Everything, including my makeup bag full of tips, was gone. Thank God for my job. I've always had one—and held onto it like a gator with a goat. It made me not my mother.

Inside the motel room, the curtains were pinned shut with a hair clip and five girls in two beds were deep in the hungry sleep of those fleeing warlords or working back-to-back shifts in heels assigned by a sadistic hotelier. I darted to the shower where I scrubbed off the chlorinated Jacuzzi film still clinging to me. Finding that my towel was staunching a sink leak, I pointlessly patted off with disintegrating toilet paper. I tugged on the gold "brunch" dress designated by said hotelier, who seemed to only employ those with a C cup—or higher—to lean over his customers in said dresses—and was back on the road in under seven.

I scrounged change from the floor mats for coffee, which I mainlined while screeching back into the exact same parking spot I'd left less than thirty minutes earlier. Leaping over a sunning gecko, I ran through the kitchen door into a blast of Spanish music and whirring fans, where the frenetic pace of the crew matched mine. I inhaled a roll from the warmer and then stepped out into the bossa nova of the poolside hotel restaurant as the rattan banquettes were just starting to fill. My manager, Kurt, waited for me with a raised brow.

"Mandy vill take you to your table." He handed me two menus as I arrived. His German accent made him sound like he was perpetually auditioning to play a *Die Hard* villain. I liked South Beach because it was full of foreigners who gave off a waft of far-off places mingled with their high-end sunscreen and couture cologne. But I did not like Kurt. "Number thirteen. Thank you, dahlink."

I surreptitiously swiped the sweat from my temples. "My pleasure. Right this way, please." Kurt and I exchanged smiles as I took the couple to their table, but I knew from his pursed lips he was displeased. He idled there.

"I'm sorry I didn't get here earlier," I told him after I returned, our foreheads almost touching while we peered down at the seating map as if it were worthy of study. "But I was on time."

"Earlier *is* on time."

"You're right," I affirmed. Remaining on the safe side of Kurt's binary good graces required constant affirmations.

"You vant to be head hostess you have to act like it. I am trusting you, Mandy. You have a head on your shoulders—unlike zese booby twigs." He flicked a finger at a waitress gripping a tray of cappuccinos as a brusquely passing businessman nearly felled her. "I have to make a shit. You seat zese fatsos," he murmured as he smiled invitingly at the portly reddened family approaching the stand. I smiled at the nanny who trailed them, given away by the maid's uniform she couldn't have been voluntarily wearing to the beach.

As Kurt went to relieve himself, I commenced my repetitive loops of the sprawling restaurant floor. You could have fit three of Kath's Catfish Heaven in that place. I had started picking up after-school shifts when I was fourteen, and all of us who worked there, including Kath, did everything from scraping the fryer to scooping potatoes. But, as physically grueling as the work had been at Kath's, I never found myself counting down the minutes. Certainly not while staring at girls my own age hunched beside beach totes that cost more than Mom's trailer. Here I'd watch as, sunglasses covering half their faces, they gazed at the menu, debating if a thirty-dollar salad of microgreens would tide them over. They would raise slim arms, encased in gauzy cover-ups, to finger their statement necklaces while discussing the stress that limitless leisure inexplicably induced.

The lulls between meals were the worst part of the day. They gave me too much time to think about what I'd left behind. I missed Grammy. I worried my eight year-old brother, Billy, was skipping summer school. That, without me there to buy it, there wasn't enough peanut butter for him to make himself a sandwich. That I wouldn't have enough gas to get to and from the Majestic before Kurt flipped my check at me at the end of the month. That South Beach itself was a mirage where everyone was just as aimlessly close to the edge as Tallyville.

But on that Saturday there weren't any lulls. The restaurant was half-staffed because there was some big event in the ballroom, a fundraiser for the senate race. Kath's Catfish Heaven style, every one of the staff was running around doing every thing.

At some point I passed through the kitchen and the apoplectic head of Room Service grabbed me. "You! Run this order up!" Putting my back into it, I shoved the laden cart onto the service elevator and opened the check to see that my destination was the penthouse. At which point that breakfast roll I'd eaten threatened to come back up.

I retraced the morning's sprint of shame. Thanks to my hometown's faltering population, I couldn't so much as grab a quart of milk without facing past mistakes. So, as I had many times before, I pulled myself up to my full height, shook my hair forward, and rang the bell. The door opened to Rooster Boxers in a hotel robe he was still pulling on. While clearly trying to channel Hugh Heffner, he was presenting more Big Lebowski. *If I never see another frat guy in a hotel robe.*

"Dude." He grinned with surprised delight as if the hotel had just sent up a complimentary stripper.

"Where would you like this set up . . ." I unclenched my jaw to finish the mandated script. "Sir?"

"Oh-ho-ho, sa-weet." He looked like he wanted to high-five someone, but there were only the two of us in the vestibule.

"If you prefer me to leave it here—"

"Come on in. You know the way." He strode ahead and I pushed the cart to the dining table where I quickly popped the sides up from under the linen. "Nice uniform." I sensed him coming up behind me and stood just as the master bathroom door opened to the sound of a running shower. The guy who'd been on the terrace earlier strode out—naked.

"Shit!" he said, darting back into the bathroom.

"Westerbrook!" Rooster called to him.

"I . . . uh . . . needed my razor, Trevor." He stepped back out, securing a towel around his waist, his toffee face turning a satisfying plum color. "Did you take it?"

"Look." Trevor pointed at me. "Mandy—from last night."

"Yeah, hi." He nodded. "So did you . . . uh . . . find your purse?" His genuine curiosity seemed to take his friend aback. Trevor studied us.

"All right!" I lifted off the lids. "Eggs Benedict. Chicken and sage sausage. Blue cheese burger. Fries. Double espresso and vanilla milkshake. If you could just sign?" I handed Trevor the check, but he just kept grinning. Because he was high.

"We should meet up later."

I wanted nothing more than to give him the look a girl like me has to perfect. Lips pulled taut to both ears as if by piano wire, eyes dead-on. A firm, pleasant, "No fucking way." But I couldn't risk rattling his cage.

"What time do you get off?" He cracked himself up at the double entendre.

"Nine." Ten. "We're going to the Lido Club." We weren't. "You don't need to sign. Just call down when you're ready for them to take the cart. Enjoy your stay."

"Enjoyed it," Trevor said like he was peeing on me.

"Dude," Westerbrook admonished him, his embarrassment amplified. Unable to even look at me he grabbed the check and scribbled his signature.

"What?" Rooster balked, stuffing a fistful of fries into his mouth. "Just sayin', I'm looking forward to seeing what she does for dessert."

I took the check and turned for the door, Rooster's friend at my heels. "Sorry." He fumbled to open it for me. "Trevor's a fuck-up. We're fuck-ups."

"How nice for you. I'm working."

"Westerbrook" tipped me a hundred bucks, which I discovered on my way downstairs. I did not return to hurl the leather fold at their grease-flecked faces because my taillight needed fixing and I wanted to turn my cell back on. So I took his daddy's money. *That's what I do for dessert.*

Back at the kitchen the check was plucked from my hands and two brimming pitchers were put in their place. "Water! Ballroom! Now!" Clenching the handles, I followed the string of servers to the corridor where I was the last one through the padded doors. Silverware clinked as waiters scurried to finish setting the round tables.

Suddenly the speakers screeched. "The good people of Florida should vote to reelect Senator Watkins because what this country needs is—" a man's voice boomed. "Okay! Mike's on, now we're cookin' with gas." I looked up to the stage at the far end of the room.

"You sounding like the Wizard still doesn't make me believe you!" a woman playfully called out.

"Because I'm pussy footing around here," he said with frustration.

He crouched down at the front of the stage as the blond walked up to him. He dropped his head to hers, and she spoke softly to him before pointing him back to the microphone. He mugged being dragged back to the podium by a cane.

"Remember, I know when you're not saying it straight," she called up to him, crossing her arms in her black blazer while I moved slowly around the tables, filling each glass.

"You do?"

"A wife knows when to call bullshit."

He grinned at her. "A wife knows a hell of a lot more than that."

"Don't waste your flirting, Tom," she said, a smile in her voice. "I'm already sold. Okay, hurry now, before all the people get here, say it to me plain and simple, just like you said it to me on the beach. You're just introducing the man. Shoot from the hip. People should vote to reelect Senator Watkins because America needs . . ." she prompted.

"To get . . ." He gripped the podium, thinking intently. "We just need to get . . . a map."

"A map," she repeated dubiously.

"A goddamn map, Lindsay. Too many people want better, but they have no fucking idea how to get there. They're living just one paycheck ahead of real destitution." His whole countenance darkened. I stopped even pretending to pour and just listened. "They have kids who want to go to school, but they can't because they're stuck home taking care of sick grandparents—or siblings. They're too focused on surviving to think about thriving. How can we make this all just a little bit easier on them? What can we take off their plates so they can give their kids a fighting chance? How do we give them a clear path forward? It's a fact of nature, no—it's damn physics is what it is—a body in motion stays in motion. People deserve genuine motion." He brought his hands down flat on the podium and shook his head. "And one of these stuffed shirts ought to give it to them already."

A waiter had stopped setting a nearby table and was frowning at me. I hadn't cried in front of anyone since third grade when I taught myself exactly how many steps it was from the school bus—or our door—to the sanctity of the nearby woods. I'd silently count with a jutted chin until the cover of foliage made it safe to collapse. And I sensed a collapse was imminent.

I rushed out of the ballroom to the ladies', which was blessedly empty. Twisting the stall lock behind me, my head dropped with tears whose force took me by surprise. Up until that moment I'd been harnessing every molecule to convince myself I was in motion. But I wasn't. Not really. I was just in a breathless state of stuck, leaping from one trestle to the next in front of a barreling train and mistaking that for travel. Maybe I wasn't in my mom's trailer, or at Kath's, but I was standing in someone else's bathroom, wearing someone else's clothes, surrounded by strangers. And a guy I was stupid enough to believe was anything other than the same old shit had stolen every penny I'd earned.

The bathroom door flung open. I tried to catch my breath as someone rushed to the sinks. "No," she murmured. And then louder, "No-no-no."

I gulped and tugged at the toilet paper to wipe my face. I heard Grammy in my head. Amanda Beth, get it together. *Now.* But I couldn't, I couldn't.

"There's no reception in here?" the woman muttered.

In the gap between stall the door and the wall I saw beige heels and freckled legs, the edge of a white skirt.

"It's—no. You have to go out to the ballroom." I sounded raspy and clogged from crying. I cleared my throat.

"He's not worth it," she said halfheartedly to me.

"Right, no it's not—just I'm . . . um . . . I was listening to the guy practicing his introduction in there and everything he's saying is—America should listen to *him.*" *Get it together.* I unlocked the door. "Sorry to babble. I'm fine." I blushed as I realized it was the blond from the conference room, the speaker's wife, her black blazer now tied around the waist of her white dress. "Are you okay?" I stepped out.

"No . . . I'm . . ."

That's when I saw it, in the mirror behind her, a deep stain spreading below the blazer. Stunned, she looked down and we both saw the red trail snaking down her legs.

"I've so been there." I touched her forearm. "Don't worry, I'll get you—"

"I'm not prepared . . . for this." She fumbled with her phone. "I just need to call my doctor."

"I'll get you a tampon."

She looked at me like she couldn't decipher my meaning.

"There's a housekeeping station. At the other end of the corridor."

"A tampon isn't going to . . ." Her mouth twisted. "This isn't . . . we were trying . . ." She clenched her eyes shut. "His speech," she instructed herself. "Is in thirty minutes. And I have to get back in there. That's what's next."

"Wait here." I motioned to the handicap stall. "I'll run to the staff room and get you a clean skirt."

She shook her head, nonetheless stepping inside. "We're here at the hotel. Room 817. If you wouldn't mind?" She reached in her blazer pocket and pulled out a key card with a trembling hand. "Just the black skirt in the closet."

"Not at all."

I sped-walked past the arriving attendees, greeting each other with hearty handshakes. Upstairs, I slipped the card in above the Please Service sign and went to the closet. I found the black skirt, but then it occurred to me that someone in her situation might need fresh drawers. I unclipped the hotel's plastic laundry bag from its hanger. Hesitating for half a second, I lifted the suitcase lid and, among the tossed contents, found a pair of underwear and hose to put in the bag. In the bathroom I collected a few washcloths stacked beside a faded Hello Kitty pencil case filled with make-up—I grabbed that, too. I saw the needles and vials in the trash, but nothing in my life had given me reason to know their purpose. Infertility wasn't exactly Tallyville's most pressing concern.

Looping past the housekeeping office on the main floor, I grabbed sanitary supplies, which I snuck through the thick flow of luncheon attendees and back to the bathroom. Two women in pastel suits were drying their hands.

"I have your things," I said as soon as they left.

The stall door unlatched and she looked out at me, tear streaks marring her foundation but her composure otherwise returned. "I can't thank you enough."

"No problem." I passed her the clothes. "And here." When I handed her the bag, she looked into it and then back at me. "Oh my God, you're amazing."

Assuming she wanted to be alone—I certainly would have—I was about to leave when she said, "Will you wait and take the bag back up?"

"Of course."

A few minutes later, she emerged in her new outfit and pulled a face at herself in the mirror. "I'm a hot mess." "Not at all," I said, taking the bag.

A man's laughter just outside filtered in. She ran a hand over her hair and then tugged out the pencil case, which seemed to threaten her resolve for a moment before she reached in and took out her powder. "Well," she said to us both with an eye toward the door. "Let's just say a prayer of thanks for the predominantly male population of the South Floridian Lawyers Association, shall we? They don't tend to notice the fine print on us wives." She swiped her cheeks with blush. With her large brown eyes and fine features she was very attractive, but now that I looked closely I would have said older than someone who would want to have a baby. Where I came from she would have been grandma material.

"It does seem to be a lot of guys."

"Funny, that's how they sign their Christmas cards." She smiled at me. "Well this was above and beyond the call of duty . . . I don't even know your name."

"Man—Amanda." I pushed myself to use my full name. "Luker. Sorry to be simpering when you came in. I really appreciated what your husband was saying out there, is all. About motion. And stuck towns. Obviously he's talking about much more than me and my stupid problems—"

"He's talking about whatever it is you're facing on our government's watch. And he means it. Spread the word."

"Yes, ma'am."

"But not about this."

"About what?" I cocked my head at her and she grabbed my

hand in both of hers, squeezing it with more appreciation than I could remember getting from a grown-up.

"One foot in front of the other, Amanda." She threw her shoulders back and walked to the door as if refreshed. "That's all a girl can do."

I made it through the rest of my shift, standing at attention for guests lounging under the misting machines as the staff ferried tapas just outside the perimeter of relief. Adding to the temperature, a pinhole of hope burned in my chest. The feeling was reminiscent of when Diego opened his laptop at the Tallyville Super 8 and showed me the work he was so proud of, his face animating with the passion of someone who so badly wanted me to see what he did.

And this hope went further back—to the first time I checked out a stack of books from the library with Grammy standing behind me, nodding proudly with her ever-present rattan purse dangling from the crook of her elbow. "There's more," she said, meaning we'd come back every week, but I took it to mean more than Delilah and the trailer and a street that nature reclaimed at its end.

On my break I stuck my head in the ballroom, but by then everyone was long gone. I picked up a program from the stack by the door to find the last name of the man who'd introduced the senator. Davis. Tom Davis.

As soon as I clocked out at ten, I grabbed my keys and wallet and went to the Business Center. Built before the world could be run on one's phone, it was rarely used except by the occasional guy surfing for things he didn't want record of in his search history. I had taken to using it as I once used the library, like it was mine alone.

Parking myself at the first computer, I tugged down the zipper that had been digging into my ribs all day and typed in Tom's name as I held the lamé to my chest.

In the first image I found, he was clad in a suit and stood by a flag, looking like a businessman with a sweep of black bangs, his blue eyes warm and smiling. In the flatness of the photo, nothing distinguished him from those at the hotel restaurant who cut into steaks with elbows raised or stared into space while their wives kept the family vacation to a low roar.

But here's what I found out; he was a good guy. A whiz kid who'd worked his way through school on merit scholarships and became the state's most formidable trial lawyer. He'd written for his law review and later for local papers, impassioned op-eds identifying missed opportunities for communities to support struggling families. He'd won massive settlements for class action suits against tobacco and chemical companies. Afraid the opposition was going to vote for torte reform, he'd thrown his influence behind Watkins, making strong inroads into the Florida political scene. And, this is the part that made my arms goose-pimple, he grew up a few towns over from Tallyville, and there wasn't anything in that direction to be proud of.

One foot in front of the other.

He'd met Lindsay Palmer, of the Jacksonville Palmers, at college—then they'd gone onto law school together and had built a joint practice. In her wedding picture, her curls looked a little big, her dress a little flouncy, her lipstick a little pale, but, despite the dated fashion, she was still strikingly beautiful.

Then I Googled them both and a batch of articles came up that I hadn't expected. Their daughter, Ashleigh, had been killed a year earlier in a car accident. She was sixteen. Before the news clip I clicked on could play, a voice interrupted me.

"Feet hurt, huh?"

I startled to see Westerbrook had rolled a desk chair out from behind the last cubicle. "I didn't know anyone was down here." I clenched my elbows to keep my dress from flopping open.

"Me, neither. You don't have to go."

"I'm done, actually, so . . ." I didn't want to zip up in front of him. But I couldn't move my arms if I didn't.

He was wearing linen pants and carrying his dress shirt flung over his shoulder. I realized that it had met with a dark cocktail—a bitch of a stain for whoever's problem this guy's laundry was. "Do you think we'll ever be fully dressed together?"

I cringed. "That wasn't—I don't normally . . ." Why was I apologizing to him? "At any rate, I'm not into sharing office space with those about to whack off."

"That makes two of us. Is that your poison?" He pointed to the screen behind me. "Pretty dark stuff."

I paused the video. "No, it's—no. That's the guy who was speaking here today. Tom Davis. He was compelling. But I didn't know about his daughter."

"Horrible. " He shook his head at the news story.

I shut down the computer.

"I should probably get back to work," he said reluctantly.

"Right."

He pointed at the desk and I craned my head around the corner to see a spreadsheet. "We're supposed to be heading out drinking, but I forgot to get this done today."

Keeping my dress pinned to me, I bent to pick up the shoes I hadn't realized I'd slipped off. "They do."

"Sorry?"

"Hurt." I gave him that one.

"That sucks. Hey, aren't there those little gel things you can slip in there? Like, deflated implant-looking things?"

"How would you know that?"

"I have a sister—step." He clasped his hands. "Do you? Have siblings?"

"A brother—half," I said.

"Me, too."

"Which part?"

"Top part."

I blushed. "No, I meant—"

He was smiling at me. "I'm Pax, by the way. Pax Westerbrook." He stood and extended his hand. I awkwardly shook it with my elbows at my side.

"Amanda Luker."

"So do you want me to turn around so you can zip up before you go out there?"

"Yes," I sighed, giving up on pride.

"Dude." I heard Trevor open the door behind me and froze. "I waited a fucking hour and the bitch didn't show—"

"Yeah," Pax said quickly, "She's—"

I turned around. Trevor stared at Pax's naked chest, my unzipped dress and bare feet, like I was still topless. "Oh, I get it."

"She was just—" Pax started, but was interrupted by Kurt rounding into the room behind them.

Shit.

He took in the three of us and his eyes narrowed. "Amanda, vy does security have you going into a room on the 8th floor and coming out with a bag zis afternoon?"

"I was, um . . ." I stepped past both guys to where he stood in the doorway. There was no way to explain myself without mentioning Mrs. Davis.

"Um? You can't be serious. I told zem my Mandy wouldn't be messing around. I covered for you." He eyed the two guys, his face setting in that hard expression that was the precursor to his ripping someone a new one.

"I was just using the computer, doing some research." I tried to get him to remember I was one of the good ones.

"Oh so *that's* what she is," Rooster seethed. "A hustler."

"Trevor," Pax said tightly as I felt myself go rigid.

"You should ask her where your watch went," Rooster pushed. "You know she tried to charge me last night."

"What?" I balked at his blatant lie.

"Admit it. You took it."

Pax looked to me. "You did?"

"Fuck you," I said before I could catch myself.

"Zat's it," Kurt hissed.

Panic surged. "Kurt, please, you know I would never—"

"You're fired."

"Kurt, I swear to you." He tugged away as I tried to touch his arm.

"I suggest you leave ze property before I call security."

"But what about my check?" *How* could this be happening?

"You'll have to call ze office on Monday." He straightened his collar. "Sings can get lost. I don't know."

"Kurt." My chin jutted out, counting commencing.

"I tell you, Mandy, but you don't listen. Shit on me, I wash my hands of you." He gazed at his nails. "Now get your thieving ass out of my sight."

Chapter Two

DESPITE FEELING LIKE I'D BEEN HURLED to the depths of a well, the morning sun still found me in Mom's trailer. God knows why it wanted to, but it persisted in shining through the crack in the tin foil taped to the windows. If I were a shaft of dawn, I'd have sought a patch of grass to fall on—maybe one of the marigolds that grew wild by the side of the highway, a full nest of eggs, or a penthouse terrace overlooking the ocean. I would not have gone willingly into Delilah Luker's double-wide.

I lay on the living area's pullout couch and fought the same urge I did every morning in the two week's since I'd slunk back—the desire to roll over and hold my little brother for just a few minutes when he still looked like a baby and smelled like soap, before his breathing lightened, his eyes opened, and his kinetic boyness took over. But I knew if I didn't move it and put breakfast on, I would never get him to the road in time to catch the bus. Delilah assumed he was handling it, just like she did when I was his age and, all of twenty-four herself, she thought an eight-year-old could cook.

I brushed my teeth while I waited for the shower to turn hot and stared at the peeling vinyl. I'd spent the first night back from

South Beach wiping off every inch of the place with a bucket of bleach and while it still felt grimy, at least it no longer looked fairy-tale neglected. Billy had been staying with neighbors a lot, I learned, because Mom had someone. That's all she would say. Someone. "Mom," I called toward the bedroom. There was no answer. "Delilah!"

The couch springs screeched as Billy hopped up. "Mom." I heard him push her door open, then the bathroom. "Not here," he said.

"Excellent. Get dressed and I'll make eggs." Before I'd left with Diego, I'd signed him up for a summer session so he could get extra help with his reading. If he fell behind he'd be even less into school than he was already.

"I want to stay home with you." He squeezed past me to pee.

"As if." His sandy blond hair was a mess, as if sleep were a hat he'd just tugged off. I smoothed his bedhead and said, "That place may be a shithole, the teachers may suck, and your whole class might have buggers, but you have to keep at it or . . ." I felt the tepid shower.

"Or what?"

"Dude, you're going to college if it kills me."

"You went to college," he said, flushing.

"But you're staying till they give you that degree. Wash hands." I pulled him back inside by the shoulder. "One of us isn't working at Mickey D's the rest of our lives."

"Free Happy Meals." He dried his hands on my T-shirt.

"Well, yes, there's that."

"Mandy." His eyebrows shot up like the space rockets on his underwear. "Are you gonna work at McDonald's?"

"No. Even they don't want me. Thank you for proving my point. Get your clothes on." I steered him to the outfit Mom had left out for him on the table and pulled the accordion door shut.

While he folded up the couch, I stood in the shower a minute longer than I had time for and wondered why, as far back as I could remember, I'd *always* wanted something else for myself. Did our neighbors feel that way—or did their ambitions end at the county line? And why hadn't I had a big brother or sister who would've whipped my ass before letting me drop out of community college? Although, considering Delilah was sixteen when she had me, an older sibling was probably not, in fact, what I would have wished for.

After I dropped Billy off, I headed out to follow up with the handful of places that hadn't said an outright no to my inquiries. To save gas I parked and walked in my flip-flops from one end of town to the other, but all I turned up was a nickel and an offer of a beer from letchy Dan Stevens, whose wife had been my ninth-grade math teacher. I never liked her, but I still wouldn't screw her husband just to get a job rustling up his coffee. Although, with only the GED under my belt, and Kath holding a grudge at my quitting in the first place, I was getting scared that Dan was going to end up being my best offer.

I stood on the uneven sidewalk, which sprouted weeds between every stone, the sun on the back of my neck like a finger poking me. I *needed* to get out of there, which required saving money, which meant getting a job, and staying put exactly where I didn't want to be. The frustration made my eyes sting.

Just then my phone rang. I didn't know the number.

"Hello?" I answered eagerly.

"Is this Amanda?" a man asked.

"Yes." I tried to fill my voice with a hirable quality.

"This is Pax Westerbrook. We met at the—"

A sound like a motorcycle idling escaped the back of my throat. "I know who you are."

"You remember?"

"It's not like your name's Dave."

"Right."

"Calling to make sure I'm well-and-truly fired? I am. I'm well-and-truly fired." I actually kicked the lamppost base with my toe.

"Um, I was just—sorry, this feels stupid now—I wanted to see if you were okay."

"Why?"

"I feel super shitty about what happened—I found my watch and Trevor admitted you didn't actually, you know, solicit him."

"To Kurt?" I clutched the phone. "He told the hotel?"

"No, uh, actually, just me. He can be an asshole when he's been drinking, but he's not a bad guy."

I rolled my eyes at the empty street. "Okay, well, thanks for calling to clarify that—"

"I want to make it up to you," he said hastily, before I could disconnect.

"Make it up to me?"

"Please. I want to. I'm in West Palm—I could come down."

Was this guy asking me out? Seriously?

"Well, I'm back home now, so . . ."

"Oh. I just thought I could—"

"Why now? Why not step in when my manager was reaming me out?"

"I didn't know what to think. Look, Trevor was out of line," he conceded the one thing he seemed willing while completely not answering my question.

"Your friend accuses me of being a thief and a hooker, *which you believed*, and all you can say is that he was out of line?"

"What else do you want me to say?" He was suddenly defensive. I couldn't believe it.

"Okay, look, dude, if you needed to clean your conscience, consider it gleaming. I'm fine. Never been better. Your wonderful friend was just having his period and it's all good. So you take care now." I hung up.

I didn't know why Pax Westerbrook was getting such a rise out of me—just thinking of his uselessly stunned expression as Kurt led me away by the elbow reminded me of the worst of the guys who Mom had paraded through the trailer, like they were big men there to skin something for dinner and make it all right. But when Mom freaked out because the lights went off or Billy had a fever, when reality slammed into the aluminum sides like a gator's tail, they just shoved their hands deep in their pockets and looked sheepish.

Sheepish. That's what he'd been. I had no space for it.

I headed back to the trailer. Halfway there I spotted Mom's Buick at the edge of the Walmart parking lot and pulled over. She was sitting in the front seat, tears forming black gullies that trailed beneath her sunglasses.

"Hey," I called tentatively as I approached.

"Did Billy get off all right?" she asked, not looking at me or questioning what I was doing there.

"Yes. You okay?" I leaned down in her open window.

"Did he have his green shirt on—they were supposed to wear green today." She pulled a Wendy's wrapper from her purse and blew her nose.

"He put on what you left out for him."

"And there was enough baloney for his lunch?" she asked, as if I was the spouse who'd forgotten to buy more.

"I'll pick some up today—now, I'm here," I realized. I had been trying to ration my visits to Walmart, because once I walked every aisle, touched every towel and sundress, that would be it. I would have nothing else to look at. Budget cuts had long since closed the library. And the cable was off so I couldn't even watch stupid TV.

"Thanks, Mandy. I'm just making a run to the bank to get change before the lunch crowd." She had her diner uniform on.

"Okay." I accepted her answer, which explained nothing whatsoever about what was going on. "Did he dump you? The 'someone' you're seeing?"

She shook her head. Then she pointed to the dashboard, where a pregnancy test seemed to be cooking, its cross turning a deep pink.

"Fuuuck," I said in a low, long breath. I came around and got in the passenger seat. "What're you gonna do?" I asked stupidly, even though I'd passed three billboards telling me Jesus watches the unborn in the last mile. There was nothing to do.

"It'll be okay," she said.

"God, Mom, how?"

"I don't know."

I had figured I was in for ten more years to get Billy to voting age and the hell out of here, but now I felt like my parole had just been revoked.

"How are you managing Billy when I'm not here?" I asked, even though I didn't want the answer.

"Well, you are here." Ever Delilah, even knocked up in a parking lot, she pulled her visor mirror down, palmed her face off, and unzipped her makeup bag. I thought of Lindsay Davis and her Hello Kitty pencil case—two women armoring themselves with a smudge of paint. "And, despite what Little Man might've told you, we manage just fine—if I'm working the late shift I pack his lunch and leave out his clothes the night before. He has never missed a single day of school." What I didn't snap back was the diner closed at nine—it was the bars that were open late, and a coordinated outfit was the least of what he needed. It was her one consistent thing—that the three of us looked pulled together when that screen door slammed shut on the mess behind us, no matter the amount of spit shining required. No matter that there was nothing to eat for breakfast before we left. "Any luck with the search?" she asked.

"No. And that douche who got me fired—well, technically friend of douche—just called me."

"What did he want?"

"To 'make it up to me,'" I snorted.

"Why don't you go see what that means?" She reapplied her foundation, scowling at the wrinkles she had smoked and sunned into existence. When I was fourteen, I asked Grammy how come she didn't have brown spots or deep crevices around her mouth like her friends and she said, "Don't smoke, wear a hat." I quit that day and put my sitting money toward a bottle of Banana Boat.

"Are you serious?"

She turned to me, hands on the steering wheel like we were going somewhere. "Mandy, a rich kid offered to do something for you. Anything is better than what we got going on right now—which is nothing. Life will hand you very few turns on the Ferris wheel—this might be one of yours."

We had a few more knockdowns about my calling him, but what I remember is her saying that bit about the Ferris wheel; that must've been the thing that decided it. Pax invited me to his family's house four hours away. On the ocean. Where I was supposed to give my name "at the booth." I'd never been to a house guarded by more than a pit bull before. I was sure when the uniformed guy asked for my ID I wouldn't be on the list, but Pax had remembered and I took that as a sign that maybe I wasn't about to have a bucket of blood dropped on my head.

I'd read all of Stephen King in seventh grade. I was like that: I'd find something in the stacks and just binge on it, all in a row, but *Carrie* was my favorite. Only child of a single mother, obviously. I think it comforted me because with all of Delilah's faults at least she was not *that*. She wanted me to date. And she never asked anything so dumb as, "Why don't you bring 'em round the trailer?" She'd just have me swing them by her job where she'd give us a free soda, or whatever, depending on where she was working at the time, and send us on our way. She talked to the guys I'd bring by like they were regular people—didn't flirt with them or overprotect. It was kind of her finest hour. She couldn't make a parent-teacher conference to save her life, but the boyfriend thing she'd always been good at. And she didn't really have anything to worry about—even if she'd been capable. After watching her I held guys at a distance, like a diaper I was running to the pail.

Pax's house was on South Ocean Boulevard, a coveted stretch of coast just down the way from the Lauder family and Donald Trump. Past the booth the front gate, high and curlicued, looked like something off the cover of a romance novel. At my approach it swung open, revealing a long drive, at the end of which was the white stuccoed Westerbrook mansion, crawling with help, like a wedding cake left out at a picnic. I pulled up beside a truck where people were unloading tables and chairs. On the lawn that rolled down to the surf, a parquet dance floor was being assembled. Taking a breath, I hopped out in my cut-offs and flip-flops, which I'd chosen after rejecting every sundress Delilah threw at me, because if I'd shown up looking like I was trying to impress him and then he was as big a dick as I expected, the humiliation would finish me off.

The entrance had a staircase you could leave a glass slipper on. The double doors opened and out came a girl about my age wearing a shift the shade of mint chip ice cream and carrying a clipboard. With her pointy nose and chin she was very pretty in a controlled sort of way. "Can I help you?" she asked as she clopped gracefully down in her low-heeled sling backs. "Which team are you on? Then I can tell you where to park."

"Team?"

"Catering, setup, bar?" She flipped her pages.

"Oh, sorry, I'm here to see Pax, actually."

She dropped the clipboard, blushing. "Apologies."

"Hey, honest mistake. You have a ton of people here."

"I think he's sailing with James. Is he expecting you?"

"He said three. Who's James?" We rounded the corner of the truck, and she saw the duct tape holding my Honda together. She tensed back up.

"Did he stiff you?"

"Sorry?" I asked.

"He does that all the time—running out on bar tabs or forgetting his credit card. I don't think he has any malicious intent—I think he's just wasted. I can write you a check."

I was not there for a handout. I shouldn't have been there at all. "This was a mistake—please tell him Amanda—or actually, don't." I opened my door, silently asking it not to fall off its hinge.

"Don't what?" We turned to see him striding from the back of the house in white shorts, his tan torso bare. "Hey, you came." He smiled at me. "And you've met Pym."

"Not formally," she corrected him.

"This my stepsister, Pym. Pym, this is Amanda, the girl I was telling you about." She and I smiled tightly at each other. "Why are you dressed like that?"

"I'm in charge today," she answered smugly, "I had to look—commanding."

"Where's Cricket?"

"You know your mother—she likes to waft in at the last second, expecting everything to be running smoothly while she's been applying her Shalimar and adjusting her Givenchy, but God forbid the tablecloths are the wrong length—I'll be hearing about it until Christmas."

"Big event?" I asked, letting the door close behind me.

"Political fundraiser," he answered. "Why are you carrying a clipboard?"

"Because the fucking Wi-Fi is out," Pym said evenly, "so I'm having to do this all on paper and if you ask me one more question I will shove it up your ass." I decided Pym might have some likeable qualities. "Now I have to go make sure the hors d'oeuvres are being prepared without garlic—the senator's entire family is allergic." She tried to stride purposefully off, but her tiny heels sunk into the grass with each step—she'd have been more "commanding" in flip-flops.

"So, I'm glad you came." He rocked from his heels to his toes and back again while I crossed my arms, to guard against whatever effect he wanted meeting him here to have. "I . . . uh . . . talked to my mother, who talked to the head housekeeper, who thinks we're about to have an opening."

"An opening?" I asked.

"It's a good gig because we're only here less than half the year and with such a large staff you don't have to clean much. And if the head housekeeper likes you, in a few years you could maybe move up to the Connecticut place—or even Aspen if that's your thing."

"My thing?"

"Yeah." He slid his hands into the back of his shorts, which made all his muscles flex. "Oh, and you have to submit to a background check, but that's just standard."

Once again I was stunned. I'd spent four hours of gas money for *this*. "You're offering me a job *cleaning up after you*! *That's* how you're going to make it up to me?" I spun for my car.

"W-well, I just thought, hostess, and . . . and you brought the cart, and—"

"Oh my God." I threw the door open and flung myself in. It was by far the best—and only—offer I had going, but there was no way. Fucking Delilah's pride. It made its presence in me known at the most inopportune moments.

He put his hand on the door. "I was just trying to help."

I looked up at him, struggling to close my gaping jaw and say something. "*Help* would've been stepping in, putting your asshole, yes, *asshole* of a friend in check. Barring that, help would've been maybe *asking* what I wanted to do next."

"What *do* you want to do?" he asked intently.

"I don't know yet." I was brought up short. "Look, maybe all I'm qualified to be is a maid—and I will do it with my head held high. But I would like to have been asked if *maybe* I was dreaming just a little bit bigger than that. You look like the kind of people who could put in a word for someone."

"Oh, God. We are—we can. I'm sorry, please stay." He seemed genuinely mortified. "This was a mistake—let me make *this* up to you." He waited for my answer, looking like he might jump on the hood of my car to stop me from leaving.

"By pimping me—where do we go down from here?"

He laughed. Then I laughed. He placed his palms flat on the car roof, arms outstretched. He smelled like the ocean. "Hey, that guy'll be here."

"What guy?"

"That guy you were Googling at the hotel—Tom Davis. Tonight he's introducing Senator Watkins. We're hosting a fundraiser for his reelection campaign. You should stay."

"After my background check?"

"I'm serious. Stay."

"Thanks, but I'm not doing another eight-hour round-trip to get my prom dress."

"That's it." He snapped his fingers. "*That* is how I will make it up to you. I will take you shopping and introduce you to Tom Davis."

"Oh, yeah, that is just like a job."

"Great. Let me grab a shirt."

I sat in the drive and waited for him, daring myself to peel out. But all I could hear was the fairground's barker beckoning me to get on.

Pax's sports car was so low to the ground it was hard not to flinch every time an SUV passed—it felt like it would ride right over us. When I looked at him, the phrase that came to mind was something from *Grease*: Pax was the living end. The tan, the car, the sunglasses, the way the wind tousled his hair—he was beautiful like a dolphin is beautiful, like certain things in nature attain momentary perfection. *He* was perfection. And I was in the passenger seat with it.

"Mama always told me never to ride with strangers."

He shifted gears. "Technically, we've seen each other naked so I think that makes us something other than strangers—plus I witnessed a life-altering event."

"Kind of like you helped me give birth in an elevator."

"Kind of."

"Only you were the one pressing the emergency stop button."

He smiled as he turned onto Worth Avenue. "You hungry?"

"Always."

He swerved to a stop in front of a little café and came back a few minutes later with two milkshakes. "I don't like to go into these places empty-handed. It makes them so much more nervous if you're carrying food."

"Where, exactly, are we going?" I asked as he pulled back out and then up to one of the stores down the block.

"Wherever Cricket's charge accounts take us."

"That's funny," I said, getting out as he tossed the valet his keys. I sipped my milkshake, letting him hold the door for me, like this was a date.

"What?" he asked.

"I call my mom by her first name, too." It was strange to think we had anything whatsoever in common. "Delilah."

"Does she live up to her name?" he asked, referencing its biblical origins as the air conditioning and scented candles made me shiver, something unsettling about such a sweet fragrance in a simulated winter.

"No, sadly, more often the guys are *her* undoing." The carpet was Kelly green, the walls a vintage floral. It felt like a glimpse of the world Grammy had aspired to and Delilah reactively spurned. "This feels fancy," I said. "I don't need anything this fancy."

"Look, if *only* my friend had gotten you fired we'd be at Chico's right now. But this is a double make-it-up-to-you." He was funny, I admitted to myself as I touched the fabric of the cocktail dresses, trying to imagine wearing anything that cost three-month's pay. An overly made-up woman eyed us as Pax gesticulated with his shake.

"Don't you need to be back at your house helping Pym with the party?" I asked.

"Nah." He plunked himself down on a tufted ottoman and leaned back. We were the only two customers. "Pym's a bit of a control freak. Tonight I'll do my thing. Be Paxton Westerbrook, whatever the fuck that means." His face darkened for a moment. "Hey, I can tell you're not going to get into the swing of this. Miss, excuse me." He called the anxious woman over. "My friend, Amanda, here needs a dress for a fundraiser at my parents' place tonight. Can you suggest a few things?"

"I'd be delighted."

"Something simple," I added, hoping that translated into cheap.

"Okay, fine," he conceded. "No feathers, no rhinestones, and nothing that lights up."

As I headed into the dressing room, I wondered if perhaps this was what he wanted—to dress me up and then undress me. But he made no move to come in. A sliver of me was disappointed.

"That's it," he said. "That's the winner." It was a mink-brown halter, made out of silk. It clung through the hips, and then spun out into a circle skirt that ended at the knee. Elegant, classic, and sexy.

"Very light to pack, great for travel," the clerk said. I felt like maybe she was mocking me. "Do you need shoes?"

"No."

"Yes," Pax said over me.

"I feel like something horrible is happening," I said when she left to fetch me some heels.

"Not the reaction I was expecting, but okay."

"I mean, like, my accepting this dress and the shoes somehow makes what happened okay, how Trevor behaved—how you behaved. I feel like I've been bought. For a few hundred dollars."

"Hey." He stood up and looked me squarely in the face, the glint in his eye extinguished. "I've done a lot of stupid shit. And this could've just been one more thing—it almost was—that just gets stuck in my head like one of those pointy things you jab in a lobster claw, one more embarrassment. But I—I don't know why—I couldn't let you be that. So I'm trying." He stared in a way that paused my breath. "And failing, clearly, but I'm trying. Okay?"

"Well, in that case, I think I also need some underwear that won't show."

"You got it."

I don't remember what we talked about as we drove back—just that, given how different our upbringings had been, he was surprisingly easy to talk to. Pym set me up in the pool house to shower and change and I found myself listening for the click of the bathroom lock—would he let himself in, slide in behind me under the steam?

I knew that was the Delilah part of me talking. That what I *needed* tonight were introductions to people I could never otherwise get my résumé to, if I'd even had a résumé. What I *had* was two hours to change my life.

I blew out my hair and headed up the walk, trying to channel the girls in dresses, just like this one, I'd seated a thousand times. A server waiting around the hedge with a tray of champagne-filled flutes directed me to the house.

"Hello, good evening." Pym was standing on the stone patio, greeting the guests as they arrived. "You look great," she said.

"Thank you. So do you." She was wearing a black version of the dress from this morning and had swapped out her pearl studs for discrete diamonds.

"Mom, this is Amanda Luker, Pax's friend."

Cricket turned and I instantly felt like a leaf with a gale force wind bearing down on me. It wasn't just that she was tall, easily six feet in heels, it was that she had an energy like a cat on the savanna—the kind that makes gazelles freeze in their tracks and stop breathing. "Nice to meet you." She extended a hand and shook mine vigorously. "Where is he?"

"Maybe helping James get ready," Pym suggested.

"Ugh," Cricket said, "I told the nanny to put his clothes out for him. He shouldn't have needed any help."

"Younger brother?" I asked.

"Eight and an absolute devil," Cricket said, looking over the crowd, fingertips to her sternum. "He'll be trying to steal the change from people's pockets."

"Isn't that what we're all doing?" Pax asked, coming up behind her. "This is a fundraiser, right?" Cricket smiled as he leaned over her shoulder to kiss her cheek. She slid a hand into his hair. "Hey, you look awesome," he said to me as he broke from her embrace.

"Thanks." I could have returned the compliment. He was wearing tight seersucker pants and a custom-fit white shirt. Whoever designed his clothes could not have hoped for a better body than his to be displaying in the world.

"Pym, dear," Cricket said, surveying the party, "I don't like those hurricane lanterns—can you have them swapped out?"

"Of course," Pym said, the way I used to say *of course* to Kurt when I really meant, suck it.

Once Pym had excused herself, Cricket turned her full feline focus on her son. "Have you seen the bore?" she asked, pulling the ruffled neckline of her cocktail dress slightly open. I wondered which of their guests had earned this distinction.

"I think he's hiding in his study."

Cricket rolled her eyes. "He is the most dreary man on God's green earth." They laughed together. "All right, I better circulate. Amanda, nice to meet you," she tossed off, but as she left she threw a look to Pax that ordinarily I would have said meant, *Don't forget you're leaving with me.*

I had seen so many mothers like this at the hotel—single, travelling with only sons who had grown to resemble the ex-husbands who had broken their hearts. Having never relaxed into the mom role because they were still aggressively on the market, they flirted with their sons out of habit—who flirted back because it was all they knew.

I didn't want Billy to end up in that role.

"Who's the bore?" I asked.

"My stepfather—Taggart Westerbrook—yes, I took his name. Raw bar?" Pax asked, extending a hand toward where the crowd thickened.

"The magic's gone, huh?"

He placed a hand lightly on my lower back to steer me, sending a low current through my skin. "According to legend my father swept her off her feet, fireworks, the whole Cole Porter shebang with a good deal of drugs thrown in. Then left her in Marrakech seven months pregnant. I don't think magic was what she was looking for on round two. Let's get some oysters."

We wove into the crowd toward the table laden with all manner of ocean creatures and abutted by ice sculptures of the state flag. Not knowing how to respond to Pax's explanation, I simply said, "People always ordered those seafood towers at the hotel, but I couldn't understand it. I mean, I get expensive cooking, but why would you spend a fortune for groceries on ice?"

Pax grinned and waved his arm like a magician's assistant. "Et voilà. Groceries on ice."

I smiled and took a shrimp. Which was admittedly delicious.

"So, how long did you work there?" he asked, slurping an oyster.

"Four months."

He pulled a W-monogrammed napkin from the pile to dab his chin. "And what would you like to do—in all seriousness."

"Join the navy—see the world."

"Really?"

"No." Truth was, beyond *out of there*, I didn't have a concrete vision. I knew I'd be wearing a blazer, I'd have a desk of my own, responsibilities. I was good with the books at Kath's—maybe something in money? I shifted my drink to my other hand to take a passing pastry puff. "What about you?"

"Oh, you haven't heard?" he said sarcastically. "I'm being groomed to take over Westerbrook Equities."

"Like monkeys?"

"Yes, just like that. Whoever can pick the most grubs off my stepdad's fur gets to be CEO."

"That's how I got my hostess job."

He clinked my glass with his. "Want to meet Tom Davis?"

"Oh, I couldn't," I said, suddenly shy for perhaps the first time in my life.

"Come on." He led me across the dance floor to a cluster of men in seersucker suits and women in sherbet-colored dresses. We elbowed our way in.

"I'm sorry, Dale," Tom was addressing an older gentleman. "But you're going to have to explain to me what the fuck a bootstrap is." The crowd laughed. Lindsay grinned. In a peach-toned cocktail dress she looked better than she'd been at the hotel. Her face had color and her smile was full and warm. I tried to duck my head a little, not wanting her to see me and be reminded. "I mean it. I went to the same public school as my parents. When they graduated it still had a Math Club—can you imagine that? We had two stoplights and a Math Club. By the time I passed through, VH1 was already trying to save the music and now they have kids zoning out in class because their houses are meth labs. How do you keep the teachers giving a crap in that kind of environment for that kind of pay? My parents got a bootstrap. These kids aren't getting shit from us."

"Forget Watkins," someone said, "You should run, Tom."

He blushed. "Nah, I'm a long way off from anything like that."

"You sure?"

"Sure." Tom took Lindsay's hand and squeezed it. They smiled—not at each other, but into each other. The way couples look at the altar. Then he turned back to his enthralled crowd. "Now, if you'll excuse me I need to make sure I have my note cards in order."

The Davises started to walk away when Pax took two quick steps after them. "Mr. Davis, sir." He turned. "Pax Westerbrook. We're delighted to have you here this evening. I'm sure my sister has everything organized to the minute, but is there anything you need?" He was suddenly formal. Groomed.

"For the Rays to beat the Red Sox tonight—any update?"

"He really wants to know," Lindsay said wryly.

"I do," Tom admitted.

"I will get right on that. This is my friend, Amanda Luker."

I was awestruck. Later I'd learn that people were tempted to pin Tom Davis' appeal on his Kennedy good looks, but it was more than that. He was so perpetually at ease he made those around him feel that things could be easy, that solutions—even for epic problems— were only one discussion away. That, and his eyes were always smiling, like he'd just caught his breath after hearing a really good joke.

He shook my hand. "Pleasure to meet you, Amanda. This is my wife, Lindsay." She startled as she registered me.

"Nice to meet you." I took her hand, trying to telegraph that whatever happened in that ladies' room was nobody's business as far as I was concerned. "I heard a little bit of your speech last month in South Beach," I said to Tom.

"I wouldn't have taken you for a class action lawyer."

"I was—refilling the water pitchers." I didn't want Lindsay to think, standing here in this dress, I was trying to be anything I wasn't—or that I was trying to sleep my way to being Cricket.

"Well, thank you. I get a very dry mouth when I'm nervous so you helped a great deal." As Tom spoke Pax actually squeezed my hand. "Well, thanks again for having us, Pax. Great to meet you, Amanda. You two kids enjoy yourselves tonight." Oh God, I wanted to, but instead I just felt a vibrating sense of urgency. In seven months my mother's dependency on me would expand exponentially—again. I had to find a life preserver before she scrambled on my back.

Pax and I walked to the periphery of the dance floor. "So this company you're being groomed to run. Do they need anyone to make coffee?"

"I think they have those pod machines now."

"Seriously, I can type faster than a water moccasin. I know Excel and QuickBooks. My Mom had a job at a dealership for a bit and the other assistant taught me."

He put his finger on his chin. "I actually *might* know the right people." He seemed delighted. "Let's look for the man with the bow tie." We wended our way through the crowd while I tried to swipe something off every passing tray. Tomorrow it would be back to bologna sandwiches. I observed the crowd observing us. Even though Pax seemed to deliberately tune it out, like the celebrities at the hotel, I knew he had to be aware of how the women were looking at him. Hungrily. Wondering who he was escorting around the party.

Finally, we found the man with the bow tie, an older gentleman named Roger who slapped Pax on the back by way of a greeting, sloshing Pax's champagne onto my bare toes. "Your mother looks lovely, as always," he told Pax.

"Amanda, this is Roger Barkingdale. He runs our Palm Beach branch," he said proudly. "Roger, this is Amanda Luker. She's looking for a job and I thought we might have an opening in admin."

"Any relation to Elizabeth?" he asked me.

"No—I'm from Tallyville," I answered, assuming that clarified he had not passed me on the polo grounds. "But I'd be happy to relocate for the right job."

"Where are you working now?"

"I'm—"

"She's between things," Pax jumped in.

"Well, have your resume and college transcript faxed to my office and I'll see what we can do."

"I've actually been working in the hospitality industry until recently, but I've completed a semester at our community—"

"She's hardworking," Pax interjected again. "I think we could at least give her a trial. I can vouch for her."

Roger looked me up and down, his wattles covering more of his collar as he leaned down toward Pax and lowered his voice ineffectively. "Without your stepfather reluctantly covering your ass I'd have fired you ten times over, so I hardly think you're in a position to 'vouch' for anyone. I don't know what you get up to when you roll in late and leave early, but I don't think you should bring it here, to your mother's doorstep, do you?" He moved away slowly, favoring one hip.

Pax didn't turn to me—or apologize for Roger. I thought of another party—eleventh grade—Matt Dwyer and Bobbie Pitts wanted to get one of the dance squad girl's attention, so they picked up the cooler to fling its contents in her direction—only they stumbled under the weight of the beer-sodden ice and doused me.

"Come on." Pax grabbed my arm, his affability suddenly gone like a dog hearing an intruder. He deposited me at the start of the wood walkway to the sand. "Wait here."

"Where are we going?"

He doubled back to swipe two bottles of champagne from behind the bar as his mother took the microphone to welcome everyone.

"Won't we miss Tom introducing Watkins?" I asked as I followed him down the uneven steps.

He plunked himself in the sand just below the dunes. "You don't want to be up there," he said as I stumbled down to him in my heels.

"I kind of do, actually." Then I realized maybe he wasn't embarrassed for himself, but angry at me—maybe he thought I'd ruined his night. Over the waves I could hear everyone applauding as Cricket handed the mike to Tom Davis.

Pax took a long swig.

"Really?" I asked.

"What?"

"You're just going to sit here and get trashed?"

"So?"

"So, you're ridiculous." I wanted him to apologize to me or shrug it off. At the very least stick it out at the party. "You walk around in an Abercrombie ad and now one guy is a dick and you're pouting."

"You don't know anything about me."

"You're right. I don't." I wanted to strip that dress off and throw it in his face. The moon on the ocean was beautiful, and I wasn't working. I was here—with him—and this should have been different.

He picked up a stick of dried sea grass and made an arc in the sand. "I guess I should be touched the bore's been vouching for me—however 'reluctantly.'"

Pax didn't even notice I'd been called a ho—again. It was all about him, which just made me angrier. But now wasn't the time to tell him off. I couldn't afford to give up on networking and I didn't have the guts to walk back out there alone, so a very un-me thing came out of my mouth. "I'm sure he just cares about you and wants to give you time to find your footing."

"What Taggart loves is breaking ninety on the golf course, Pym's GPA, and when the Dow crosses fifteen hundred. Look, he's not a bad guy—he adopted a junkie's kid—everyone around here thinks he's a saint."

"Your dad was a junkie—is?"

He snorted. "When you have as much money as my dad you can get your blood cleaned every day. He'll live to be a hundred."

I nodded. He wanted me to feel sorry for him. But whatever kind of trapeze act his life might have been, I saw a big fat safety net under everyone in it.

He took another long draw and looked up at me. "Shit, you're so hot in that dress. I didn't bring a blanket," he said as if he expected one to just appear. Maybe things just appeared in his life—I had. "How do you feel about getting sand in your hair?"

As. If. "Does that line work?"

"Usually."

"Dude, I would give an-y-thing to have a job I couldn't get fired from. A family that could send me to college. I bet you've never been hungry. Or left alone to figure out how to take care of a kid a third your age. You have first class problems, princess."

His eyes darkened. "The night we met you were so insulted when I tried to hold the limo door for you that you went in on Trevor's side instead—which is how you kicked off that mistake. I may have too much, but it's taught me how to take what's on offer."

"Well, *I'm* not." I stomped back up the steps and found my way to the house as the senator was finishing his speech. I quickly cut across the lawn to the white-jacketed valets. "I don't have a ticket," I told them. "But it's the only one with a duct-taped door."

As I stood there waiting, fuming, disappointed, furious at myself for thinking this could end any other way, one of the staff showed another his phone. "Shit," he said, voice low. "Isn't that the guy they're raising money for tonight? Watkins? Damn."

"What?" I asked as the party behind us got suddenly silent. A hush rippled through the crowd.

The guy extended his phone to me. "Somebody hacked the senator's phone and found a lot of pictures of boys—sorry."

My car came belching over. About to get into the driver's seat, I saw the Davises rushing back down into the thrum of tables from the veranda, with their arms linked, and I tried to imagine having a partner. I'd never felt that—romantically or otherwise.

I also had no idea what the fuck a bootstrap was, but I had an inkling that it was probably myself.

Chapter
Three

Seeing Delilah sucking saltines the next morning, her skin once again the same green as the ratty couch blanket, sent me out of the trailer as fast as my sneakers could go. By nine I was already slapping the offending dress and heels on the counter of the post office. "Hey, Vera." I puffed at my sweat-slickened bangs. "What's the cheapest way to mail this?" I looked at the rack of Priority Mail envelopes. Had it been an option, I'd have plopped Mom in one, too. *Dear Pax, Real life from me to you.*

"Fancy." Vera eyed my booty over the newspaper, the reading of which she metered out to last until closing. "You don't want 'em?"

"No. Nope. So . . ." I twisted my lips to the side. "Yeah."

"Shame." She drummed her flamingo-hued nails, and I recognized Tom Davis's face in the photo beneath them. She clapped her hands excitedly, bringing my attention back to her. "Sell 'em on eBay, how 'bout that?"

"Delilah already made that suggestion." Yelled it out from the bathroom floor, to be precise.

"Bet she did," Vera said with an implication I'd long since learned to ignore.

"So how much?" I hated that I cared enough to send his

purchases back. It was exactly the wrong amount of caring. But the satisfaction in imagining Pax's chagrin was the only potentially attainable thing I had going at the moment. Usually, I wasn't that girl. I was the one who'd worked her way through The Shining in the passenger seat of the Buick while her mom waited for some guy to leave his own house. That woman put more energy than she applied to just about anything into analyzing what those asshats did in the steps to their cars. As if a lighter-flick, phone-check, or wedgie-tug revealed something relevant to her, or us—it never did.

But I just couldn't stomach the idea of Pax thinking he'd given me a treat yesterday. Or writing me off because he'd brightened my sad little life with a dress he'd picture me storing in my sad little closet and embracing in Brokeback moments of regret. My life would not be sad. It would not be little. And he sure as hell was not cause for regret. "I want it gone. How much to West Palm?"

"Hold up, now. Lemme see." Vera hopped off her stool, her toes bulging over the soles of her flip-flops as if sprouting from the green plastic leaves on the straps.

The fan, decades into its losing battle with the humidity, kept pace with Vera's geisha shuffle. "Fifteen dollars and seventy-five cents, Priority. Or eleven fifty, First Class." I did not have twelve dollars to spend on this.

"Really, nothing cheaper? How much for a hitchhiker heading south?"

"Seven bucks for Parcel Post. That's for books and magazines, but I won't tell if you don't. Best I can do."

It was a quart of milk, two loaves of bread, and a torn package of eggs. Two gallons and three quick hand pumps of gas. I needed money to make my point that I didn't need money. The luxe fabric slid over the edges of the plastic scale like a jellyfish attempting escape.

Get it together, Amanda

~

I had hoped by the time I saw Grammy I'd have good news or, really, *any* news, so I'd avoided telling her I was home. But after seeing Vera, if Grammy didn't already know, she would within the hour.

Walking up to her little Victorian always made my chest rise in anticipation of the comfort that would greet me there, complicated as it was. In that house, designed for the air to cross through before machines could be plugged in to force it, order awaited me. I knocked on the porch's screen door, pressing my forehead against the mesh to peer into the breezeway. "Grammy?"

She came out from the kitchen, hands wet, stopping when she saw me, an irrepressible smile breaking through her obvious dismay. Grammy knew how hard I tried, how much I wanted—she wanted it all for me. When I was struggling to make enough money at Kath's to stay in college, she offered to take out a reverse mortgage. I couldn't let her do it—if only because I needed the security of being related to at least one person not in imminent danger of losing her home. When my grades started slipping from exhaustion, she held her tongue and when I told her I was leaving with Diego I know she hoped for the best but feared . . . well, here I was.

"Hi," I said in a small voice. Drying her hands on the apron she wore over her work dresses, she unlatched the door and held it open.

"Come here." She reached up to hug me to her, the faint scent of gardenia and baby powder making me rest my eyes for a half second.

"Missed you," I said into her soft shoulder.

She pushed me back and cocked her head sternly. "Now don't you mistake my being happy to see you for my being happy to see you."

"No, ma'am."

Everything was exactly as it always had been, the shades three quarters drawn, the little living room we never sat in adorned with a vase of jonquil from her garden, the wood floor creaking with each step—making the sneaking out Delilah did as a teenager impressive on a certain level.

I followed her gray pin curls to the kitchen where I knew she'd be drinking her coffee before leaving to answer phones at the dentist's office. When my grandfather had been alive, he'd had strong opinions on the subject of married women working. He'd apparently had strong opinions on just about everything. But as long as I could remember, Grammy liked having a place to go every day. And even in Tallyville the cost of living had outpaced social security pretty sharply.

On the Formica table sat the basket with her pressed pillowcases, waiting to be taken upstairs, just one of the little rituals that defined her. Delilah did not believe in ironing. If my grandfather had strong opinions, Delilah had equally strong beliefs. And she did not believe in anything Grammy.

At eighteen Grammy, known only as Barbara back then, had had "the good sense" to marry Richard Luker, a man always found where he was supposed to be: either keeping the books for Harding Citrus Suppliers or at church if it was a Sunday. I never met him. He died a month before I was born, "from shame," Grammy supposedly told Delilah. Had there been someone to point a gun at, he would have seen to it that a wedding with his knocked-up daughter would have occurred, but my dad was apparently just, "some guy passing through."

Both of them had told me that Grammy tried to get Mom to come home after I was born, but on *her* terms. Which, knowing Delilah, was pretty much like saying don't come home. Grammy had tried to help out with me—and later with Billy—but her help always came with a lot of questions—"Is Mandy getting enough milk?" "Why don't you get her shoes with some support?"—that would send Delilah into a rage: "I am perfectly capable of taking care of my own goddamn children!" (She was not.) Which would make Grammy tear up.

While it wasn't a frequent occurrence, being around Grammy and Mom at the same time felt like standing in an electrical storm. I told myself that I didn't mind that Grammy had attempted, not so quietly, to wash her hands of Mom. A part of me needed to know such a thing was possible.

"Vera says hello," I ventured as Grammy wrapped her sandwich in wax paper. "I'm sorry I didn't stop in earlier."

She nodded me over to the table as she lay down a crisp linen place mat. I took a seat. Cold tea was poured over crackling ice and two Stella D'Oros were taken from the jar. I could never reconcile that Mom had grown up with things like full cookie jars. Although, as she'd be the first to tell you a few drinks down, it wasn't the cookie jars she was running away from so much as their getting thrown at the wall. My grandfather's impatience with Delilah being Delilah didn't start at my conception.

Grammy stood at the end of the table while I took a long sip. The fact that she wasn't joining me or returning to her coffee meant that I was to explain myself. I searched for a spin on my failed departure.

She spoke instead, "Your momma should have left you well enough alone in Miami."

"Pardon?"

"You were getting yourself settled. She had no right to rope you back into this mess." So she knew. She shook her head, her face dragged downward by the pregnancy, her daughter compounding a disaster Grammy had failed to contain the first two times.

"She didn't. I came back on my own."

She studied me for signs of lying, looking no more relieved at finding none.

"I'm between things," I said quickly, cringing. We both knew where I'd gotten that phrase. The disappointment in her eyes was unbearable. Averting them, mine landed on the newspaper at the other end of the table. Tom Davis. I craned to read the headline. "Tom Davis Running for Watkins' Seat." It could have been any story, any headline, but I knew him. At least I hoped I did.

"On my way, I mean." I would have said anything to make the present circumstances not be what they were. "To something pretty different, actually."

She waited for me to continue.

I wanted it to be true. "In government."

"Government?"

"Yes, that guy was speaking at the hotel where I was working." I pointed at the paper. "Tom Davis? He's running to take over from Watkins, who—"

"Yes, I saw it on the news—these politicians are disgusting."

"It's a last-minute thing so there's a lot going on." It *was* last minute. There probably *was* a lot going on. I mitigated the risk of failing her lie detector. "I'm going to join the campaign."

She took this in. We both did. It was so outside my wheelhouse I might as well have said I was developing an app.

"So then you're just passing through?" She weighed the credulity of my proclamation, but I could hear her hope.

"Yup, just came by to make sure you weren't kicking up your heels." I did my best impression of her. "I don't want to hear nonsense about you playing hooky. People talk you know, Grammy."

She let out a laugh and then swiped her fingers under her eyes. She went to remove my empty glass but instead put her palm to my shoulder. I reached up and grabbed it, the strength of her grip always surprising as she squeezed tightly before letting me go.

~

Since I hadn't even been able to scare up a job at the Tallyville dump, I'm not sure what made me think I was about to land one on a statewide campaign. My municipal experience consisted of the mayor wiping barbeque sauce from his cheek while audibly debating stuffing my tip in my bra. But as Grammy had tacitly confirmed, Delilah's growing belly threatened to collar my neck, so reality testing was off the menu.

Besides, I didn't invent showing up at a political office with sugarplum visions of creating a just and ordered world. As Tom Davis succinctly put it, kids aren't being given shit. So campaigns are run on the backs of the young and unsaddled, fueled on our fervent belief in a future more tolerable than today. But it was more than that. Until I saw Lindsay navigate whatever had transpired for her in that bathroom, and then the grassy circles of the Westerbrook's party, I hadn't yet come across a woman I wanted to be. I definitely hadn't met a couple I wanted to emulate.

I left Grammy's that morning with fifty dollars pressed in my hand and a ham and cheese pressed into waxed paper. The money filled my gas tank and the sandwich placated Billy, or so I needed to believe. Then I left the trailer park—as I should have that first time—in the driver's seat.

For those who've never been to Palm Beach, steps from the ocean you find spectacular wealth. Inland from that, decaying poverty. And further in still, gated communities of varying pretense linked by stretches of box-store dotted highways. The hastily assembled Davis for Senate office was in a strip mall between a laundromat and a Christian bookstore that was sporadically open. I reached the office in a teeming downpour, the grooming I'd done in the rearview washed away in the few puddle leaps required to make it inside.

Among the mess of cartons and half-assembled office furniture, everyone seemed to be attached to a phone and all of them talked at once. I must have stood there soaking the linoleum a good ten minutes before it registered that I wasn't on anyone's radar. And neither were the two women in rain slickers and the guy slouched on the wall with his arms crossed. Their impatience instantly oriented me.

I squeezed out my hair, wiped my hands on my skirt, and turned my hostess smile in their annoyed direction. "How can I help you?"

Who knows how long they'd been ignored because I had to repeat myself before they all jumped to talk at once. The elder woman was there to complain about campaign signs wrecking her lawn. The younger was supposed to pick up handouts for her church social that had already started. And the guy had been waiting an hour to do an interview for his college newspaper. I found the complainer the bathroom, got cups of water for all, and— massaging them with apologies—gingerly interrupted staffers until I'd located assistance for each one. Turns out the receptionist had cut out to grab a smoke at some point and, understandably overwhelmed, never returned.

Just like that, I was the newest volunteer at Davis for Senate.

I wasn't the only one who'd heard him speak and felt like Tom was reading his or her mind, but the other zealots were law students whose employment opportunities were drying up faster than the ink on their school acceptance letters. Used to logging brutal hours, they knew how to keep their brains sharp for the long haul, but not how to be disarmingly pleasant while doing so. Between Kath and Kurt I'd developed the muscles to complete a Miss America pageant while dodging scatter shot. I knew how to triage those with plummeting blood sugar and soaring expectations, how to make a table where there was none, and how to simultaneously plunge fries into boiling grease, scoop ice cream, ladle soup, take an order, *and smile.*

And thanks to Delilah, I knew how to make things stretch. Paper towels for a coffee filter—a damp one to freshen that stale pizza in the microwave. Cold Popeyes chicken and mustard packets transformed into a quick salad. I had an MBA in making a dollar out of fifteen cents. Which is about what that campaign had. We were the scrappy guys with our sleeves rolled up, jumping in at the zero hour. Tom, who I caught glimpses of as he scurried to and from fundraisers and rallies, an entourage perpetually talking at him, was encouraged to make the most of his outsider status. It allowed him to be the fresh thinker he was.

That bustling office on South Dixie Highway was the exact opposite of where I'd been my whole life—everyone was there because they wanted to be. As braced as I was for the other staffers to cop an attitude with me, it was hard to imagine a doctorate could have garnered more respect than a well-timed Pepsi. There were just too many fires to put out for anyone to get bogged down with my credentials. I alternated sleeping in the back of my car, when it was cool enough, and the floor under my desk. I was the only volunteer who sort of, kind of, really lived there, so I may have essentially been marooned in that strip mall, but I was practically high from the experience.

Lindsay Davis rarely came by because her smile was needed in a thousand other places. Her and Tom's whiteboard schedule, which was perpetually being redrawn, indicated that the campaign required as much from her as her husband.

Even still, at the same time every month days were x-ed out for her and Tom to go to their IVF clinic in Jacksonville. I couldn't help fantasizing about giving my pending sibling to her and solving all our problems.

If she remembered me from either of our two earlier meetings, she didn't let on, but she did notice the orange flowers growing by the road that I'd taken to cutting and arranging in the greeting area. Those, plus a few magazines and a bowl of candy and, as Grammy had imparted, people felt greeted instead of shuffled.

"Oh." Lindsay said one day, stopping on the way to Tom's office. "Right." She nodded, taking in my handiwork. "Smart."

Outside the walls of Grammy's Victorian that adjective had never been assigned to me.

September arrived, forcing the departure of a handful of staff for their fall semesters, which meant those of us who remained shifted up. While my title still didn't entail a salary, it did embolden me enough to move from the floor to the sagging couch by the copier. By then, I'd also become skilled at sink showers, reminding myself that any Jane Austen heroine made do with a bowl and a pitcher.

It was surprising I was the only vagabond who'd drifted into our offices since there was always an open box of donuts and a pizza on offer. Other than the donuts being more dependable than whatever Delilah could scare up, it really wasn't much of a stretch from how I'd grown up.

When we won the special election and Tom became the official Democratic candidate, I bought a postcard for Grammy at the neighboring bookstore with a picture of Mary and Joseph attending their newborn. Pressing a Davis sticker on it, I wrote, "Love, Amanda Beth, (newly appointed) Head Volunteer of the Inn." I was finally part of something bursting with potential that wasn't my mother.

One afternoon, about a month later, I was making my way back across the steady traffic that separated us from the Office Max, four bags straining with discounted printer ink slapping at my calves, when I saw the Davis's car pulling in from a fundraiser. They were on their way inside when Lindsay froze, her hand still in her purse. "It's not here," she called to Tom and he spun back.

"Everything okay?" I asked as I approached, blowing my bangs from my eyes.

"No." Lindsay shook her head in concern. "It's not."

"How can I help?" I asked.

"Let's not lose time on this," Tom said, checking his phone. "I'll just run back to the luncheon and grab it."

Lindsay took me in for a second before reaching out a splayed hand in revelation. "You know them. She knows the hosts, Tom."

"Let's just send a staffer."

"I'll get someone for you." I headed toward the office door.

"No." Lindsay stopped me. "I don't want—I know her," she said to Tom. "She's discreet."

She did remember me. "Amanda," I said, seizing the opportunity to reintroduce myself. "Head volunteer." I put down the bags to extend my hand to Tom.

"Yes." He shook it firmly. "The Amanda who figured out how to open the window in the bathroom. Your reputation precedes you."

"There was gum on the hinge."

"Well, we're damn glad to have you."

"Happy to be here." I tried to temper my grin.

"We've met before, though, right?"

Eager to get me on my way, Lindsay interrupted him, "Sorry, but, Amanda, I've left Tom's talking points at the luncheon. In the hostess's sitting room—right on her desk, where I set down my bag. One of the programs that . . . I'd rather not have it just sitting around. We have a meeting now or I'd go back. John will take you, but if you could just slip in and grab it we'd be grateful."

"No problem, let me just run these in and—"

"I got it." Tom lifted the bags, his arms dropping. "Oof. You're tough." Lindsay grabbed the blazer draped over his forearm before it hit the asphalt.

"Scrappy," I demurred.

He laughed. "Thanks, Amanda. Seriously."

"Yes, seriously." Lindsay opened the car door for me. "Just bring it by our hotel on your way back if you could."

I happily stepped into the backseat of the sedan, which immediately peeled out. Of course, the minute I replayed the conversation I realized where I was headed. We only had one luncheon host in common—the Westerbrooks. I looked down at my jeans, wishing I were at least wearing a blouse, instead of a T-shirt. But the odds of avoiding Pax were in my favor. It was the middle of a weekday, for God's sake. I figured the guy must have a meeting, golf game, or hangover. Besides, the whole point was to get in and out without drawing attention to the fact that I'd been sent.

John's talk radio droned as he took me over the bridge and under the towering palms. He dropped me at the Westerbrooks' and I slipped into the loop of people breaking down the luncheon. I tucked my head as I made my way quickly through the kitchen to the dining room. Through the wall of French doors I saw a tent off the pool where women milled about air-kissing good-byes. The Westerbrooks were hopefully still out there. And in Pax's case, *out there* out there. Spain, ideally.

Whatever Lindsay assumed, my last visit hadn't seen me past the foyer so I had no idea which room was allotted for Pax's mother to sit. (Mine preferred a busted recliner close enough to the TV to change its channels with her toe.) Planning to dodge behind an urn if necessary, I quickly traversed the grand hallway. I passed a living room, a library with a wall of duck prints, a concert space containing only a grand piano, eventually arriving at a pale coral room that had to be my destination. On one side of the door was a tufted settee facing a marble mantle and on the other, a curving antique desk between sumptuously draped windows that looked out over a shaded patio. The ocean sparkled in the distance. I couldn't imagine what their other houses looked like; what kind of dwellings would make them ever want to leave this one?

Among the sterling desk accessories I found a program from the luncheon and turned it over to see notes scrawled on the back. Suddenly, I heard someone coming. Grabbing the tasseled fringe of the drape, I went to step behind it, but the idea of being discovered hiding there was too mortifying. Across the room I spotted an open archway next to the fireplace. I raced through it only to discover that it was not an exit, but a deep alcove of glass cases. Porcelain figurines were displayed on every shelf, slender women holding infants, picking flowers, dancing. And I was trapped beside them. Stepping back into the shadow, I regretted not just staying put and explaining myself.

"Tom's a doll." In the reflection from the glass cases, I saw Cricket enter the room with Taggart. In a fitted robin's egg suit, she was slipping off her earrings.

"I'm worried we were a little premature throwing him into this. He says what he thinks to a fault and he's so green he'll take advice from damn near anybody," Taggart said gruffly. He dropped in a chair beside her desk and extended his loafers as if to inspect them.

"Isn't that what he's supposed to be doing right now, taking advice?" She slid open a desk drawer and withdrew a leather-bound date book.

"As long as there aren't too many cooks," he mulled. "He does seem to actually believe what he's saying. Haven't seen one of those in a while."

She said something as she perused the binder.

"Mmm," Taggart answered, staring at his lap. "Hot, though."

"It was."

"Not as bad as August."

"No." She flipped through the pages. God, what if they were hunkering in? *Do husbands sit in these rooms for any length of time?* I wondered. *Is that allowed?*

That's when I realized that the couch, with it's floral back to them at the desk, had a person on it. In washed out red pants and a pale pink shirt, he practically blended in. He was sleeping. He was Pax.

"Exactly what I'd thought," Taggart tsked, taking the book from Cricket. "We'll be in Greenwich for the Round Hill dinner."

"If you prefer I can do Round Hill on my own," she said airily in a way that sounded like a deep-seated wish.

I watched Pax's slumbering face. It was completely relaxed and he held a chintz pillow to his chest as if it were a teddy bear.

"No, we'll just cancel the other thing." Taggart frowned.

"Fine," Cricket said to the window. "Whatever you think." They sat like that for a moment, but I wouldn't characterize it as a comfortable silence.

All at once Taggart stood and walked out, shutting the door a little too forcefully, startling Pax awake. His eyes opened, landing directly on mine—like he expected to find me there.

I shrank back as much as the alcove would allow. Pax lifted to dart his eyes over the couch, then jerked back down. Cricket slowly returned the date book to its drawer. Her earrings held in her palm, she opened the French door, sending a waft of salty air into the room. She stepped onto the flagstone patio and clicked the door closed behind her. Pax spun upright. "It is you, right?"

I let out a defeated sigh. "Yes."

The door from the patio opened again, sending Pax leaping in beside me. "Why are we hiding?" he breathed into my ear. He smelled faintly like cologne. I wanted to take a step back—and was simultaneously pleased there was nowhere to step back to.

I shook my head. The door closed again.

"All clear." He pointed to where Cricket had taken a seat on the veranda and was flipping through a magazine on her lap. He pivoted in the alcove to face me, blocking my view. "To what do I owe the pleasure?"

"I'm not here for yours."

"And here I was hoping it was my turn to hide."

He was too good at this. "The Davises sent me. I'm working on the campaign and I was just collecting Mrs. Davis's things from the event."

"Did she leave a Lladró?" He nodded to the figurines behind me. "We have a few to spare."

"Cricket doesn't seem like the type."

"They were the first Mrs. Westerbrook's. Pym insists we keep them right here, but really she thinks they're god-awful—she just does it to torture Cricket. So what are you looking for?"

I lifted the program as if it proved something. "I didn't want to disturb your parents."

"A hurricane couldn't disturb my parents." He looked at me a beat too long.

"Do you often sleep in your mother's sitting room?"

"Is it endearing if I say yes?"

"No."

He grinned. "I'm not a fan of the speeches. It would have been impolite to go to my room."

"Your people's rules don't make any sense."

"But stuffing one kind of bird into another, then deep-frying it, does?"

"Only someone who's never tried a turducken would ask that." I tapped his chest with the edge of the program. Against my better judgment.

He grabbed it. "Wait, so you're working for Davis?"

"Yes." We both held on to the paper. "Volunteering, actually. At the moment. So . . ."

"At the moment," he repeated. His skin was still flushed from sleep, his eyes a little heavy. His hair called out for smoothing. We hadn't been this close, for this long. I wanted to lean in and take his lower lip between my teeth. Which was irrelevant. "Look," he said. "I'm sorry about last time. It was crass."

"It was." Damn it. I didn't expect an apology. "You weren't surprised to wake up and see me standing in this glorified doll closet?"

He shook his head.

"Why?" I pressed.

His cheeks flushed a deeper pink, matching the decor. "Didn't know I'd woken up, I guess." He let out a laugh and then released the program to rub at the back of his neck, averting his eyes.

"Oh," I said. *Oh.* Despite knowing better, the Delilah part of me that had always sought out impossibly happy endings—only in the Dewey Decimal System—wondered if maybe there wasn't some kind of potential here.

I hadn't touched anyone, hadn't been touched, in months. I'd been so good, avoiding the come-ons from the law students, keeping my head down. I just wanted to slip my tongue between his lips, touch his stomach. I wanted to take what he had to offer. Even if that's all it was—especially if that's all it was. I tilted my chin and gave him the glance, an invitation.

A look of discomfort flickered across his face that sent mortification flooding into me, like a syringe had been emptied into my spine.

"Mandy."

"I should get going." I went to step around, but he caught my arm.

"No—I didn't mean—"

"Pax?" It was a girl's voice. I stepped back into the alcove.

"Coming," he called, striding out to head her off.

"What are you doing in here?" she asked, like she'd found him trying on his mother's clothes.

"You know I'm not up for all that."

"You're just like my father," she scolded with familiarity—flirtatiousness. I couldn't not peek. A shiny brown ponytail, a dress in the vein of Cricket's. She straightened his couch-ruffled bangs and then reached up on her pumps to give him a kiss.

He swerved awkwardly and then coughed to cover. "Are you heading out?"

"Pym and I are going to hit a few balls. See you at the club at seven?"

"Great."

"Don't forget to bring your tie this time." She gave him a pointed peck and walked out. He turned to me, but I was sure to speak first.

"She seems like the type who'd insist on a blanket."

His eyes dropped to the floor, his frown reminiscent of Taggart's. "Allison insists on a lot of things."

"Well, good for you," I said as graciously as I could muster.

"I didn't think I was ever going to see you again."

"And now you have. I'll find my way out."

My cheeks were still beating as John pulled into the Davis's hotel on the inter-coastal. I hated showing my hand. *Hated* it. At least he knew I'd gotten myself out of Tallyville. So I could, you know, cower in his house like an idiot.

Allison. I mentally sneered her name, picturing her hitting her balls, her short polish-free nails perfectly aligned on the racquet. If that's what he wanted then whatever. They could sit and discuss where they'd "summer" until they drooled. It's just—he seemed to detest that scene—and then there *she* was, the scene's sorority president. Whatever she meant to him it was enough to keep him from kissing me—the girl who washed her hair in the same sink as her underwear. *The volunteer.* "At the moment." Why had I told him that?

I was so caught up that I didn't take in where I was until

the elevator deposited me on the highest floor and I stepped out onto the landing. The door opened just as I lifted my fingers to knock. Lindsay, wearing an oxford shirt of Tom's over a bathing suit, was backlit by the sun flooding in from the floor-to-ceiling windows lining the vast room behind her. "You got it?" she asked eagerly.

"Yes."

I handed the program to her and she waved it over her head like a winning ticket. "Lesson learned." She ceremoniously ripped it in half and dropped it on the front hall table. "Those women bring out the worst in me."

"Me too," I admitted.

"Phew!" She did a little shudder. "Can I get you some iced tea for the ride back?"

"Maybe a bottle of water?"

"You got it. Come on in." I followed her over to the open kitchen. The patio doors were slid to the side and the lush breeze swept around us. Gauzy curtains lifted up like flicking sails.

"God, this view is amazing. The campaign really set you guys up."

"We got this," she corrected me, handing me a chilled bottle. "Since this is really where the fundraising is happening—we needed a base. Our home is in Jacksonville. But we're thinking about selling it—starting fresh." She gave me a sad smile that conjured the opposite.

"Has Tom always wanted to do this?" I changed the subject to what I assumed was well-trodden ground.

"He's always been passionate about these issues, but I don't know that we imagined it would lead *here*. Not that you can know where anything's leading." She took a breath that looked like it hurt. "Let's just say the phrase 'now or never' suddenly took on a visceral meaning last year."

"They certainly have you booked up," I tried again.

"Oh, I wouldn't have it any other way. I know booked. I worked eighty-hour weeks while trying to make the dance recitals. I tried to keep working, but sitting at that desk the thought at the back of my mind all those years was *I have to get home to Ashleigh.* Sometimes I still space out and accidentally turn into her school parking lot." She made a heartbreaking attempt to smile for my comfort. "So being down here, doing something so wholly *new* feels great. And being a senator's wife—wow, that would be something else entirely. Good, important work to do, snow, seasons. A literal change of scenery."

"Of course." I got it.

Her gaze shifted past me to the water outside. "But yes, this view is amazing," she reminded herself. "Okay!" She pulled her hair up into a ponytail. "Now that the 'avert crisis' box is checked, I'm going to squeeze in a swim before I meet Tom. I'll ride to the lobby with you, just let me grab my cap." She went into the bedroom, and I returned to the front door. As I waited I glanced down at the torn luncheon program, realizing the notes were in two different people's handwriting.

Taggart might be the most boring person we have ever met, Tom wrote in his scrawl.

Yep, Lindsay responded in her graceful script.

She's such a spitfire.

Pay attention!

You think she messes around?

It'd be like fucking a broom handle.

"Amanda."

"Yes!" I straightened as she approached, tucking a dangling dark blond wisp under the white rubber. I wouldn't have wanted Cricket to find those speaking points either.

She stood in front of me, hands on her hips. For a second

I wondered if I was in trouble. "Consider yourself officially employed."

"Really?" I asked, stunned.

"You've more than proven yourself at this point."

"Wow." It took me a second to follow her into the wood-paneled elevator. "I mean, thank you so much. You don't have to clear it with Arthur or Tom or someone?"

She gave me a funny look as she leaned over to hit the button for the lobby. "I've cleared it with me."

I nodded, not breaking into tears of gratitude as we dropped down. Not throwing my arms around her as we parted. And not calling Pax the second I was alone to say that any urge I'd had to find out what we could be had officially passed.

Part II

Chapter
Four

A YEAR AND A HALF LATER AND MY LIFE looked very different. I drove a brand new Ford Focus to Senator Tom Davis's downtown Jacksonville office every day. I had a federal job, the kind I was supposed to wear pantyhose for, with my own cubicle, a row of bobblehead dolls—and health insurance.

I woke every day in my one-bedroom rental wondering when the trappings of my new life would become as mundanely invisible as the trailer's threadbare sofa had once been. When would rolling over on a real bed of my own stop feeling luxurious? Or showering in a bathroom so big it had a vinyl-covered double sink? Every detail was dream-vivid, from the four-burner stove to the shower curtain liner I could afford to replace whenever it got moldy. But it wasn't just dizzy appreciation that made each loop on my Target towels stand out, there was also an anxious compulsion to memorize every detail for when it disappeared, and I tumbled back to Delilah, a fear I couldn't seem to shake.

It had come so close to that in the days after Tom won the election. Most of the staff had peeled off to look for law jobs while the two with the strongest credentials were plucked to move to Washington and run his operation on the hill. I'd spent the final hours dismantling campaign headquarters—piling the unused lawn signs into bags for recycling, untangling and disassembling the phone system we'd rented—wondering how many nights I could survive in my car before I had to turn it toward Tallyville—when Lindsay noticed me taking my clothes and toiletries to my sagging trunk. "Tom!" she'd called out, eyes on mine. "Have we finished staffing Jacksonville yet?"

Those are things you don't forget.

"Mornin', Manda," my colleague, Charlene, said. I used my full name, thinking the extra syllable gave it authority, only to find that up here people had a slightly thicker Southern accent that cut it back down to two.

Charlene had been at the office through three senators and she knew which days you did not want the lunch at the commissary downstairs and how to get the ladies' room serviced when the plumbing failed. With her soft face and size sixteen drip-dry pink suits, she looked like someone who wanted to get back to her nails, but she was ruthless when it came to getting anything done for a constituent. Which could not be said for our colleague, Rufus.

"Senator Davis's office, how may I direct your call?" I heard him answer droopily, his hands pushing the pockets of his cardigan past his knees. He was ostensibly my age but acted like someone's miserable grandfather, like he'd come to Florida just to get a jump-start on his cranky golden years.

"A-man-da." Clive said my name like he was breaking into song, the same way he always did, sliding like Justin Timberlake past my desk, the same way he always slid. "A bunch of us are going for drinks after work—want to come?"

"Oh, I'd love to but I have plans." It was the same excuse I gave every Friday. Clive, with his chin dimple and sapphire eyes, could not understand it. Only a few months out of Yale he had been talked into taking the position by his father, who considered Tom Davis as a good a rung as any to start Clive's own political climb. But Clive was unfortunately a little hampered in the impression-making department by the fact that he thought pretty much the entire state of Florida was beneath him, with the exception of me, who he was determined to get beneath him. For some reason he behaved as if the office were a desert island and he and I were therefore obligated to perpetuate the species. I'm sure I was the first girl to shrug off his offer.

"Yeah, I'm not going to stay out late." He tried to backpedal into casual. "I have the kids in the morning," referring to the boys he mentored in a basketball program for children with incarcerated parents. "Can't let them down."

"No," I agreed.

"Okay."

"Okay." I smiled, letting him walk away baffled once again.

Most likely, given the long hours and meager singles scene in Jacksonville, I wouldn't have turned him down, but I had a covert vantage point. It was strange in such a small office that he didn't know that I was the admin to whom our e-mail-monitoring firm forwarded all flagged material. I knew that after mentoring said kids he was going to go back to his place and "beat off to Alexis Texas." I knew that he called his dad a pussy and that only the day before he'd told his old roommate from Yale that he wanted to "spluge" on my face.

As long as he didn't engage in illegal activity, or anything that could harm Tom's reputation, I didn't need to take action. Not going out for drinks was action enough.

"Hello?" I picked up a call transferred to my desk.

"Drinks tonight?" It was Rebecca. She worked for a real estate law firm a floor above and we'd met in the salad bar line my first week. I hadn't really had close friends growing up. Not knowing who my daddy was meant the girls whose daddies had run off could put me below them on the pecking order of shit. Delilah said they were just jealous of my looks—whatever the reason I learned early on to avoid them. So I was surprisingly delighted to discover that Rebecca was actually "Becky" from a flyswatter of a town and she was also determined to live a food stamp-free life. I didn't have to sugarcoat anything with her.

"Strong ones," I answered. "And burgers. Meet you downstairs." The light on my phone blinked and I jumped calls.

"Are you sending her money?" Grammy's opener wiped the smile off my face like she had reached out with one of her starched handkerchiefs.

"No."

"Amanda Beth, don't you lie to me."

"I'm sending money for Ray Lynne, but that's not the same." Almost a year old, Ray Lynne had been a tough baby, hard to soothe, a light sleeper.

So I dreaded Delilah's calls—always late at night, her voice small and flat, Ray Lynne inconsolable in the background. Billy couldn't possibly sleep through it. "Just twenty bucks. For Pampers, Mandy," she'd ask, and I knew she was staring straight ahead, getting through the request, same as me.

"Amanda," Grammy's voice broke in exasperation. "She will never take responsibility if you make this easy on her." Nothing about those calls was easy for either of us. "She needs to learn how to hold onto a job."

"She will never take responsibility—"

"Exactly," she said. "It's foolish, you wasting your hard-earned money."

"I was going to say no matter what you or I do." I tried to reassure us both that I was doing the right thing. "That's my other line, can I call you tonight?"

"Okay." She sounded like she was trying to calm herself. "You get back to work."

"I'll call you later, I promise." I disconnected, my vision flattening. This wasn't going to get any easier as Ray Lynne got older; I knew that much from Billy. The more I took care of her—even from a distance—the more care I would be expected to take.

I pulled out my phone to stare at my bank account. I believed there was a number high enough that would put me at ease, enough money not to be broadsided by Delilah's miscalculations, but whatever it was I wasn't anywhere near it. I'd lived my whole life in a state devoted to vacation; I wondered if I would ever know what it was like to take one. The persistent red light flashing on the desk phone had me leaning toward no.

"Hello?" I said, answering the call.

"Amanda, it's Lindsay Davis."

"Mrs. Davis." I sat straighter. "How are you?"

"No one should have twins at forty-five. This was a terrible, terrible idea."

I could hear their wailing as I took a quick swig of coffee to regroup. "I'm so sorry. Can I help you?"

"My nanny hurt her back. She can't come in. She can't send anyone. She may, I realize as I'm saying this, be quitting. I would quit. I would like to quit." Her voice bounced as she spoke, and I heard that familiar pause of a mom switching her kid to her other hip. "Chip has been up for three nights. Collin has an ear infection. I'm so tired my skin hurts. It wasn't like this with—" She paused. "Before. She was so easy." Lindsay made a long breathy *haaah* sound. "I promised myself I would never say stuff like that, wouldn't compare, but I am so fucking tired."

"How can I help?"

"I'm supposed to leave for the airport in five hours if I'm going to make Tom's supporter dinner tonight. My friends are busy with a luncheon and my parents are travelling." She was thinking it through as she spoke. "I can't leave the boys with someone they don't know—we'll all have to go together. In the tiny plane. Shit. How can I call the agency with them sobbing their guts out in the background—who would come? Please. Help me find someone."

I knew how to do this—I'd been doing it forever. "I could go with you."

"What?"

"Trust me. I know everything there is to know about toddlers in confined spaces."

Lindsay had been all set to move with Tom to DC when he was elected, but they discovered the pregnancy within days of his win and she was put on bed rest shortly thereafter. Once the twins arrived, she'd opted to stay close to her mother and friends as she found her parenting footing afresh.

For the first year Tom had shared a place with a few congress-men who also had young children and flew home a lot, but in June he'd found an apartment of his own and the staff had worked around the clock for a weekend to get it set up.

I'm not sure what I was expecting the Davis Riverside house to look like. It was not small, certainly, not by Tallyville standards. But tiny compared with anything else in the neighborhood. And they seemed to be bursting out of it like a roasting tomato.

She met me in the foyer, which was crowded with toys and strollers. "Come on in." She looked around, the way you do when someone arrives for the first time, seeing messes that had blurred into camouflage. She stepped backward, bumping her calves into a plastic music table. "God, yes, we should clear some of these out of here." I looked up at the wall, where someone had rolled stripes of paint, testing shades of earth tones. "Oh, yes, that."

"Are you repainting? I like that mushroom color." It had a check mark on it—it seemed to be the winner.

"We'd thought we'd maybe—well . . ." She lifted her hands into her hair. "It's a few years old to be truthful. Every year we thought we'd move. But I was working and Ashleigh had band and then Ashleigh had PSAT prep, then SAT tutoring—every year it seemed like something. And even though Tom—we had more money—I just didn't know where I'd find the time, because you know it's all on the wives. I'd be the one looking at houses, ordering the movers. So we decided when Ashleigh started college I'd make the time." She looked away. "Now we can't bear to be here and can't bear to leave. But you're helping, right?" Her voice brightened. She scooped up Chip and blew a raspberry on his cheek. "And this time—I'm not missing a second of this." She looked exhausted. Worse than any day on the campaign. Her hair was dirty. Her robe had stains on it.

"Here." I held out my arms for him. "Let me take them and you go get ready."

I took the kids into the living room, which was filled with even more rainbow-colored plastic. Two of everything. Collin had been a pound bigger at birth and the differences were obvious. Chip was excited to try walking by holding onto the couch. Collin just wanted to bang things together—a rattle with the coffee table, a book with my leg, a plastic block with Chip's head. Collin was either going to go grow up to be an abuser or a cage fighter.

"Okay, I think that's the last of it," Lindsay said. After we got everything loaded into the front hall, I saw that same Hello Kitty pencil case sticking out of her tote. Lindsay must have noticed me staring at it. "Ashleigh gave it to me for a business trip when she was little—of course I didn't use it. I had a Chanel one. I was a grown-up. I found it after." The limo honked, saving me from figuring out what to say to that.

The plane belonged to a donor of Tom's who had put it at his disposal. Despite its walnut paneling and "concierge," it was no bigger than a tube of toothpaste and I quickly went from feeling thrilled that my first flight ever was going to be private to wishing we were in a cargo plane. Especially since the accoustics were magnifying Chip's screams as if he were shouting down a paper towel tube. The upside was that trying to keep the kids from drinking their bottles before takeoff so they'd drink during takeoff distracted me until we'd suddenly reached our cruising altitude, the air thinned, and the twins passed out.

Then I realized Lindsay was crying on the seat across from me. "Don't mind me." She swished her palm in front of her face. "I'm overwhelmed and perimenopausal."

I handed her a cocktail napkin.

"Thank you for handling Teddy Huvane's septic issue," she said as she blew her nose. "He's an old friend of Tom's from law school."

"No problem. I was happy to help."

The city of Miami had declared eminent domain and had dug a trench on Teddy's property to run a gas line—severing his septic line in the process. But then the city tried to say it was the county's problem; the county said it was the city. Teddy was going in circles and about three seconds from building an outhouse on the mayor's lawn. Then I remembered seeing an article in the Miami Herald about how the mayor had a thing for Sharon Stone, who was scheduled to testify in Congress about funding stroke research. I got him flown up and Tom made the introduction. The mayor expressed his gratitude by fixing Huvane's septic line.

"Charlene says you're indispensible."

"Aw, that's sweet."

Lindsay dabbed at her eyes. "She has never once paid anyone a compliment so don't dismiss it."

"Thank you."

"I'm sorry you're always seeing me when I'm a hot mess."

"You are not a hot mess," I answered, stunned she could see herself that way as she sat there in her khaki cigarette pants and a fitted blazer with contrasting trim. Even with the thirty or so extra pounds from her pregnancy she was effortlessly chic. The children were wearing color-coordinated outfits. Everything I'd helped her pack in their diaper bags was organic. "My mom is a hot mess. You are super together."

She considered me for a moment. "I bet your mom is beautiful."

Simultaneously flattered and embarrassed, I knew any mention of my appearance from a woman feeling underwhelmed by her own was a hot stove. "My mom never got anyone elected."

"Speaking of which, can you pass me that black duffle? I need to go through the briefing binders. People are really loving Tom, but he needs to be more strategic right now if he wants to propose his own bills later in the session. Aligning himself with the senators who have the ear of the president might have to take priority over voting along party lines."

"Can I look?" I asked as she reached into the bag, not sure if they were confidential.

"Of course! I didn't know you had an interest in the actual nuts and bolts of policy."

"Well, I want to be useful. While I love Charlene, I don't necessarily want to *be* Charlene—staying the same while everything and everyone around me moves on." I took a risk admitting this to her.

She slid her glasses on. "I doubt that could ever happen to you, Amanda."

Tom was stuck in meetings so Lindsay and I schlepped the kids through the sweltering evening heat to his new apartment off Dupont Circle. I held Chip in the elevator as we all cooled off and Collin tried to walk up Lindsay's leg.

"Have you seen it yet?" I asked.

Lindsay shook her head while Collin made another run at her. "I want to start spending more time up here—I thought I could handle them on my own in Jacksonville, but I—well, I can't. And we miss each other. It's too hard to be apart for so long." She smiled and shrugged. "So I told him we need a family place in DC starting this summer and here we finally are. I think this is going to be good." She nodded to herself the way tired people do. "I think it's going to be a fresh start."

Lindsay opened the apartment door while I dragged out the bags and car seats. Then she kind of froze in the entryway, looking back down at the keys in confusion.

"Mrs. Davis?" I asked as the kids toddled in ahead of us—Collin heading straight for the glass coffee table with the shiny metal sculpture at its center. It was flanked by leather couches facing an enormous flat screen perched on a dangerously low console. Other than the framed pictures of Lindsay and the kids, with its parquet floor, galley kitchen, framed sports jerseys, and wobbly standing lamps, it was an unremarkable bachelor pad.

"I'm just . . ." She didn't finish as her eyes landed on the photo of Tom hugging her on election night. "Okay, so this *is* . . ." She walked to the door off the living room, opening it to a small bedroom while I headed off Collin. The next door opened to the bathroom and the last to a linen closet. "Can we at least get the AC on," she said sharply. "I feel like I'm having a panic attack."

I'd *never* seen her this thrown before, not even when we met as she miscarried.

"Hey!" We turned as Tom brought the last of our bags in from the hall, his face glowing with excitement. "I'm so sorry I couldn't meet you at the airport, babe. How was the flight?" Suddenly the full picture of what he was seeing seemed to register. "What are *you* guys doing here?" He dropped his blazer, scooped up Chip, and nestled his face into his neck, making him squeal in delight.

"Didn't they give you my messages? Carla quit." Lindsay tapped her knuckles on the glass dining table. "I thought we agreed on a two or three-bedroom place."

"Linds." He pulled her into him with his free arm and planted a kiss on her forehead. "I didn't want to be rattling around in something big all by myself during the week. It's bad enough not having you here."

"What if you weren't by yourself?" she asked.

"Huh?"

"What if we came up more?"

He looked around, but it wasn't clear for what. "Let's discuss it later. So, what's the plan? We bringing them to dinner?"

Chip was practicing his shout, and Collin had found the remote control and was banging it on the coffee table. Lindsay bent to replace the remote with a toy from her pocket. "Amanda, here, has come to my rescue. She's going to stay with the kids tonight and— shoot, Amanda, I thought there'd be a room for you. For them."

"Sorry, I didn't know. Let's see . . ." He looked around. "That couch pulls out."

"Oh, great," she said sarcastically.

"That's so fine for me, I swear," I said. "And I can make a bed for the kids out of pillows and blankets."

"That'd be great, Amanda," Tom said.

Lindsay turned to him. "What happened to the toys I had sent up? I gave Rhonda the link to the cribs I wanted."

Tom was kissing Collin's ears and making him giggle. "I don't know, honey. Talk to Rhonda."

Rhonda Johnson ran Tom's staff and life with a relentlessness bordering on zealotry. In the Jacksonville office we frequently compared time stamps on her e-mails, marveling that she was reminding us at 3:00 a.m. to be sure Tom's lucky suit made it back on the plane with him or that he wasn't to be spotted eating a burger the weekend before the Safe Foods Act went to the floor.

"I will," Lindsay said.

"I better shower." He placed Chip gently back on the parquet.

"You all set?" Lindsay asked me. "Take anything from the fridge, assuming there is anything, and we'll order in for you guys before we leave." She followed him into the bedroom while I tried to pry Collin's hands off an ashtray. "I saw you on C-SPAN yesterday," she said, the thin wall barely muffling her voice.

"What did you think? Too strident? Those guys had to be called out. I'm sorry, but they did."

"And Jon Stewart showed a clip of you last night."

"Yeah, I know. I'm official now."

"You're getting better, but I think you could be punching the jobs angle harder. I made some notes on the briefs you left at the house."

"Honey, I have advisers covering that sort of thing for me now," he said wearily. "Can we just relax and have a nice night? Do the feedback thing later. I just missed you so fucking much."

I could hear them kiss and looked around for a stereo. But a few seconds later, he came out wrapped in a towel and went catty-corner into the bathroom with a disarmingly embarrassed wave to me. I know perhaps I should have been feeling awkward for being there, but growing up in a trailer, then babysitting in others, I was used to being present for things I shouldn't have been, because there wasn't really anywhere else for them to be happening.

Tom and Lindsay were the blue print for everything I wanted to have one day—right down to a deep attraction undiminished by miscommunication. Discovering that they sometimes annoyed each other yet were still together after twenty plus years just made me love them more.

"Hello, Rhonda." I heard Lindsay on her phone as soon as the shower turned on. "Fine, thank you. I just wanted to see why none of the things for the twins that I e-mailed you about ended up in the apartment . . . No, I appreciate that Tom had instructions, but if those instructions conflict with my instructions in the future I'd appreciate you notifying me so we can all be the on the same page. I do not like surprises." She took a staggered breath as she listened. "Look, let's just be frank. I know you think I'm the stupid wife who cares about nothing more important than where her children sleep, but until I got pregnant *his* schedule was planned around *mine*. I edited every speech, set the campaign's agenda, and sat in on every hiring interview—including yours—so I'd appreciate a modicum of respect. Terrific. Bitch." I assume Rhonda had already hung up.

They came home late and tipsy. I kept my eyes closed, a reflex from growing up sleeping five feet from the front door. "They love you, Tom. It's that simple. They love you. You're the future of the party—you heard him—the future of the party."

"I'll be the hangover after the party if we don't get some sleep."

"You sure you're tired?" she asked flirtatiously.

"Yes, honey, I'm sorry, but I am dead on my feet." He kissed her. "Rain check?"

"You know where to find me."

In the morning, using my socks and lip gloss to make puppets, I tried to keep the kids quiet, but it was like throwing my body on a landmine. "What time did you order the plane for?" Tom asked as he made coffee and Collin somehow spilled the beans all over the floor.

"You know, honey," Lindsay answered, scrambling with me to sweep them up before any found their way into the twins' mouths. "I think I'm gonna send Amanda home by herself today."

"Great! You guys should definitely stay the weekend. I have a ton of briefs to read, but we could take them to the zoo if it's not too hot. And maybe Rhonda could find us a sitter and I can take you for a drink on the water—"

"No, Tom, I mean I think we should stay. Monday I'll get us a nanny and a realtor. Let's do this for real, Mr. Future of the Party. We should be here for you."

"Oh, okay, that's—wow, yes, terrific." The beans crunched underfoot as he tried to hug her.

Generously, Lindsay insisted I take the private plane back. As soon as I boarded I put my feet up, downed my warm nuts, and called Becky. After quoting the end of *Working Girl*—"Guess where I am"—I shared my news. "Lindsay wants me to 'manage' the move."

"That sounds like housework." she said.

"Well, yes, but, honestly, I don't think it works that way in politics. It seems like it's all hands on deck 24-7 to make their lives happen. I mean, Clive said when Tom moved into that apartment that he had guys with master's degrees in economic policy schlepping his sports trophies up the back stairs."

"Okay, I do not know this world."

"I don't either, really. But now I've seen Tom Davis in a towel, so I have to be easing into the inner circle, right? And trust is currency." I dug for the last cashew. "But I *need* chances to prove myself. If Lindsay moves up to DC—she's my only real connection, I could end up marooned in Jacksonville."

"Hey," she said sharply.

"I just meant professionally."

"I get it. Steal me a tiny ketchup bottle, uppity cow."

"Will do."

I was still ruminating about the potential implications of Lindsay's request when the plane landed. I climbed down the stairs to the hangar with Becky's souvenir ketchup in my purse.

"Well, I'll be."

I spun around. "Pax Westerbrook." I smiled, putting my hands on my hips. He was loading his bag into the hold of a small plane opposite. He still looked like an ad—only now it was something more like a Breitling—the kind of thing where a guy in a white button-down and reflective shades walks a blazing tarmac.

"Amanda Luker. I see life has been kind."

"What? Oh, this?" I pointed behind me. "I just clean it."

He laughed. "Same Amanda."

"Not remotely."

He looked me over, taking me in. "Where's home these days?"

"Twenty minutes from here down 295," I said as the Davis town car pulled in to get me. I really could not have improved the moment if I'd had the ear of God himself.

"Listen, I was just up here for the morning to see some clients, but I'll be back in two weeks—can I take you to dinner? Please?"

I was sure if I'd been privy to his e-mails I'd probably have unearthed things that would make Clive seem like a Cub Scout, but I wasn't. All I had was Pax's smile and the way he looked at me. And after the humiliation of our last encounter, I wanted him to see that I'd worked my way up to being—well, if not quite an equal—at least someone who could buy her own dress.

It was champagne-colored cotton—the dress I chose—with gold thread woven around the hem. It was stunning, but casual, the kind of thing a woman wears when she wants to look like she didn't get a pedicure, a leg wax, or spend a little time in the sun on her lunch hour the day before.

Pax had suggested a restaurant on the water in nearby St. Augustine, a beautiful resort town with the distinction of being the oldest city in the United States—first settled in 1565. I'd been there for a couple of Davis fundraisers where I was stationed with my clipboard outside buildings that looked like they'd been picked up from Europe and plunked down here by tornado. I was a little excited to see what going inside one felt like.

I spent the drive on the phone with Lindsay, confirming the background checks on her nanny candidates, commiserating about her first DC broker, who had the weird habit of saying, "I'm knocking this out of the park," when she wasn't, and reassuring her that I'd personally gone around Rhonda and ordered a set of briefing binders for her that would arrive first thing Monday morning. Ever since I'd flown back from DC, we talked on the phone five or six times a day. Lindsay was becoming like a friend—one who I was desperate to impress. I'd have run to DC with her family pictures strapped to my back if she'd asked.

"Where's he taking you?" Lindsay said.

"It's called The Reef."

"Romantic. That's right on the water. Good for him."

"I'm a little nervous."

"Don't be. He's lucky you're even giving him an hour of your time. Call me tomorrow when you know when the new mattress is being delivered." Whatever bed Tom had bought was slowly putting Lindsay into traction.

"On it." As I hung up I wondered why Rhonda had never sent Lindsay the binders. Had Tom told her not to? I pulled into the parking lot and handed the valet my key. I was nervous about what to do until Pax arrived, but then I spotted his broad back on a barstool. "Hey." I hopped up next to him, surreptitiously swiping my damp palms on my dress.

"Hey." He smiled his beautiful smile, and I felt that same electrified punch I always felt. Part of me just wanted him to take my hand, lead me back out to his car, and rip my not-trying dress off.

"May I show you to your table?" A woman appeared beside

us with menus and he picked up his glass so we could follow. She seated us by the window right on the beach. Like his smile, the ocean was something that never lost its potency for me.

"So, how are you, Amanda Luker?" he asked as he perused the menu.

"Well, I'm not sharing a bed in shifts so that's a start."

"Did you really do that?"

I nodded emphatically. "South Beach. We rotated every eight hours based on who was covering nights and who was on breakfast. It was—Russian."

He laughed. "Is that where your family's from?"

"God, no, I don't think we're from anywhere but here. America, I mean. We probably brought people room service on the Mayflower. No, I went on a Russian lit jag junior year." He raised his eyebrows. "It might seem like the farthest thing from Florida you can imagine, but actually a subdivided Moscow apartment and a double-wide have more in common than you'd think."

He laughed again and reached for his drink. "So who was smart enough to snap you up?"

"Tom Davis."

"No—still? That's great."

"I'm in his Jacksonville office and I'm helping Mrs. Davis with the transition to Washington." Despite the fact that it had been two years, I still relished finally telling him.

"Introducing her around, that kind of thing?"

"Sending her underwear north, that kind of thing." As grateful as I was for us to re-meet with a private plane behind me I was never going to put on airs for him. "But I love my job. I never knew it was possible to love a job so much. I mean, in Tallyville work was just what you got through till you could go drinking, but now I can't wait to get in every day. I'm learning so much about how to actually get things done for people—three weeks ago we passed a tax proposal in the state legislature to incentivize Disney to open another park. And it's everything from that to protection for the citrus farmers to the Burmese python epidemic to stronger unions for hotel workers." I smiled, my confidence regained. "So where have you planted your flag?"

He grimaced. "You know what, let's order first." He waived the waitress back over, then, without consulting me, asked for another vodka stinger, a bottle of champagne, the seafood tower—with a wink to me—and the surf and turf for two.

"Is that how you impress the ladies?" I asked as the waitress retreated. "What if I was a vegetarian now?"

"I'd expect you to politely pick on the side dishes."

"Is that what Allison did?" I shot back.

"Wow, good memory. Allison is a girl who likes to be taken care of," he said. The present tense was not lost on me. Was this a date or just a makeup for the makeup?

"So, how's Pym?" I changed the subject as the waitress showed Pax the champagne label.

"Effortlessly running the charity social scene in three cities. It's funny, because with all her education and commendations, she doesn't really work. She buys dresses that make her look thoroughly unfuckable, she's photographed wearing those dresses, and she raises money from other people who want to be photographed wearing dresses. But Taggart thinks she is the fucking second coming." He tasted the champagne, then nodded his approval.

I wondered if he'd felt this hostility to Pym two years ago—and I'd missed it. Or perhaps it had grown.

"She gets an alcohol sponsor to donate a case," Pax continued, "or some friend to donate a signed football to the silent auction and Taggart acts like she's just split his stocks."

"Well, there's something to be said for trying to be the best at what interests you—I mean, at least she's not half-assing it." I smiled. "How's James?".

"Cricket's already looking at boarding schools." He emptied half his glass without even pausing to toast.

"Oh. Did you go to boarding school?"

"She popped me in for a year when she first met Taggart, but then she pulled me out again when she needed someone to talk to at dinner."

"And James doesn't make small talk?"

"James is Taggart's mini-me," he said by way of an answer.

As the waitress delivered our seafood tower, my phone rang. "Forgive me," I said.

"Tom?" he asked.

"My other boss." I twisted away in my seat. "Billy?"

"Is chicken supposed to be pink on the inside?"

"No."

"It's not like a burger?" he asked.

"No, it's not like a burger."

"I told Lyle it was like a burger."

"Billy, did you eat raw chicken?"

"Just a little. I'm fine."

"You don't sound fine."

There was a short pause before he spoke. "I just need to sweat it out."

"What time is Delilah getting home?"

"Let me check the stars and give you an estimate," he quoted Grammy.

"Ugh. She have Ray Lynne with her?"

"Neighbor's gonna drop her off in a few. I'm *fine*, Mandy." All of ten years old, he was still feisty, like I had called and interrupted *his* evening.

"I know you are. You keep me posted, okay?"

"Okay."

I turned back to Pax. "One more second." I dialed Delilah.

"To what do I owe the honor?" she answered.

I tucked my head and put my hand over my mouth. "Your son is about five minutes from having undercooked chicken coming out both ends."

"He's just being dramatic because I said he couldn't go out on the nights I needed him to watch Ray Lynne."

"Mom, he sounds bad."

"Mandy, I need the tips—Saturday's my big night."

"Never mind. I'll call Grammy."

"Don't you dare." She all but reached down the line to slap me. "I have this under control."

"That's what Billy said." I hung up and turned back to Pax a second time. "I am so sorry. One last call. Grammy?" I said as soon as she answered. "I need a favor." I wasn't totally sure how it was my favor when I was the one three hundred miles away, but I begged her to go anyway. She didn't like being at the trailer park after sunset. "Just have Billy call me when you get there, okay?"

I turned back to find Pax with a bemused smile on his face. It reminded me of the people around the hotel pool who would watch the guys trimming the hedges like they were an exhibit. "What?"

"Nothing. You just . . . uh . . .have a lot going on."

"All in a day. So, what *are* you doing?" I saw that he'd finished another glass while I'd been triaging.

"Second-in-command at Westerbrook Equities, Palm Beach branch." He was talking to his empty plate. "I've finished my Series 7—rocked it—and I'm thinking b-school in a few years." He suddenly sounded like somebody else, like he'd gained twenty pounds and twenty years between sentences.

"So you're getting along with Rodger?"

At that name his head sprung up. "That asshole wanted to push me out, so I just shoved myself in his face." He punched the air with the heel of his hand. "I'm sitting on his bed when he wakes up in the morning, I lie across his desk all day, and if he goes to take a shit I hand him the paper."

"Vivid."

He shrugged and I noticed his cheeks were flushing. "It worked. Reluctant respect. He said in a few more months he'll feel comfortable recommending to Taggart that I'm transferred to the New York office so I can apply to Columbia and Stern." He made the schools sound like prisons.

"That's great."

He scowled, his face suddenly ugly, like when Billy was trying to get me to yell at him because what he really needed to do was yell back. But this wasn't Billy.

"Yeah." He refilled his glass, polishing off the bottle. "I thought about what you said."

"You did?"

"About the opportunities I have."

"Oh. Right."

"And I've been ramming my dick down their throats ever since."

I nodded. Not only were my lips pressed together and arms crossed but I had also wrapped my legs closed, down to my twisted ankles. The only thing left to do was either lift the metal tray and use it as a deflector against his vitriol, or pull my napkin over my head and hope he forgot I was there until he drank himself under the table. I wondered if he was as boorish with Alison.

"Pax?"

"Yes?"

"I'm going to the ladies'—don't get up." Although he wasn't.

I walked straight out the door and handed the valet my ticket.

It was a highly unclassy thing I was doing, but it had been a highly unclassy encounter, despite the lighting and the music, the bubbles and brine.

"Ugh," I said out loud as I waited for my car. Pax had been adrift, and now he was going hell-for-leather toward a career that blatantly made him miserable. For a second, I felt bad for him again, because maybe he didn't have anyone in his life to tell him that, and maybe I should go back in and Jiminy Cricket his ass.

But then I thought of all the sad sacks I'd had to have breakfast with over the years, the talks Mom gave them over Froot Loops about getting their shit together, and I realized that Pax Westerbrook was not where I should be putting my energy. Lindsay was right—he had been lucky to get an hour of my time.

I would drive straight to the Davises and spend the night finishing their packing.

Chapter Five

It was New Years Day of a presidential election year and everyone working in politics was about to start obsessively handicapping every contest coast to coast, district to district. Gambling addicts loitering around the track have nothing on minions inside the beltway.

If the Republican incumbent, President Gaitlin won reelection, then Tom and the other Democrats' ability to affect change would continue to be stymied. But my attention was shamefully elsewhere. While my colleagues set up betting pools on potential front-runners and forwarded the latest parody videos around the bullpen, I was preoccupied with cookies.

Cookies.

And I just wanted to stop.

In fourth grade Delilah was in a grueling "between things" stretch, and I decided, in order to help myself hang in being her daughter, I needed to create an incentive system. The idea occurred to me while reading *How to Eat Fried Worms,* in which a nerdy kid gets himself to do exactly that by setting his mind to triumph over his bullies. By doing odd jobs around the park, I managed to buy myself two boxes of Nabisco Pinwheels and hide them beneath the couch. After school, if the antenna—and her boyfriend—were working, I'd watch an hour of soaps, struggle through homework and then, at 5:00 p.m., take one chocolaty wheel from the package. Twisting the marshmallow from the cookie, I'd savor both like I was being filmed for a commercial.

For a whole month I had something to look forward to that was under my control. In the sweltering, overcrowded, rowdy classroom and then on that bus crammed three kids to a seat, all that mattered was the clock ticking closer to my prize. A cookie was waiting. Until the day my fingers reached the end of the package, at which point my resolve deflated like a sliced Mylar balloon.

The date with Pax had left me with that finished-package feeling, which surprised me—I hadn't realized I'd been saving the idea of him as some sort of prize for myself.

But, I discovered, as I dreamed about him night after night, he was somehow enmeshed in the Scarlett-O'Hara-gripping-the-earth moment I'd had at the post office a few years back. The end of the hope of having him disoriented me. *And we didn't even hook up.* I hadn't gotten to eat the cookie and somehow I had eaten the cookie.

Which led me, on the heels of that crappy dinner in St. Augustine, to the bartender with the surfer abs who was as eager to have a girlfriend as I was to be one. We always went to his place and I was always happy to wake up in my own. Plus, keeping our daylight interaction to a minimum helped me deal with the fact that conversation was not what he was bringing to the table.

Lindsay dubbed him the "Bodtender" as the two of us sliced Davis family photos out of bubble wrap in her new Georgetown home. She asked if I ever wanted more. I told her the truth: I didn't want to be distracted. "Good for you," she said approvingly. My chest inflated with pride like a damp sock on a blow-dryer. Her "good-for-yous" felt like chisel cuts incrementally uncovering my legitimacy.

It had taken a string of Sundays marching through fusty old homes before Lindsay finally found their new place. It looked like any other DC townhouse from the street, but the previous owner had removed the back wall and replaced it with glass facing a yard for the boys to romp through. In addition to the furniture, Lindsay ordered a new set of everything—bedding, linens, lamps. It seemed like what she needed most was to fill this house with items that had yet to conjure any memories. They did, however, come with cardboard. A forest of cardboard. We unpacked so many delivery cartons that fall, it felt like we worked in a stockroom.

Even after the last box was flattened and bundled at the end of the drive that Christmas, I still made the trip at least once a week, shuttling between the Davis's worlds in a trench coat that felt alternately flimsy and stifling at opposite ends of the journey.

Yet, tiring as it was, I loved hanging up the phone or stepping back onto the jet knowing the results of my efforts had an obviously stabilizing affect on their family, giving Lindsay the foundation to support Tom, who provided order to others. What's more, Lindsay welcomed my solutions and acted on my suggestions. She wasn't counting on my babysitting money—she was counting on *me*.

By Super Tuesday Senator Charles Merrick of Maine was far ahead of the other Democratic hopefuls, all of whom had stumbled at some point like stallions hitting potholes. But while his pedigree was impeccable, Merrick's patrician demeanor quickly became an unanticipated challenge. He blathered on in front of the cameras like a professor happy to lecture an empty chair, stumping even the most accomplished image consultants. The search was on for a vice-presidential running mate with the interpersonal skills that Merrick was missing.

It wasn't long before the twenty-four hour news networks started floating Tom's name. They agreed that what he lacked in experience he more than made up for in charisma and pithiness. He could fold up a talking point like a paper airplane and sail it into a slogan. And, most importantly, he was southern, born and beloved in a pivotal swing state.

Suddenly, the election had my full attention. Of course I was excited that Tom could be, as they said, "a heartbeat away from the presidency." But I was personally terrified because if he became VP he'd be replaced as senator in a special election by someone who would bring his own staff—which would leave me unemployed in politics with no college education. And I was still sending Delilah money every month for Ray Lynne, money I should have been putting aside for night school.

Tom warned us that we weren't to get caught up in the "search soap opera," but it was impossible not to think he was being road tested. In May his schedule rapidly filled with campaign events. The Davis staff found ourselves at the beck and call of Merrick's advisers, which was not dissimilar to when Mom dated the married guy with the car dealership. If Merrick fancied fly-fishing at the asscrack of dawn, the Davises were there with their waders on. If Merrick wanted to see how climate change policy would play in the Midwest, he had Tom introduce it in a speech that could tank *his* career.

But no confirmation. For every event with Tom, Merrick also appeared in public with the governor of Iowa and Congressman Ramirez from California, who could deliver the Latino vote. The office was so tense that Clive broke out in hives. Then in early June Tom and Lindsay flew home to host a fundraiser dinner for Merrick in Jacksonville. It was after midnight by the time I got the campaign materials back to the office. Nearly one in the morning by the time I got home. I was just brushing my teeth when the phone rang. "Did I wake you?" Lindsay asked tentatively.

"Not at all."

"And you're not with the Bodtender?"

"Definitely not."

She sighed. "I thought with the kids in D.C. I was going to sleep for fourteen hours straight, but I can't even close my eyes."

"I'm sorry. Maybe a Tylenol PM?"

"Merrick's camp asked Tom to stay for a drink after the fundraiser," she hedged. "I'm kind of coming out of my skin."

I spat my toothpaste. "How can I help?"

She was waiting at her front door in navy pajamas, holding out a glass of wine for me. "Oh, I'm good," I demurred.

"Amanda, you drove over here in the dead of night so I can get a grip. At least let me give you a drink."

I took a polite sip and set it down on the entry table with my wallet and keys. "So, we're getting a grip?"

"Look at this." She pointed at the neglected paint samples still striping the foyer wall. "This house makes me want to put a pillow over my head and ask you to hold it."

"That'd get a no."

"I'm so glad you're here. Come upstairs. There's just so much to be sorted, so much to be given away." All the lamps were on in their bedroom and CNN was muted. The contents of her walk-in closet were laid out on every surface.

"Wow."

She pointed at each pile. "The suits I wore pre-twins. Those dresses—I could starve myself for a year and *maybe* fit one thigh in. The era of bathing suits is definitely out for the foreseeable future."

"I'll get some bags from the kitchen."

"Great."

I ran down to where the counter held bins of mostly junk mail that I'd been collecting for them over the last months. I grabbed a box of garbage bags and jogged up the stairs as Lindsay emerged from her closet with an armful of jeans.

"Load number one," she called and dumped them in. "Everything on the bench goes, too." Rolling up her sleeves, she pulled out every dresser drawer and even went through their ski clothes, becoming, as one does on such a mission, more ruthless in her tossing with every mounting pile. We filled five bags and were half way through the sixth when she came out of her closet with a massive box. "My wedding dress," she said, blowing an errant hair from her face.

"Oh, you should keep that."

"One of my future daughters-in-law might want to make a tablecloth out of it?"

"Definitely," I said as I followed her into the hall. She balanced the box against the wall while fumbling to open the door across from her bedroom.

"Oh, here!" I grabbed the box just before it dropped. The door gave way and the hall light spilled onto the pink carpet, and the end of a four-poster bed. Lindsay, who had been in motion since my arrival, suddenly froze. She took a half step back, her chest visibly rising. She blinked for a moment.

"You don't have to sort everything tonight," I said quietly.

"Where will you bring all this?" she asked into the darkness, the way one distracts a child with mundane questions as all hell is breaking loose.

"Goodwill. There's a drop box around the corner."

"Do they still have those Dress for Success programs? Give-the-homeless-a-suit-so-they-can-get-a-job sort of thing?"

I didn't say that they weren't all homeless. That some had perfectly fine trailers and just needed to look decent for an interview at the car dealership where they'd end up dating the owner. "Yes, I mean, they did in Tallyville."

"They don't need cocktail dresses. That's something Nancy would do," she said, meaning Merrick's wife, the heir to a cattle fortune. "You take them."

"Me?"

"Yes, take the cocktail dresses. You're the right size."

I was two sizes smaller but I would never have said that. "Oh, I'm happy to bring those to Goodwill, so you can get a deduction."

"No, you've been a great help. I'd like you to have them. Ashleigh was always borrowing my things without asking," she said into the empty room, "We'd have such fights. I'd ground her. Then Tom started covering the dry cleaning for her so I wouldn't know and I just—" She abruptly took the box from me, dropped it inside, and pulled the door shut. She turned to me, catching her breath. "Take them, okay?"

We heard footsteps coming up the front walk and Lindsay jogged down the stairs before I could answer. Tom cracked the door and, seeing us coming, swung it wide open. "You're awake!" he exclaimed, strolling in with the deliberate motions of a man who'd been drinking. I stopped halfway down the stairs. "What're you ladies up to?"

"So?" Lindsay asked eagerly. She stopped on the last step, putting them at equal height. "What did they say? Did they decide?"

"Everything. Nothing. The DNC still wants Stapleton." The governor of Iowa. "They talk in circles, but goddamn do they like to talk." He attempted to hang his blazer on the banister twice before getting it right then swung his arm around Lindsay. "How are you still upright?"

"Are you joking?"

"Oh." He dropped his chin. "Bad news, babe, they only want me joking when there's an audience. Will you be my audience?"

"Did they give you *any* sense of timing?" Lindsay asked, putting a steadying palm on his chest. I tucked my head and walked past them to get my keys.

"They have a final requirement."

"Final?"

"That's how they put it."

"And?"

"If they choose me I have to resign from the senate. They don't want me 'conflicted.'"

She blinked at him. "That's crazy. That leaves you nothing to go back to." I was stuck there, holding my keys and phone, not wanting to interrupt to say goodbye, but not having been dismissed.

"You heard them, I'm going to be vice president. I don't need anything to go back to, right?"

"But what if you're not? We worked so hard to get you there—to be in a place where you could make a difference. That was the goal. They can't ask you to gamble that."

"They're not asking—they're telling. And if that's what it takes to be able to make an infinitely bigger difference for infinitely more people, so be it. And, Linds, for the next few months they want us here—in the home we raised Ashleigh, that's how they put it."

"You'll be on the trail. *I* will be in the home we raised Ashleigh."

"I should say good night."

"We can do this," Tom said, his voice slurring.

"But I don't want to," she said, tears splattering her pajamas. "I don't want to live here." She pulled his arm off her.

He stared at the floor. It seemed to take a moment for Lindsay's statement to sink in through the whiskey. "I don't understand. You want me to tell them to just forget it?"

"Tom, no! I'm just—it's a lot of uncertainty, a lot of risk, and it's been weeks of this and you aren't telling me anything about when I'm supposed to—"

"The minute I fucking know one fucking thing about what I am fucking doing I will tell you."

"Tom." Her eyes flashed to me.

He sat heavily on the stairs. "Babe, I'm useless. Please can't we figure this all out tomorrow?"

"Tomorrow." She took a controlled breath. "*We* have to fly back up to DC for Chip's physical therapy appointment. They're going great, thanks for asking, his coordination is almost at Collin's level. Then *we're* going to the preschool meet and greet at the school you have yet to visit. After which *we* have to buy the new caps for swim class in minnow green because our kids are minnows now and that starts Friday. So, no. Now is the time *we* have to talk about you leaving the United States Senate." She turned to me, realizing I was stuck by the door. "Amanda, you all set?"

"Yes. Good night, guys." I let myself out, none of us optimistic it would be.

In the morning, Tom's selection as Merrick's running mate was officially announced—my phone buzzed with the news only seconds before I watched it on television. Tom was leaving the senate.

My heart collapsed like a cheap beach chair.

This was it. The end of health insurance and needing a suit. I was going to be back at Jacksonville's equivalent of Catfish Heaven. I would never accomplish anything with my life to earn another cookie. I stayed up all night running the numbers, figuring out how long it would be before I lost my car, my apartment.

For three days I watched everyone around me update their resumes on the sly and slip out for "personal calls." I had no calls to make. Every person who could put in a word for me was frantically asking everyone they knew to put in a word for them.

Sunday morning I was researching state schools and seeing if I could waitress my way all the way through this time when I got Lindsay's text.

S.O. Fucking S.

The Davises were bringing the Merricks to Sunday service with the minister who'd married them and had christened all three Davis children. It was to be followed by an "intimate luncheon" at their Riverside home—and a 20/20 interview.

Apparently, Lindsay frantically filled me in, the caterer was so rattled by the secret service casing the house and the weed he'd forgotten to remove from his glove compartment that he had gulped down half a bottle of sherry. Even the unflappable Rhonda was overwhelmed. With my solvency hanging in the balance, I suited up and raced over.

But no sooner had I benched the chef and delegated a meal Kath would have been proud of, than ABC's lighting equipment promptly short-circuited the cooling system. I called four electricians, promising double to whoever got a generator installed first, then ran out to buy bomb-sniffed box fans for every room. When I got back Merrick's staff was showing the segment producer every conceivable furniture configuration that might achieve 20/20's Floridian vision. "Fuck! Not one fucking palm tree print? What the fuck?" (And back to K-Mart.)

Lindsay was the first through the front door, where she was promptly felled by a displaced ottoman. Mrs. Merrick, one hand on her Hermès scarf, the other wrapped around her waist, made her way in as if stepping around dog shit. "How quaint!" she called over the whir of the fans.

"Oh, thank you!" Lindsay said as I helped her to her feet. "You'll have to come back when we're not under siege!" She gamely led her guests around the barricade of furniture to the dining room. Charles Merrick automatically took Tom's place at the head of the table, causing Tom to stop short. Lindsay nudged her husband to a side chair and handed him a glass to raise.

He cleared his throat. "It's a real honor to welcome you both to our home and, of course, be given this opportunity to support you." Merrick cupped his ear as I shifted the fan from blowing napkins in their faces. "We're giving this everything we've got!"

"I should hope so," Charles Merrick said, picking at the black-eyed peas. Suddenly, the generator chugged to life. Cool air streamed from the vents. Lindsay dropped her head back in relief and Nancy Merrick asked for salt. Clinking silverware was the only sound that followed.

Lindsay told me later that she'd already given up. To explain the Merricks, Tom invoked Chris Rock: there was Oprah-rich, and then there were the people who signed Oprah's checks. The Merricks were the check signers and privately put off by the masses whose votes they were courting. Masses who thrilled to Tom's rallying cry.

You would never have guessed any of this once the 20/20 cameras rolled.

Just before sitting down with Elizabeth Vargas, Merrick gamely rolled up his sleeves and Nancy unwound her scarf. I watched from the back of the living room as the banter between the two couples took on the ease of old college friends, prompted by Lindsay, who exuded warmth enough for all of them.

She was spectacular.

As the last ABC van pulled out and I picked up my purse, Lindsay turned to me. "We've been told Tom needs something called a body man. Basically someone who'll trail him minute by minute—a kind of personal assistant on steroids. I've been wracking my brain, running through all the guys in the state offices, but, of course, you're the woman for the job."

"Really?"

"You'll be switched onto the campaign payroll starting tomorrow." Campaign payroll! I was simultaneously limp with relief and stiff with elation. "And Amanda?"

"Yes?"

"Do you own a suitcase?"

I bought two. One for overnights. One for the longer hauls. That evening the click of the Davis front door shutting was the starting gun on an energy-drink-pounding, vending-machine-dining, chair-sleeping marathon that blessedly left me without a brain cell to think about anything I was missing—Pax or the idea of him included. I was either in a vehicle, a tiny plane, a motel, hotel, or scrum of suited security, handing Tom cough drops, tissues, notes, local baked goods, the bag to throw them up into, fresh shirts, and a thousand other things a man perpetually selling needs. At one point I realized I'd reached into the wrong carry-on and he was wearing my deodorant. His knees became inflamed through jumping onto stages from fields, factory floors, and parking lots. His hands grew swollen from relentless shaking. His voice constantly gave out. But Tom thrived on it. "I can do this, Amanda," he would say to me, buoyed, yet again, by the realization. "I can really help these people." I'd have to remind him to lie down so at least his body could rest—"Yes, even if you can't sleep"—just like I used to do with Billy.

Not that I would have opted to step away, for even a moment, had I been greeted as he was wherever we went. Men in expensive suits stuttered to ask his opinion, babies were lifted for his kiss, and women of every age—well, it reminded me of the scene in Indiana Jones where Harrison Ford practically lectures a room of students out of their panties. As a senator, he'd always had interested audiences, but now people were rapt. The thousands at his rallies wore such fervent expressions it seemed they were trying to beam him into the White House with their eyes. If Lindsay's praise had made me feel like a grown up, this must have made Tom feel like a God. It was, by any standard, intoxicating.

The Democratic convention was in Boston that year, a city that was experiencing an unexpected heat wave. From their box,

Lindsay, the twins, and Tom's parents, all of them dressed in the same royal blue as Tom's tie, waved to the cameras with glowing smiles. I watched with pride as Tom finally introduced the world to the vision I'd heard in that South Beach ballroom. When he was done the building shook with cheers for four solid minutes. Standing backstage with the rest of the team, I couldn't help crying.

I was sending Billy a picture of my view of the crowd when my phone buzzed with a text.

Are you here?

I stared at the number I'd never let myself add to my contacts.

Here, where? I typed.

Earth. Boston. Convention Center.

I didn't think I had any adrenaline left after the last few months, but I was wrong.

Backstage, I wrote him.

I believe you owe me a dinner.

I smiled despite myself. *Who is this?*

Meet me by the fountain across from the entrance.

I bit my lip.

If you can get away. My phone buzzed once more. *And also, please.*

Tom was done for the night, and when I told Lindsay that Pax was in the vicinity she shooed me out, saying that all she could think about was getting herself and the kids into bed. I smoothed the red dress from her that I'd had altered and dug in my purse for lip gloss. Outside the air was heavy, forcing me to slow as I cleared the vendors and news trailers.

It had been a year since I'd last seen him and I wasn't sure what to expect. Was he still bitter and miserable? And then I spotted him standing by the spraying water. He was in jeans and a white T-shirt, his oxford shirt draped over his arm. Our eyes made contact and he lit up like the dance floor under our feet that first night. I didn't think I could take having to let go of the idea of him a second time.

He strolled over and I saw that his face was perceptibly thinner, his eyes clearer. "Wow, are you speaking at this thing?" he asked.

I put a hand self-consciously to my stomach. "I'm a little over-dressed for . . ."

"Standing by a fountain with a jerk," he finished for me.

"Yes."

"Thanks for stealing away."

"Sure." I reminded myself to drop my hand to my side.

"So you game for dinner?"

"Well, apparently, I owe you."

He looked down at his tennis shoes. "Honestly, I would have left myself that night if the laws of physics permitted." He raised his gaze under his thatch of lashes.

"I need to get back soon." It was a start, but I still gave myself an out.

"Yes, ma'am. Well, let's just walk. There are a few restaurants not far."

"What are you doing here?" I asked, falling into step with him. "I mean, other than your obvious patriotic and civic duty as president of your local chapter of Hedge Funds for Merrick."

"I . . . uh . . . got out of the business." He pointed me across the street.

"Really?"

His cell buzzed and he checked it as we strolled. "I got a job. Working for someone who is neither my stepfather, nor has ever seen my stepfather naked."

I turned to face him. "Are you implying your father and Rodger are lovers?"

"Golf buddies. I wanted to stay out of the locker room nepotism."

"Wow," I said as we turned a corner and the crowd thinned.

"I'm working for the financial reform lobby."

I stopped. "You're kidding."

"I am not."

"That is downright Shakespearean of you, Paxton Westerbrook."

"I know." He smiled.

"How's Taggart taking it?"

He ticktocked his head like a metronome. "Mom says he's trying to be proud. How about Ethiopian?" He pointed at a place up ahead as his phone dinged with another e-mail. He took it out and typed a quick reply. "Always wanted to try that. Can you imagine any of my parents' guests eating with their hands? They even have designated utensils for corn. Maybe Indian?"

We wound our way up to the cobblestone streets of Beacon Hill, stopping for pizza, as it was the safest date food he volleyed. We started talking and, like that afternoon on Worth Avenue, I don't remember what we said, only that it was effortless. The check sat untouched for an hour. After we pried ourselves away, skipping dessert and opting for ice cream at his place, we headed toward his Airbnb digs for the weekend, the top floor of a narrow brownstone. The stairwell was stifling, and I was starting to sweat. While my sheath dress had been appropriate for the arctic conditions at the convention center, now it just felt confining.

"This place was free last minute, but I think I'm the only person who overlooked the no AC thing," he said, unlocking the door. The apartment was decorated sparsely—microsuede couch, Ikea table, a few textbooks on financial theory. I guessed the owner was an MBA student away for the summer, trying to turn some quick cash by renting the place.

"You want a beer?" Pax stepped into the sleek galley kitchen and opened the refrigerator.

"Beer's great, thanks." I walked over and we both stood for a moment too long before the open door, letting ourselves cool.

He handed it to me and grabbed a water for himself.

I looked at him questioningly.

"Given my dad's predilections, I've imposed some strict cut-offs for myself," he answered.

I nodded, impressed, and touched the chilled bottle to my chest. He watched. I wanted to take my dress off—ask if I could borrow some boxers. Clearing his throat, he pulled out his buzzing phone. "I'm turning this thing off." He placed it on the counter. "Way too much going on—" he caught himself. "I mean, I'm sure it's nothing like what you've been doing."

"I'm so inside Tom's schedule—it's like there are certain things I'm just trying to hold at bay."

"Such as?"

"Like." I dropped my head back. "He disappears for ten minutes every day around eleven." Pax laughed. "It's just TMI. I have bought that man foot powder, but I do not want to start holding his digestive schedule in my head like it's the Associated Press briefing rundown."

He handed the bottle opener to me, but I decided not to pop the top off, not wanting—or needing—to dull anything about this moment. "I'll just use it as an ice pack, if you don't mind?"

"Music?" He opened his iPad on the kitchen counter. His screen saver was a sunset picture of him with his arm around a blond who looked like Pym, who looked like Allison, who would one day look like Cricket. Something sultry came low from the apartment's speakers.

"So, are you seeing anyone? Not that I would follow a guy with a girlfriend up to his fourth-floor convection oven."

He looked down at the picture as if noticing it for the first time. One side of his mouth turned up. "No, Amanda. I'm not."

"Just taking a poll," I said feebly.

"That's my cousin." He pulled out the carton of ice cream I'd lost the appetite for and two bowls.

"Oh God, don't bother—let's just eat it out of the carton."

"I would never have texted you if I was," he said, passing it over with a spoon.

"Well, you seem to be doing many things you'd never do."

Again the half grin. "It's too hot to talk."

"It's too hot for a lot of things," I countered.

He took another long sip and then placed his water on the granite counter before walking toward me. "We can fix that." My breath grew shallow. He slid his hand into my hand and led me down the hallway. "So . . . Amanda, Amanda, Amanda. Why is it that when I quit Taggart's firm last year you were the person I pictured telling?" He pushed open the door to the bathroom. It was tiled entirely in black with a shower that ran the width of the room. He stood in front of me. I didn't move, didn't avert my eyes. A bead of sweat made its way down his collarbone. "Why is that?"

Having been haunted by the same need for recognition from him, the answer became suddenly clear. "Because you want my respect."

He let out the tiniest "ha" of acknowledgment, a borderline exhale. "That's what I want," he confirmed. His expression was serious. Intent. "And this." He reached out and turned on the water, then he spun me away from him, raising my hands overhead to the cool tile wall. He ran his fingers down my arms and arrived at the dress's zipper. He tugged it gently as his lips grazed the nape of my neck.

I dropped my arms and my dress fell away to the floor. I tried to reach behind me to touch him. "Uh, uh, uh," he admonished, replacing my palms to the tile. His fingers traced my arms once more before sliding around my ribs to cup my breasts. I groaned.

He turned me around, taking my hand, and leading me right into the shower, the cold water instantly soaking his shirt. It was there, under the spray, as I unbuttoned him, that our mouths finally found each other, equally hungry, equally desperate. "Please," he implored, staring into me. "Please get out of my head."

"No," I said into his mouth, my hands moving into his wet hair. His lips sank into my skin, the edge of his teeth grazing me as his warm tongue found its way inside the lace of my bra. He sank down onto the floor, pulling me on top of him.

I awoke a few hours later to the sound of his beating heart, his hand cradling my neck with a tenderness that made me feel unnervingly fragile. I tried to sit up in the bed without waking him, but he stirred as I stood. "Sorry."

He lifted onto his elbows and inhaled, his eyes widening as he reached for my arm. I stepped out of his grasp.

"I really have to get back," I said. "Davis has a teachers' union breakfast. And then a thousand events and we leave right after he introduces Merrick tomorrow night—tonight."

"Where to?"

"Des Moines."

He thought for a second. "I'm heading to Chicago on Tuesday."

"We'll be in Columbus by then." It'd been so much more intense than I'd anticipated having Pax inside me. Before sex had been something I brought half of myself to—at best. Some part of my brain was always elsewhere—solving some problem that wouldn't let me go. But with Pax I'd stopped thinking. And certainly I'd stopped thinking about what should happen next.

He swung his feet to the floor. "Send me your schedule and I'll get my ass to one of your stops."

I stepped close enough that my breasts were in his face. "Just the ass? Because I'm growing pretty fond of the whole package."

"Leave my package out of this."

Laughing, I leaned down and kissed him. He slipped my hair behind my ear.

"Are we really going to?" I didn't dare finish the question.

"Let's do this!" He invoked the Merrick-Davis slogan, swinging a fist into the air—without completely clarifying what "this" was. I wasn't ready to ask.

But when he said that incredible ass would be there—it was, waiting to transform some god-awful stopover in some god-awful hotel into something amazing. From Tulsa, Oklahoma, to Bend, Oregon, we took each other with a fervor that only seemed to compound with each pilfered night.

And it was so much better than a cookie.

Chapter
Six

I WAS SO AWAKE. DESPITE NOT having slept for more than four hours at a time in weeks, I was seeing the world around me in high def, fueled on caffeine, sugar, nicotine gum, and unbearable hope. It was impossible to believe that for the first twenty-four years of my life I hadn't set foot on a plane—when only that day I'd woken in Iowa, flown with Davis to Jacksonville for him to cast his vote on camera, then finally up to Portland, Maine, where the Merricks lived. There, we waited for the election results, the ceiling of the hotel ballroom a few floors below netted with three thousand balloons.

What will living in DC be like, I wondered? Would the transition team help us find apartments or would I move into Pax's place, which, thanks to my crazed schedule, I still hadn't even seen? The thought caught me off guard; I sloshed the drink I was carrying for Tom over the back of my hand. It was the mocktail I mixed for him ten times a day: half Coke, half Diet Coke, exactly three cubes of ice—and a cherry if I could hide it under the ice.

Well, why not move in with Pax? I asked myself as I handed the cup off to Tom's left hand—since the knuckles on his right were too bruised from being shaken for him to hold anything. "Mr.

Vice President." As had become our half-joking ritual, I dipped my head. He saluted.

I was about to embark on the next phase of a career more exciting than anything I had ever remotely hoped for myself. Whether home turned out to be with Pax or a place of my own, maybe it didn't really matter; I'd be so busy I'd hardly be there anyway. While the staff manically clicked through the suite's cable news stations, I went to get Tom's snack. He liked deviled eggs—but scraped flat so the filling didn't squirt upon biting. As I fixed the eggs that Room Service had not prepared to his preferred white/yolk ratio, I tried to picture living with Pax and realized I had no idea what that kind of commitment looked like—other than Mom's revolving door, my examples were the late-night brawls in neighboring trailers that ended in black eyes.

"Amanda," an aide summoned me from the doorway. I rushed past the secret service to find Billy, Delilah, Ray Lynne, and Grammy waiting in the hall. I was so excited: for them to be here on this historic night, that I could afford to fly them up, and that I was finally getting to see them after so many months. I threw my arms around Billy. "How was your flight? Did you like it?" I asked him. He'd had another growth spurt—at eleven he wasn't going to be my "little" brother much longer.

He pulled a gallon freezer bag containing a dirty shirt out of his backpack. "Ray Lynne barfed on me. Thanks for the heads-up about the Ziplocs." I could have written a book on flying with toddlers by that point. Lindsay's nanny and I had the routine so down a married couple could not have done better.

"It's so great to see you guys," I gushed.

"Oh my God, I have literally never been so cold in my life," Delilah said. "People live like this?" Beneath the denim jacket that provided little protection against the snow, I recognized her "funeral" dress—a short-sleeved black jersey number she got at Target. She'd retouched her roots so recently the skin at her hairline was still pink from the bleach. "*No one* wanted to let us up here. And I say that as someone who checks IDs for a living. Can I smoke?"

"Not in the hotel. And if they let you out, you might not be able to get back in—it's getting pretty crazy."

"I should've bought one of those patch thingies. Think anyone here has some nicotine gum?"

"In my purse."

"I'm firsty. And hungwy," Ray Lynne added from Mom's arms.

"And I'd like to sit down," Grammy said as she unbuttoned her cardigan. She was favoring her good hip.

"Okay, let me get you guys to your room."

"Who's winning?" Billy asked.

"Way too early to tell." I put my arm around him.

"Amanda, is that your family?" Lindsay called from inside, crossing to us. In her blue boucle suit she looked so perfect—she'd been camera ready since 6 a.m. I was momentarily embarrassed that my family looked like what they were, people who'd navigated multiple airports with a two-and-a-half year-old to be with me. I made introductions, saving Mom for last. "And this is Delilah." They shook hands. I could see Mom sizing Lindsay up—the woman who had wooed away her daughter.

"I was just going to take them down to their room so they can get a bite to eat."

"Nonsense," Lindsay waved them in. "We have enough food in here to run for the White House all over again and no one has the appetite to touch it."

"Oh, we're not really dressed for—" Grammy said, shrinking back in her soft pants and cardigan, but Delilah kind of squared her hips.

"Oh, please, you've just gotten off a plane. Would Ray Lynne like to look at a book?" Lindsay took her from Mom and steered

Billy in by the shoulders. She had a glow—I could already imagine her in a *Vogue* spread timed with the inauguration.

"Damm, Mandy, this is so exciting." Delilah pinched my arm like I was ten as we followed them into the suite. "Are you gonna live in the White House?"

"Oh, no—very few staff sleep on site, if any."

"Well, I'm telling everyone you're moving to the White House."

I smiled while I fixed Grammy a plate. Ray Lynne had joined the twins for story time with their indefatigable nanny. "Tom Collins?" I asked Delilah, picking up the gin.

"Here, let me do that." Delilah took the bottle from my hand and picked up the ice tongs, calling on the skills she picked up three jobs ago.

"Ah, I see someone knows how to fix a drink," Tom said as he joined us. While Merrick was parked in front of CNBC looking like he was trying to pass a kidney stone, Tom was still working the room, campaigning when there was no one left to convince.

Delilah pivoted to him, smile cranking up. "Never bartend a bartender."

He laughed. "Amanda, you didn't tell me your mom could be your sister."

She laughed and hip bumped me. "Mom, meet Tom Davis, the *imminent* vice president of the United States."

"What can I fix for you, Mr. Imminent?"

"Is that a Tom Collins?"

"Yep."

"Make it two."

"Coming right up." She flipped a lemon off the back of her hand and caught it.

Smiling, Tom appeared impressed. Or after being offered his three hundredth corn dog, he didn't know how to stop being impressed. "First Shot Girl, you're hired."

She grinned. I gritted my teeth.

"Mom, I'm sure Ray Lynne is exhausted. Why don't I show you and Grammy to the room so you can tuck her in?"

"I've just spent the entire day buckled in next to my mother. How about you let me enjoy one drink?"

"Fair enough."

As Tom returned to Merrick, I went into the adjoining sitting room, where Tom and Lindsay's parents had been banished and where story time was being held. Before I could scoop my little sister from the floor and help Grammy up from the couch, Tom's mother, Belle, paused me.

"Amanda, do they have any crudités or hors d'oeuvres out there?"

Lindsay's mother, Anne, flared her nostrils at Belle's mispronunciation, which made it sound like she had asked for "crude whores." Poor Belle. Sitting next to one another on the couch, Anne and Belle looked like one of those *In Style* spreads of two identical outfits, the nice version and the cheap one. Of course, Tom must have given his parents money, so her suit couldn't have actually cost less than Anne's. In fact, it probably cost more because I once heard Lindsay say that her parents wouldn't accept anything from her. But from her brassy blond hair next to Anne's subtle butter color, to the garish hues of her silk scarf next to Anne's elegant hunter one, Belle Davis looked, well, tacky.

"I'll bring you some," I said.

"Amanda, did I tell you my grandfather was in the state legislature?" Belle looked up at me girlishly, her eyes rimmed with a little too much mascara.

"You didn't." She had. Twice already.

"It will be so nice to have a Davis back in office." She wrapped her poppy-colored nails around her knee and raised it. "His whole life I've told Tommy he was born for this."

"Amanda," Anne brayed as I brought back a plate of carrot sticks for them. She had a commanding voice. "Can you get that PR person to come find me? No one has answered my question yet."

"About?"

"What I'm supposed to say if anyone asks me who I voted for."

"Why? Who did you vote for?"

"Well, we voted to reelect President Gaitlin, of course. In case they ask, I don't want to lie. But I don't want to embarrass anyone."

"You voted for Gaitlin?" I tried not to sound horrified.

"Amanda," Lindsay's father said gruffly. "We have been Republicans all our lives and we are not going to switch our party affiliation now."

Belle gave Tom's parents an incongruously sweet smile, as if she hadn't understood.

"A mother needs to have a strong hand in raising a child," Anne continued. "Lindsay always siphoned off too much of her time and energy for Tom—helping him build his practice, helping him meet the right people." I was confused, used as everyone was to hearing that phrase describe women who had chosen their families over their careers. Hadn't she done both?

"Lindsay should be home raising those new kids she wanted so badly," her father declared. "Not being put to work all over the damn country."

"I think she enjoys it," I suggested meekly.

He made a humph sound.

"Okay, well," I said brightly as if we'd been discussing voter turnout in Dubuque. "I will be right back if anyone needs anything."

Downstairs in their hotel room I made up the sofa bed for Billy and tucked Ray Lynne into the queen she would share with Mom. "Grammy will sit with you while you fall asleep." I kissed her nose as her eyes fluttered shut. I leaned over and breathed her in—gummy bears and that soil smell of sweaty kids. "How'd it go today?" I whispered to Grammy once Ray Lynne's breathing deepened.

"She flirted with every man flying alone, ring or no. She had it in her head any man who could afford a ticket—was one. I suppose I should just be happy she didn't join the mile high club today," she sighed.

"Grammy!"

"I've read Danielle Steel."

I laughed. "How's Billy doing?"

"As best as can be expected." She pulled out her sudoku. "He shouldn't be running after a toddler." I couldn't disagree. "He needs a man around. Someone to show him what's what." Apparently Mom was on the task.

My phone buzzed with a text from Pax. *Um, am I in the wrong hotel suite? Was I supposed to go directly to the White House?*

Don't move! I'll be right up! I wrote.

"Grammy, do you mind staying with her?" I asked.

"I'm just happy to be here," she said. "Go. Work."

I raced back up to the (fingers crossed) Presidential Suite where Pax dropped his garment bag to sweep me into his arms. The spontaneous human gesture was welcome by me, but, I could sense, jarring to a room full of those who had either been carefully choreographed—or been carefully choreographing—for so many months.

Tom came right over to shake his hand. "You had my vote first thing this morning, sir. How's it going?" Pax asked him.

"The East Coast polls are closing now. They're calling Georgia, South and North Carolina for Gailtin, which we expected. We're still ahead, because we're carrying the Northeast. But we won't know how things are really shaking out for another hour. And there's been heavy rain in California so there's that."

"What does that mean?" Pax asked.

"Fuck if I know, but they haven't shut up about it all day." Smiling, he patted Pax on the shoulder and went back to Lindsay.

"God, I could rip that dress off you right here," Pax whispered in my ear and I wanted to find a place to be alone with him, but then—

Delilah came out of the powder room, drying her hands on one of the Merrick-Davis napkins. "Who's this?" she asked, her smile suddenly a little flat.

"Mom, remember Pax Westerbrook? The one who had the house down in West Palm?"

She looked him over. "The one who thought you stole his watch?"

He blushed. "I'll never be able to live that down, will I?" He held out his hand. "Hello Mrs. Luker, nice to meet you."

"Oh, not Mrs.—just Delilah." I wasn't sure exactly why I hadn't told her about Pax. Even though she had always met my boyfriends, I had never really confided in her about them because I hated it when she confided back. Some women may want a mom who's more like a girlfriend, but I think they don't know what they're asking for.

"And that cute thing in the corner glued to his phone is Billy," she pointed.

"He looks just like you," he said politely.

"Oh? I think he looks like his dad—that I remember. Mandy, anyone here single?"

"Sadly, I think everyone is, except the candidates."

"I think I see a gentleman who needs his drink refreshed." She sauntered across the room. "You probably want to get settled," I suggested to Pax, hoping to move us out of the sight line of Delilah's flirtations..

"Don't you need to stay?" he asked.

"Everyone in this room wants to help Merrick and Davis. I think they'd curl in a ball to make a human footstool if either guy asked. I won't be missed for twenty minutes."

"Come here," Pax said as we crossed the threshold of his room, pulling me hard against him and then pressing me equally hard against the slamming door. In seconds my thong was on the carpet and my legs were wrapped around his waist. I thought there was no way I'd be able to come considering the fumes I was running on, but he knew just how to touch me so the adrenaline and cortisol and fear and need popped inside me like a balloon filled with Jell-O shots.

"*Now*, we'll never forget tonight. You sure you don't want to lie down?" he asked afterward, gingerly lowering my feet to the floor.

"I can't. I'll wake up next Tuesday." I tugged my skirt down and swiped up my thong. "How do I look?"

"A little fucked." He took my chin and kissed me gently on the lips.

My phone vibrated and I opened the text, not wanting to believe what I was reading. I literally shook the phone and looked at it again like it was a Magic 8 Ball.

"What?" he asked.

"They called Pennsylvania for Gaitlin. Shit." I blew out hard, possibilities we'd all held at bay demanded my attention, like a damp patch of dry wall you suddenly have to admit has rotting wood behind it. Merrick's biggest media buy was in Pennsylvania. "We *have* to take Ohio, Pax, we have to. Let's go. I feel like I need to be staring at the TV, willing this to go right." I was talking too fast.

Back at the suite Delilah was standing awkwardly by herself in the middle of the room where the energy had switched from pent-up jubilation to bracing for impact. "Mom?" I asked as Pax went to call his colleagues. "You okay?"

She was holding a drink she'd mixed for someone who was apparently now in no mood. She set it on a side table. "I guess I should go to bed."

High school. Two in the morning. Coming out of my room to find Mom still waiting to be picked up. Her pack of cigarettes smoked to stubs. *I guess I should go to bed.*

"I'm sorry, Mom." Even as I said it the thought occurred that she should be saying it to me.

"I hope I can sleep."

"I know, we're all pretty wired." I looked past her at the sliver of TV visible between people's shoulders.

"And my back."

"What's wrong with your back?"

"Dr. Hamlin—who sometimes comes by the diner with his wife—he says it's a bulging disk. Might be herniated."

"Ow."

"I don't know how much longer I can keep working on my feet, lifting those buckets of dishes."

She had my attention. "What about a desk job?" I asked.

"I haven't had one since Freddie took a chance on me at the dealership."

"What about night classes?"

"How am I gonna pay for night classes?"

"Well, what're you gonna do if your back goes?" My voice was rising. "You don't have insurance."

"I was thinking . . ."

I hated it when she said that. It was always a preamble to a revelation that required something of me, something I'd be forced to give.

". . . that you could maybe send me a little more every month. I could go down to four shifts a week, maybe take some pressure off."

"Off?"

"My spine."

I fought the instinct to step away, could feel my stomach seeking refuge up and under my ribs. When I was eight, I saw a billboard for rentals starting as low as four hundred a month. I counted Mom's tips one morning when she was sleeping. I read her pay stubs. I figured we could swing it. But the next day she was fired for mouthing off, and I realized that the dollars in the shoebox were irrelevant. There was nothing about Delilah that could be planned on, around, or for.

"Will you cover it?" she needled.

I realized I'd been expecting one of her I've-been-thinking requests from the moment I'd started working for Davis. I'd let myself hope that sending money for Ray Lynne could somehow stave it off.

"I need it and you sure seem to have stepped in it here." I watched her look over at Lindsay and Nancy Merrick, who were impeccable by comparison, even at this terrible moment.

"I can't—I'm not making that kind of—"

"I bet one night here could cover a month's rent."

"But I'm not paying for this. Mom. If your back is going, you need a long-term plan— " Unless I was her long-term plan.

"I get it."

"Mom."

"I said, I get it." She lifted her hands over her head. "Merrick for president! Wooooh!" She ignored the tight smiles as she crossed to Billy. "Come on, baby, let's go downstairs and get you ready for bed—"

Suddenly a hush fell as the newscaster announced CNN was ready to call the next set of states. We watched in collective nausea as every state in the central time zone, from Canada to the Gulf, went for Gaitlin. Even with New York's thirty-one electoral votes, they were now tied.

Pax stood by my side as it sunk in—the months of stumping, the tens of millions of dollars, the passionate endorsements from George Clooney and Lady Gaga, none of it might be enough.

By eleven o'clock we were grasping at straws. Merrick was demanding a recount of Dade County and refusing to concede. Teary eyed, Belle had taken a sedative on top of her julep and had to be helped to bed, still babbling about her family's starring role in the War between the States. "Oh, shut up, Belle. Your ancestors were barefoot and stupid, same as mine," I heard Tom's father mutter as he hoisted her off the couch.

I looked around the room, the hope in people's faces coagulating into something grim and heavy. "I'll get ice," I said to no one and took the bucket into the hall. I paused when I heard hushed voices.

"Millions of dollars—wasted." It was Lindsay's mother, Anne. Still going strong.

"Tom doesn't make the campaign finance rules, Mom." Lindsay sounded like she wanted to slump against the cooler.

"There's just so much waste. And chaos. Do you need to be trailed by so many people? Does Tom really need that Amanda walking behind him with baby wipes?"

"He does when he shakes three hundred hands a day. It frees us up to focus on the issues." Lindsay spoke over the rattle of ice.

"You put too much attention on Tom."

"He's worth it, Mom. This is all worth it." Her voice caught. "And about to be over. This will all be gone. The people, the chaos, the entourage, Amanda and her baby wipes, it will all be gone. We'll go back to our little lives just like you want—in that fucking house I cannot seem to get out of. So can you please, just cut me a little slack here, Mom?"

I backed away down the hall.

The sun didn't rise—the sky just faded from black to gray like cheap pants. I stared at Pax's ceiling from where we lay on the bed, still dressed. My bones hurt. My hair hurt. Every minute of sleep I had missed these last months was pinching my skin, demanding recompense.

At the urging of his advisers Merrick had conceded just after 2:00 a.m. It was over. Davis had no office to return to. And neither did I.

"What am I going to do?" I finally said. "I have no job. My mom is one bussed table away from needing major surgery that none of us has the money for. And there's no one else—it's all me. I don't know how the fuck I'm going to take care of them. But I have to, right?" I turned to him, my terror too much to play down. "Tell me what to do." I stared at him, desperate for consoling.

He looked back at me, his chest expanded with a breath that stalled. Whatever words he was planning to say did not make it out.

"I'll figure it out." I tried to cover, but something had shifted between us.

He squeezed my hand and laid it down. "My flight's at nine. I'm so *so* sorry to leave you like this. I thought we'd be—I mean I didn't think—"

"It's okay, I know, none of us did," I forced myself to speak. I remembered all those balloons still pegged to the ceiling. Who would release them?

Pax went to take a shower. I couldn't bring myself to turn my phone back on. "Don't you need to go upstairs?" he asked, getting dressed in a fresh suit for his noon meeting.

"Everyone is checking out. I don't think there's anything for me to do. For anyone to do. I mean, yes." My temples throbbed like there was a bullfrog in each one. "I'm sure tens of thousands of lawn signs have to be cleared and there are probably pizza places from coast to coast we owe thousands of dollars to." *We.* I would have to break that habit. "But not now, not today. I can't."

"Look, I only have the room till noon. Should I extend it so you can sleep?"

I wanted to pull the coverlet over me and black out. "I have to go downstairs. I have to face my family—get them to the airport. I thought—" I snorted. "I thought I brought them up here to witness history."

"I'll tell them you're in high-level triage—I'll get them into a taxi."

"Really? Thank you. Since I'm probably moving back in with them next week there's no need for a long good-bye."

"So DC is out?" It wasn't a question.

"I guess . . ." I didn't know how to say, *unless we get a place together and you float me while I job hunt with my GED and a stellar reference letter.*

He nodded. "Okay."

"Okay?"

He had his back to me as he returned his wallet and keys to his pockets. "This was a little crazy, anyway, I guess . . . flying all over the place, then moving to the same city. Rushed, I mean."

"Well, those were the choices." I sat up, the bullfrogs bursting. "Meet up somewhere, or move to the same place, right?"

He just looked at me, not answering. His phone buzzed. "I've got to go." He turned back. "I'll call you."

My breath swelled in my gut—and stuck. What was happening? I felt like the floor was giving and I was going to fall ten stories into Delilah's suitcase. I'd be wheeled back to Tallyville, like none of this—Lindsay, Tom, Pax—had ever happened.

"Pax, are you—are we—is this over?"

"No, no," he rushed, no smile in his eyes. "It just sounds like you have a lot on your plate right now."

"It's nothing I can't handle, you know that right?"

"I'm sure. No, I just mean—we both have full plates. Look, we'll talk."

I nodded. "Safe flight." The door shut.

"Stupid, Amanda," I said out loud. "Stupid, stupid, stupid." This wasn't the start of anything. Pax Westerbrook was never going to move in with Amanda Luker. Three thousand balloons to drop at the wake for my career and my relationship. Which turned out to just be some kind of jet-lagged hookup.

I felt a building pain between my breasts. When I was seven I snapped my arm falling in the school yard. I knew, standing there in the dust with my teacher, it would be awhile before anyone came to get me. So I decided I couldn't let it hurt. I turned the volume in my arm down to silence. And now I did the same to the thumping, throbbing under my ribs. I twisted the dial until all was stillness.

There was a knock. "Amanda!"

I opened the door to find Tom. Still in his suit from last night, he clearly hadn't slept either. But where I imagined everyone else in the building looked sour and sapped, he looked like he'd just recharged his battery back to full power. "Was helping the crew check out. Saw Westerbrook in the lobby—said I could find you here." He crossed to the windows and looked down to the street. "Secret service is leaving. We are no longer among the four most important men in the world." His eyes sparkled like he found that funny. "Now there are only two again."

"Sir?"

"Tom. I'm not a senator. I'm not a candidate. And right now I don't even think I'm technically your boss."

"Tom. I'm so sorry."

He shook his head as if I was missing the point. "I can do it, Amanda." He looked at me expectantly.

"I'm sure you can—do what?"

"Win. If that stuffed shirt could get 48 percent of the popular vote and everything that came out of his mouth sounded like a farting foghorn, I can do this. You should have seen Merrick," he said disgustedly. "He was done with us so fast he didn't even shake my hand good-bye." He grimaced before taking a stride toward me. "But I know how it works now. I've made the friends. I've made the connections. The pundits aren't blaming me this morning. They're all saying *I* was the best part of the ticket, that if it had been reversed we might have had a chance."

I wasn't sure what was happening. I had seen guys cry when they lost big on a game and I had seen the ones who doubled down, refusing to accept that they'd just put their rent money on the table. I stared into his face, not sure if I needed to herd him back upstairs to Lindsay, to cold reality.

"That's great."

"Let's flip it," he said urgently. "Let's flip the ticket."

"Okay." I was stymied. "Let's do that. Shazam. Ticket flipped."

He was taken aback. "Everyone else in this operation has turned into a zombie, but I thought you of all people would be up for this. Don't you think I should do it?"

"Of course—"

"Good." He clapped his palms together, his enthusiasm restored. "Because I'm forming an exploratory committee."

"But isn't that something people do, like, two years from now?"

"I'm not in office. I need to be proactive. And I want to send a clear message: Gaitlin, I am coming for your job. Down, but by no means out, that kind of thing."

But I felt out. So far out. I stood up, mentally slapping myself, trying to awaken the belief he was asking for.

He grabbed my shoulders. "Amanda, when you're in charge the prompter is always cued to the right speech, there's never milk in my coffee, and the reporters all think I remember their birthdays—you make this machine run. Get packed, head back to Jacksonville. Get some rest. Then report to our place first thing Monday morning."

"Really?"

"You're our first hire." I couldn't believe what I was hearing.

"What? Sorry, I sound like an idiot, but what are you hiring me to do?"

"I have no idea yet." He grinned.

"Who will I answer to?"

"No clue."

"Who will pay me?"

"Gotta figure that out. You in?"

I had started my morning with a man I had naively thought was going to stand by me. Or at least continue making space beside him that I could eventually fill. Instead I was discovering that the man who couldn't let me go, come what may, was my boss.

"I'm in."

Jacksonville was not the White House and I no longer had a federal job with health insurance, nor did I know when my next check was coming—or what amount it would be for. *But* I wasn't cancelling my car or apartment lease and taking the bus south, just yet.

That weekend after the election I picked up my phone to call Pax ten times a day. Maybe he was looking at his phone, too. Either way no call was placed. Not from him to say—hey, sorry I was weird. Not from me to ask why he was weird—because I wasn't ready to deal with the fact that he wasn't ready to deal.

By Monday I had caught up on laundry, scrubbed my place, and gotten a haircut. I was ready to go to the Davises, ready to do—something. For once I had really agonized about what to wear. How do you dress when you don't know what it is you are dressing for? "You need to wear a suit, Amanda," Becky said.

"But what if they're in sweatpants."

"Doesn't matter. It's great that Tom knows you can keep his coffee order straight, but, no offense, so can a monkey. You have more to offer than that. And after what your mom said, you need to move up a rung—or two—on the payroll."

So I settled on white linen pants and a short-sleeved blouse. When I got to their house the driveway was so full I had to park on the street. I rang the bell and Lindsay answered. "Amanda!" She looked startled but pulled me into a hug. "What are you doing here?"

"I invited her," Tom said as he passed through the entry hall carrying a tray of muffins, his sleeves rolled up. I'd assumed that hiring me had been a joint decision, but clearly I was wrong. I wondered why Tom hadn't talked to her about it.

Where he seemed refreshed and ready for battle, Lindsay still looked deeply depleted and her face was puffy from crying. "Well, then, come on in. Lend me a hand with the breakfast," she said.

Knowing what Becky would say, I nonetheless helped her ferry trays of baked goods and coffee into the living room, which, clear of the twins' toys, was now filled with the fallen soldiers of Merrick's campaign.

"Hey, Amanda," Michael Zohn greeted me. He was the brains behind Merrick's strategy, which the news networks agreed would have worked—had Merrick not been Merrick. Had Zohn just been able to shove his hand up Merrick's ass until he could operate him like a puppet.

"Shouldn't you be sleeping somewhere?" I asked.

"Yes. I should. But your boss can be very persuasive. Suffice it to say this is just a courtesy stopover on the way to the Caribbean, where I will be turning my phone off until Hanukkah."

"I'm just here because I want to be able to say in twenty years, 'Hey remember that losing candidate who made me come to his house the Monday after the election? That was crazy,'" Peter, Merrick's Head of Communcations, agreed, biting into a muffin. His skin was literally green, like he was a fish tank someone had forgotten to clean.

"Okay, let's get started." Tom clapped his cupped hands, and the twenty or so people took seats in the redecorated living room. I looked around for an empty chair, but even the window bench was full.

"Amanda," Lindsay whispered, "Would you mind keeping everything refreshed? I need to sit down."

"Are you okay?" I whispered back.

"Yes, I just can't believe we're already at this. I'm just—" she blinked hard. "It's like he can't stop being the candidate."

I swallowed, feeling guilty, because I *didn't* want him to stop being the candidate. I stationed myself in the hall doorway, where I could keep an eye on the table without making it seem like I was counting how many mini corn muffins each person was taking.

"So where do we start?" Tom asked the room.

"Well," Michael answered, pausing to swallow and taking a breath, like he could *just not believe* he was answering this question. "We have to answer the same question we always have to answer—why you? You're a half-term senator and you'll be running against the VP."

"We'd need to beef you up," Peter added.

"Find you an issue to keep you relevant."

"And on the radar."

"Climate change?" Tom quipped and everyone laughed except Lindsay.

"It needs to position you as an expert on something, as someone who is in every way the opposite of the VP," Michael clarified as if he hoped he could just leave us with that assignment.

"My heart beats, so that's one thing I have going for me." More laughter.

Across the room Lindsay glazed over.

"What about local industries?" someone asked like they were reciting the multiplication tables by rote. "What can he plant his flag in as the former senator?"

"Oranges and old people," Peter answered.

"That's what we got," Tom agreed.

"Agriculture?" someone else suggested.

"Too subsidized—too polarizing."

"Old people?" someone else joked.

"Too subsidized—too polarizing," Peter joked back.

"What about the Gulf?"

"Wait," I interrupted. The heads that weren't facing me turned.

"Yes, Amanda," Lindsay encouraged.

I swallowed. "Well, really, it's the opposite, right?" I saw Delilah in front of me—shot at forty. How would she make it to retirement? What did that word even mean anymore? People looked at me blankly. "I mean, subsidized, yes, but that's exactly why it's a good issue—and it make sense since you're from Florida—and the elderly are not polarizing." I wasn't sure if I was making sense. I had a gut feeling, but was struggling to put it into words, like I was stuck in an anxiety dream. "Everyone is old or taking care of someone old or scared of getting old."

"Exactly," Tom said, "Which is why no one wants to talk about it—it grosses people out." He started to spin back to Michael.

"Right," I agreed, not letting him. If this was it—my last chance to be more than a body man, more than the muffin girl—I was going out swinging. "Which is why you could own the conversation. In five years there will be more people over fifty-five than under it. This is your constituency—and they're not being leveraged. It hits every major issue—health-care reform, inflation, affordable housing, entitlements. Put a face on it and you target not the just the seniors, but their grown children as well who want to think that someone is going to figure this shit out for them."

"I actually like it," Peter said through a full mouth. "But we need to formalize it somehow."

"What if you open a research center?" someone suggested.

"The senior center?" Tom gibed.

"The Center for Aging?"

"Sounds like a spa."

"The Center for Age-Related Issues."

"Sounds medical."

"The Center for Human Solutions," I threw out.

"As opposed to cats?"

"As opposed to old people," I explained. "This is everyone's problem. And the name begs the question, which allows you to give the answer and get the conversation going."

"The Center for Human Solutions," Tom repeated.

"The Davis Center for Human Solutions," Lindsay corrected him. I wondered if I was the only one who could hear the resignation in her voice.

"I like it," Michael agreed. The energy in the room was crackling back to life.

"Great. Done. Nice work, Amanda."

Lindsay spun in her chair and looked at me. I wasn't sure what she wanted to say. The Lindsay of a week ago had wanted me to do anything in my power to help her husband become president. But now?

One of the aides made room for me on the piano bench. As I sat down I felt like the mechanical bull had just come to a stop. Under my arms my shirt was drenched.

The state office was gone. Merrick was gone. The campaign money was gone. And Pax might be gone. But I was still holding on.

Part III

Chapter
Seven

"Lindsay!" I called out. "Lindsay!" I raised a flap of dusty blue tarp, seeing if perhaps she was in the "room" where the contractor had temporarily plugged in the fridge and microwave. Not there. "Lindsay!" I called over the pounding of drywall being hung two rooms over. That was exciting. The drywall had been stacked in the foyer for so many months that Lindsay was starting to wonder if she was supposed to make a slipcover for it.

While leading the charge to open the Davis Center, it had taken Lindsay over a year to find a piece of land outside Jacksonville that spoke to her, another six months to hire the right architect, approve the plans, file the permit requests, and break ground. Then the construction delays started. The septic line hit rock, the electric circuit overloaded, the foundation wasn't poured correctly, and the basement flooded in the first rain. They had been promised a comfortable Valentine's move-in date, yet it was April and the house still had only one working toilet. But, even though the upper floors looked like a rib cage, the house was clearly going to be every inch the dream home Lindsay had been longing for.

Currently they were living out of three unfinished rooms on

the ground floor and hoping the nights would get warmer. "In here," Lindsay called. I found her in what could very loosely be called their bedroom slicing into large garment boxes we had carefully sealed against the dust. "Looking for something to wear to New York."

Without Merritt to lend him gravitas, the major donors Tom had hoped would back him out of the gate were still hedging, concerned, as Taggart had once expressed, about his inexperience. So Tom's team had decided that Lindsay's "coming out" party as a contender for first lady would take place over three events spanning two weeks at the end of April. Tom and Lindsay had been together over twenty years, and Michael thought her presence at his side would reassure those still on the fence. He may have been a passionate out-of-the-box thinker, but at heart he was a man who valued tradition. The first event was a red-carpet walk at the Tribeca Film Festival to promote a documentary called *Aging in America* that the Davis Center helped finance. Next was the annual benefit for the Alzheimer's Foundation, and finally Lindsay would attend the Met's Gala hosted by Anna Wintour. This year the show was a retrospective of Hervé Leger, known for his body-conscious "bandage" dresses.

"Amanda, can you help me?"

"Sure—we don't leave for an hour. If you could just direct me to Tom's outdoor gear, I'm all yours." She pointed to a box on the floor as she sifted through piles of clothes.

We'd just found out that the potential donor we were on our way to court loved off-roading. As Tom's new executive assistant at the Davis Center, I accompanied him as he crisscrossed the country to sit on any panel that would have him, befriending powerful allies in geriatrics and economics, gleaning insights and seeking endorsements. Not a week went by that I wasn't thirty thousand feet in the air watching him try to synthesize the presentations into one cohesive vision for older Americans and the people they depended on.

I was only half-listening to Lindsay as I found the clothes Tom had sent me to fetch. "My life is contractor meetings and kindergarten tours—I haven't needed anything like this since the last campaign. Maybe this one will work." She withdrew a dry cleaner bag with the maroon dress she had worn to the Merrick fundraiser at Sarah Jessica Parker's house two years ago. Like those mornings back in Tallyville when Billy would call out actions undoubtedly leading to disaster—"I'm putting the plank on the steps, Mandy! I'm getting my skateboard!"—I snapped out of autopilot. Lindsay was easily twenty pounds heavier now that she had abandoned the I-only-eat-when-Nancy-Merrick-eats diet, which led to fainting.

"You know what, Lindsay." I put my hand on hers to pause her from lifting the plastic. "This is a fresh campaign, and a fresh opportunity, why don't you go to New York a day or two early so you can buy something knockout."

She smiled at me, tacitly accepting my advice, and slid the bag back in the box. "One day—that's it. I hate to be away from the twins longer than necessary when Tom travels so much. But, I have to admit, that might be the best idea." She lifted the tape dispenser. "Do you want to invite Brian to join us?"

Did I? I wasn't sure.

It had taken me months to accept that the six weeks I'd spent with Pax weren't the beginning of anything, but the thing itself. It was so hard to believe that, after all those stops and starts, we still hadn't been able to make something beyond sex happen between us.

Once I realized it was over and forced myself to get back out there, I struggled not to compare every guy to Pax. The kisses weren't hard enough, the observations weren't funny enough, their hair wasn't soft enough. But, as Becky reminded me, even if that was true, Pax was no longer an option on the menu—and I was hungry.

Then along came Brian. Tall, with wavy auburn hair and dark eyes, he was coordinating Tom's fundraising efforts, in preparation for the official announcement of his candidacy in September. Brian's mother had built an entire wing of Mass General and he liked to say that parting people from their money for a good cause was in his blood. We'd been dating for six months, and where Pax had provoked questions of where and how and could this work, Brian and I were on the same team, in sync professionally in every way. He only knew me from now; there was no spectre of my life as a South Beach hostess for me to overcome. Just as Tom was starting over so was I—with Brian. The best part was after a day on the trail we were both just as happy to fall asleep in front of CNN.

"The campaign has a hotel room for you already," Lindsay pointed out. "I'm sure we'll be able to spare you for a few hours here and there. New York is so romantic." But was Brian? Would being in an environment that asked something more—from both of us—fray this thing between us unnecessarily? "Did I tell you Tom proposed to me in New York?"

"No." I sat on the plastic sheeting covering their duvet, sad that the question of my boyfriend joining me in New York was clarifying my feelings for him.

"Oh, this is good." Her face lit from inside like an LED box. "We went for the weekend to celebrate Tom passing the bar."

"You didn't take it together?"

"Oh, we did the first time. But the next two times Tom was on his own." She laughed. "Anyway, he'd finally passed and we were all of twenty-five, staying at this grotty little hotel off Times Square—it had a name like the Royale or something—I thought it sounded nice. This was before TripAdvisor. Our flight was delayed—thunderstorms—and we arrived in the dead of night. In the morning I said, 'Tom, do *not* get out of bed without your shoes on. The floor is moving.'"

"Oh my God."

"We checked out and walked miles and miles in the August heat looking for a hotel we could afford that could take us on the spot. We were soaked. We stank. But we were laughing. We finally found a place on Madison with tiny rooms—the Wales. The AC was broken, but we scrunched in the bathtub together and he said, 'Linds, I had a whole big plan, a carriage ride, reservations at a French restaurant, but I just want to ask you, here in this bathtub, will you marry me?'"

"I love it!" I said. "That is a great story. You should tell Diane Sawyer that story."

The light in her eyes dimmed. "Ashleigh used to make me tell her over and over when she was little. Of course one day she was about twelve and suddenly put it all together. 'Mom, did you and Daddy *sleep together* before marriage?' She was horrified." Lindsay laughed. "I like to think later she actually found that endearing."

"I'm sure she did," I said, picking up Tom's work boots—the ones he'd worn to tour wet factory floors with Merrick.

"Having some time together in New York will be good for us," she said, fingering her gold wedding band. "Tom's been travelling so much—and he's so stressed. I wish just one of these money guys would be the domino to fall already. Just one. Between living in a construction site and the kids I haven't been much help. A weekend without them might be just what we need. Think about inviting Brian." She smiled coyly. "Who knows—maybe history will repeat itself?"

"Oh God," I laughed. "I hope the Mandarin Oriental doesn't have roaches. For all our sakes."

~

In the end Chip had an ear infection so Lindsay didn't fly to New York until the morning of the first red-carpet walk. Sensing her nerves, Tom sent me back to make the trip with her. Jeanine Strathairn, Tom's recently hired public relations strategist, was waiting for us in the hotel lobby, looking tense. She was one of those people who could conjure the energy and impression of pacing while standing still. I was amazed she didn't meet us at the airport. "We have five hours to get you red-carpet ready, Mrs. Davis." That was her opener.

"I know. I got up at 4:00 a.m. to get here."

Jeanine crossed her arms over her black blouse, her oversized bag not pulling her posture off-kilter even a millimeter. I had lugged that bag around on several flights and knew it weighed nearly more than she did. "This is an important moment. A potentially defining moment." She and Lindsay were probably the same height, yet it felt like Jeanine was looking down at her.

"Which is why I am on my way to Bergdorf's right now."

Lindsay and I went straight to the evening section where I kept my eyes on the colors, avoiding the price tags like a tightrope walker avoids the drop. "What can I do for you today?" a young woman in a sleeveless white cashmere dress asked us—the kind of thing one would see on a rack at T.J. Maxx and think, "Well, of course it ended up here—what season is that for?" It's for the woman who works in air-conditioning set at Sleeveless White Cashmere.

"Yes, thank you, I need a dress for a red-carpet event tonight," Lindsay said.

The woman's face pinched against whatever she'd had injected into it. "I'm so sorry, I won't be able to help you."

"Pardon?"

"We don't carry your size in the store."

Slapped, punched, whatever you want to conjure—that's what Lindsay looked like. I stepped in. "Surely you must have clients who eat." I tried to make a joke of it. "Or who fly in to the city to shop."

"Well, of course. But they always give us advance notice so we can have things ready. That takes a day or more."

Lindsay's eyes unfocused.

"Where should we go?" I asked. "We have four and a half hours."

"Well." She tilted her head. "Saks has a Mother-of-the-Bride Department. I think they carry bigger sizes. Or you could try Lane Bryant?"

When I called Jeanine, I thought her tongue was actually going to come out of my cell. "She is not fucking walking the red carpet in some God-awful sequined old lady dress! Send her back to the hotel and I will pull every fucking string I can. What size *is* she?"

I passed the phone to Lindsay. "Sixteen," she said acidly. "Maybe eighteen. I have had three children. I have gone through menopause. Send me a postcard when you get there." Lindsay hung up.

Back at the suite Lindsay placed a defiantly large room service order and then sat silently in her bathrobe while her hair and makeup were done. The dress selection was to be the last thing. One of Jeanine's unhelpfully thin assistants arrived with what looked like the entire Spanx selection from Bloomingdale's.

"No, I hate those things. I can't breathe."

"You can breathe when you get to the White House," Jeanine answered as she walked in the door with an armful of garment bags.

"Where's Tom?" Lindsay asked. She redialed his number while we unpacked the dresses—and the compression garments. She squeezed into the first gown—a navy sleeveless floor-length. She looked so uncomfortable.

"Now I wasn't sure what she has that's nice," Jeanine said right in front of Lindsay, "So I have a little of everything. Okay, next."

"Nice?" I asked.

"Like, does she have nice ankles, or nice shoulders."

Tom walked in. "She has lovely knees," he said, smiling. "I fell in love with her knees." He kissed Lindsay and she visibly relaxed.

After trying on all six contenders she ended up back in the navy sleeveless—with a wrap to hide her "tharms," short for arms that look like thighs in pictures—something that apparently kept Jeanine awake at night.

As soon as the limo pulled away I crossed Columbus Circle. In the end I hadn't told Brian that he'd been invited to join us because when I'd played through this moment—a stroll at dusk through the southern end of Central Park—his was not the hand I kept picturing, which only made me angry with myself. I dialed Billy for my weekly check-in before I would admit that I was probably about to break up with the hardwood floor I could stand on because I couldn't shake the memory of a fur rug that got ripped out from under me.

"Mandy?"

"Grammy?" I sounded equally confused. "Is Billy over for dinner?"

"You could say that."

"Grammy," I heard him grumble. "You really don't need to answer my phone."

"So long as you are under my roof, I'll answer anything I please."

Seventh grade. Tommy French putting a slug on the back of my neck. That was the feeling that went through me—cold and wet and scary. "Billy?"

"Yep."

"What's going on?"

"Nothin'."

"What did she mean by roof over your head?"

"We're staying here."

"We?"

"Me, Ray Lynne, and Mom."

"Fuck. What happened?"

He sighed. "There are some new guys passing through—building a gas station. Anyways they were in the diner and they started making fun of Slow Eddie and Mom told 'em off and they fired her." It sounded so good, so righteous, Mom sticking up for the guy who liked to get a beer on his way home from his janitor shift. But really, probably, what had happened was these guys had been pushing her, pinching her, being gross, and she'd been letting it all slide with a tight smile until they did something she could take them on for, and I bet she went off until their eyebrows singed. Perry liked her—he wouldn't have fired her unless she left him no choice. "Anyways, she didn't realize it takes a few weeks for the unemployment checks to start coming and we owed for the last month on the trailer . . ."

"Mom was finally faced between sleeping in her car and asking Grammy for something herself," I said.

"Her back's hurting her pretty bad."

I heard Grammy in the background.

"Yes, ma'am, I'll wash up in a minute!" he called, the phone muffled to his chest. "Jesus," he muttered to me.

I looked up at the fountain, knowing as Delilah had, that the hotel room the campaign was paying for me to stay in for a week could cover the rent on the trailer for months.

"You be patient with Grammy and helpful and wash your hands a hundred times if she asks."

"Yeah."

"How's Ray Lynne?"

"She broke one of those stone flowers and Grammy tried to spank her and mom lost her shit."

"So it's going great." I rubbed my temples. "I'm in New York, but I will drive down as soon as we get back, okay?"

"New York?" he asked in a voice that suddenly sounded younger than his thirteen years.

"Yep. I'm working my ass off right here in the heart of it all. I ate a thirty-dollar cheeseburger yesterday. And I promise you, Billy, you hang in there and you will be here, too, someday."

"Uh huh." There was a crackle on the line as the satellite struggled to keep Columbus Circle and Grammy's kitchen in its sights. "Go fuck yourself." It felt like he'd spat in my face, but he was right to.

Billy gone I stood in the rapidly deepening dusk, dizzy with uncertainty.

She hadn't told me. She hadn't asked me to step in and send her money. She hadn't looked to me to rescue her.

I should have been relieved.

Should have been. But so, so wasn't. If I knew Delilah—and I did—she was saving up for a much bigger ask.

The next morning I drank my second espresso to catapult me over the slight minibar hangover I'd given myself. We were all gathered in Tom and Lindsay's suite to review the press coverage of their evening and see how Project Future FLOTUS was shaping up. Tom was just back from the gym and guzzling orange juice. Despite forgetting her Lactaid, Lindsay had gamely eaten the fettuccini Alfredo served at the postscreening dinner because she was seated next to Mario Batali, whose food forced her to spend the night making hot compresses out of washcloths. Still white, she reclined on the white bed linens in her white bathrobe.

Jeanine sat by the window, carefully scanning the society pages on her laptop. In another black sleeveless silk blouse, this one with ruffles down the front, she looked like a caricature of a naughty secretary—severe ponytail, glasses, platform heels, glossy red lips. *Tap tap tap.* Frown.

"Well?" Michael asked. Michael was always rumpled. I was sure he had arrived yesterday with that suit in a dry cleaner bag and yet he still looked like he'd slept in it.

"Not good."

"What did they say?" Lindsay asked.

"Spit it out," Tom said, grabbing a piece of bacon from the table.

"Nothing," Jeanine explained, closing her laptop. "That's just it. Not even the people who promised me coverage said anything about Lindsay—it's like you weren't even there." She was mystified.

"I wish," Lindsay moaned.

Tom sat hard on the end of the bed.

Lindsay grimaced from the motion. "Really? This is what you made me leave my sick son for?"

"Our sick son."

Lindsay sidled away from him. "I don't think our sons could pick you out of a lineup, Tom, but okay."

Tom glanced awkwardly around the room. I'd never heard her talk to him like that.

"I absolutely do not understand why this happened. But we can fix this," Jeanine jumped in. "You're on the ground now. I'm going to schedule lunches with journalists every day until the Alzheimer's event—get you on the radar. And get you a stylist."

"I just want Mylanta."

"*I* can get you that," I said. I wanted to reach out and put my hand on her ankle, like I'd touch Billy when he was upset or sick, but I knew that would be weird.

"Are we ready to get to work?" Jeanine asked, waving away the croissant her assistant, Margo, held out to her as if it were a used Kleenex.

"She's ready," Tom answered.

We had five days between events and they were, as Jeanine promised, filled with journalist meet and greets. New York could only have been a romantic sojourn for Tom and Lindsay if they considered Jeanine barking talking points foreplay. Tom was taking advantage of being there to meet with UN delegates from countries with progressive policies on the economics of aging so his days were as full as Lindsay's. And every night they courted donors.

I was only asked to attend the one dinner where Tom made a PowerPoint presentation so I could manage the equipment. As I stood on the side of the gold-leafed dining room I watched Lindsay pick at her plate, even though on the way over she had said she was starving. The potential donor's wife sat beside her, artfully moving her food around without consuming a thing. We had agreed this past week, as the schedule cycled us among three restaurants (Blue Ribbon Sushi where the women around us ordered raw fish and arugula, Michael's where they ordered the Cobb salad without avocado, bacon or cheese, and Bergdorf's where they could relax their vigilance because the entire menu seemed to consist of broth and foam) that the New York power wives looked like greyhounds. "And I'm the chubby pug," Lindsay had laughed on the first day. But I could see the competitive starvation was starting to get to her.

As soon as we got back in the car Lindsay reached under her shantung blazer and unzipped the side of her dress, trying to slide down her girdle.

"Lindsay," Tom said impatiently, a hint of disgust hardening his voice. "Can you just keep it together until we get back to the room?"

"Oh, I'm sorry, are your balls in a vice?"

He adjusted his seat belt. "I told you I'd support you if you wanted to do that cleanse Jeanine suggested. Did you even read the brochure?"

She turned to the window. The town car continued down Central Park West, me seated between them, trying to curl my shoulders into each other like a hedgehog. "I am not living off algae shakes for a month."

"Fine. Then what about coming to the gym with me?"

"Since the twins pinched that nerve it hurts to walk most days, Tom. You know that."

"I know, I know, I'm sorry." He tugged his shirt cuff from under his blazer. "But your image matters as much as mine and you might need to suck up doing some things you don't want to do."

"And *you* completely lost people in the middle of your presentation," Lindsay retaliated. "I keep telling you that bit about pension funds doesn't work."

"Michael likes it." His jaw was set.

"He's never in the room. It doesn't play. You can't deliver it right and it makes you sound stupid."

I thought of that artist—the one who paints himself into backgrounds. Maybe I could tug my blazer over my head and they would forget I was there.

We pulled up in front of the hotel and the bellman let us out. Without a word to either of us Tom went straight inside, but Lindsay hung behind under the awning. "Lindsay?" I ventured, not daring to follow it up with asking if she was okay because that would mean I knew that she wasn't. The lights changed and traffic halted at the corner. She looked past me. We stood like that, me waiting on some instruction, some summation. The taxis surged again.

"There's a Pinkberry around the corner," she said and walked away. Only if you knew to look would you have spotted that, beneath her shimmering wrap, her dress was still unzipped.

For the Alzheimer's benefit the next night, Zac Posen had measured every inch of Lindsay and had whipped up an "Oprah special" as Jeanine referred to it—three-quarter-length sleeve gray silk dress, scooped neckline, and invisible expanding side plackets that allowed for her lungs to operate as God intended. Spanx-free, she looked relaxed, allowing her natural regality to shine as they headed out the door, Tom's introductory remarks in the breast pocket of his tux. For a moment I imagined they were some bride's proud parents. I wondered if Lindsay thought the same thing as they waited opposite the mirror for the elevator.

The next morning I awoke to a text from Lindsay.

GET UP HERE. NOW.

I scrambled over the piles of paper in the dark, more printed information than a twenty-first century campaign should require, and tugged on my sweatpants. The sun was just rising as I waited impatiently for the elevator. Forty-some odd floors below the Lululemon-clad joggers were making bright streaks in the park's foliage.

I tentatively knocked on their door. "It's open!" shouted Tom. Inside, Lindsay was hysterical, tear streaked. The hotel bathrobe over her pajamas, she was upending the contents of the dresser drawers into her suitcase. "Linds, you can't leave," Tom tried to placate her. "The Met Ball is tonight—we're hosting a table."

"You can go fuck yourself. Amanda, help me pack."

Tom glared at me and I had absolutely no idea what to do. "Amanda, don't help her do anything. She's not leaving—Linds, we'll fix this."

She paused her flurry of destruction and looked at him, wiping her face with her terry cloth sleeve. "How?"

"We have a team. Let's let them figure it out."

"Figure out how not to look like *you're married to your mother?*" The words came out in guttural spurts, like rain through a clogged drainpipe. Oh God. Was the press coverage of last night's event already in?

"You don't look like my mother," he said jovially, trying to put his arm around her. "My aunt, maybe."

She tugged away. "And what time did you even get in last night? You're so concerned about appearances? You can't be seen drinking yourself under the table in the bar. It's a fucking disgrace."

Jeanine pushed in without knocking, trailed by the dour Margo. In their workout clothes they had absolutely no trace of reaction to the scene, as if tearful clients and trashed hotel rooms were all part of a day. "We just need to make you over." Jeanine waved her hand in the air like it held a magic wand, instead of an apple. "I made Katie Holmes look ten years older—I can make you ten years younger."

"Try twenty," Margo said into her iPad. I peaked over her shoulder as she parked herself at the round table by the window and rapidly clicked through the morning's headlines. It was bad. Yes, Jeanine had succeeded in putting Lindsay on the media's radar, but anything substantive she might have said on the red carpet was totally overshadowed by the cattiness of the celebrity websites. Even the *Onion* ran the headline, "Davis Using Wife as Test Case for Geriatric Policies."

"I can get someone up here to Botox you by ten. We'll make you blonder. Laser those liver spots, some dermabrasion, easy peasy—then for the facelift we can take you off the grid."

"Facelift?" Lindsay balked.

"Nothing Housewives—think Barbara Walters. Think Greta Van Susteren."

"I don't want a facelift," Lindsay said vehemently. "I'm scared of anesthesia, knives, cutting, all of it. No. My friend Wendy had one and they did it too tight—the sutures popped and she has a black ring around her face that's permanent. What about what happened to Sally Jessy Raphael?"

"We'll get you someone good."

"Jeanine," Lindsay said, catching her breath, "We're trying to convince donors that Tom and I are people who have real solutions to the public's very real problems. How am I supposed to do that with a face full of Styrofoam?"

Tom was silent—had been since his aunt comment, and I was waiting to see which woman he was going to tell to back down. Lindsay must have been waiting, too.

There was another knock. "It's open," I called.

It was the dress for the gala. Jeanine had asked Pamella Roland to make something Léger-inspired; Roland frequently dressed Christina Aguilera for the red carpet and "understands sucking shit in." I took the garment bag from the bellboy and brought it in to unzip, pulling out something that looked like a long glove.

"I can't wear that," Lindsay said flatly.

"It's all in the structure," Jeanine dismissed. "At least let's try it on."

"I'm a fifty-year-old mother of three—why can't I look like a fifty-year-old mother of three? Why can't I be myself?"

"Because," Jeanine slapped the table, "you are auditioning to represent this country and the current first lady will be leaving some very high, very expensive, very sexy shoes to fucking fill. America does not want to follow up the FLILF with Whistler's Mother."

I looked to Tom—to break in, to tell Jeanine she had gone too far, but he was staring out the window down to the traffic circle. He said nothing.

"Knock, knock!" The door opened and in walked Tom's actual mother in her travelling outfit. "Who's ready for a party?" Belle had dispensed with the pearls and silk scarves, her attempts at being an Anne manqué. Instead, in a hot pink velour tracksuit with a sequin flamingo on the back, she rushed over to hug her son. With her freshly inflated lips that bobbed on her newly unlined face like a buoy on a windless day, Belle planted a big kiss on Tom's cheek.

"How's my handsome boy?" she asked over his shoulder. "And Lindsay, you look like hell, honey. What's the matter? Is it the kids?"

Tom pulled back, seemingly struggling to suppress his reaction to his mother's new face. "Mom, we're just a little hungover from last night—those research scientists really like to throw down. Why don't you and Dad enjoy the buffet and I'll swing by your room in a bit?"

"Oh, great. I'm so excited! I bought a Louis Vuitton from the nicest African man downstairs. Do I have an hour to go to Times Square today? Your daddy and I want to get a picture with that naked cowboy."

"How about with a giant M&M instead?" Jeanine suggested, steering her to the door by the elbow. "I think I could clear that." Jeanine and Margo walked Belle out.

"I'm just going to—" I started to follow.

"Is *that* what you want me to look like?" Lindsay asked Tom before I could make it to the door.

"Linds—"

"Because she looks *cheap* and *tacky*," she leveled at him. "How dare everyone sit here and think they can make me over?" Her voice was like a circular saw. "Have they *seen* your college pictures, Tom? Have they seen your mullet and your acid-washed jeans? Without me you'd be a paralegal, living in some shitty town and saving up to go to Red Lobster."

"I worked my ass off in law school," he growled back at her.

"*Who* wrote your application, coached you on the LSAT, tutored you through L1? Who fucking paid for the whole thing?"

His eyes went to the floor. I held my breath. "You did, Linds." He swung his head like he was sliding marbles back and forth between his ears. "Look, I gotta meet that guy from Cornell. You do what you want. Leave. Stay. Wear a fucking bedspread. But to come this far just to have them use our marriage as a punch line . . . it's not going to get us a fucking cent." He shut the door firmly behind him.

I dared to look at her.

"Well." She shrugged, her voice barely audible. "Now you know everything. Will you get Jeanine back up here? I'll see you at five."

"Do you still want to visit the—"

"At five."

I knew better than to ask again or try to comfort her, so I let myself out. In my room I took six steps, dropped the key card, picked up my phone, and dialed a number from memory.

Pax answered on the first ring. "Hello?"

"Were you ashamed of me?" I asked.

"Amanda?" His voice was sandy with sleep.

"Was it my family? Do I mispronounce things without realizing it? I used to say 'nave' instead of naive because I'd only read it, never heard anyone say it. Am I tacky? Am I cheap?" All these years later, Lindsay still saw Tom as the guy who'd needed a haircut and a change of clothes in order to fit into her world. He was from "some shitty town,"—next door to my shitty town—and in some place in her brain that had gotten poked with a stick this morning—he still lived there.

"Amanda—"

"You realized I was a fuck-against-the-wall girl, not the one you build a life with, is that it? You figured it out. Well?" I thought for a second maybe the call had dropped.

"Where are you?"

I looked around the sun-soaked room for a moment, the silk decor, the extraordinary view of the city all the way out to the ocean. "I'm on the forty-third floor of the Manhattan Mandarin Oriental," as if that was where I *was*. At that moment I didn't know how to sum up my life, just my location.

"I'm at the Essex House one block away. I'll be right there."

I opened the door minutes later still in my pajamas. His cheeks were flushed from running. We looked at each other a long moment before he backed me into the room, until I was pressed against the fan-patterned wallpaper. He placed a hand on my face. "Despite every aching molecule in my body," he said quietly. "I will not fuck you against this wall because I don't want to do anything more to contribute to this crazy idea you have about what kind of girl I think you are. You are one of the fiercest, bravest people I have ever met. I think you have more substance in your gorgeous pinky finger than I have in my whole body." He broke his gaze. "And I got scared you would figure that out. You were just suddenly in such a real place—with your job and your family— and I freaked out." His eyes returned intensely to mine. "I fucked it up, Amanda. The longer I went without calling, the more of a shit I knew I'd been, and the less I could face you." He almost leaned in. I almost let him. "So you can hate me, that I can take, that I deserve, but I cannot live with you, Amanda Beth Luker, thinking that I thought you weren't good enough for the fucking Westerbrooks." Our faces fell closer together until our foreheads were touching. "I'd be so unbelievably lucky," he whispered. "If you forgave me."

I let myself sink against him as he encircled my waist, pressing me into him as if trying to merge our bones. I didn't know how he could see me when I couldn't, see myself, but in that moment—with his heart beating against my ear and the sun revealing the particles in the air around us—I believed him.

It turned out that Pax was in town because Pym had bought a table at the Met Gala, and he was courting the kind of deep-pocketed lefties who might want to back the financial reform lobby. So suddenly I was in the mall under our hotel squeezing myself into a knockoff Leger bandage dress and hoping my ponytail looked kind of Grande-esque. Then I went back up to Tom and Lindsay's suite to make sure she didn't need anything before they left.

"Amanda." Lindsay's face fell when she saw me. "Sweetie, we don't have a ticket for you. God, I wish we did because I don't think I'll get through this."

I was struggling to keep my face from falling in turn. The Roland dress she was wearing was so, so wrong. She looked like she had been sucked into one of those space-saving vacuum bags they show on infomercials. And Jeanine's makeup people had caked her in purple eye shadow.

"Pax is back," I shared gamely.

She grabbed my hand, the corners of her eyes watering. "Oh, see," she said intently, "New York *is* romantic."

"Don't cry," I said. "Your makeup will run."

"Lindsay." Her mother-in-law swanned into the room wearing what was probably an original Leger that she managed to make look like the knockoff of my knockoff. But mostly what I was staring at was the two hard semicircles of her cleavage, like someone had halved a grapefruit. Belle was so taut I expected her to turn around and reveal a series of clamps from her scalp to her ass. "Get a move on. Tom's waiting. Oh Lord, honey, at least let the girls have some air." She reached her claw-like hands toward Lindsay's breasts as Tom and Jeanine came in. Lindsay jumped away.

"I can do it myself." She reached into her dress and dug around to lift her assets out of the couture cling wrap. Suddenly she got a strange look on her face.

"Lindsay, what is it?" I asked.

"Jesus," Tom barked from the door. "Can we just go already? We're late."

"There's no point if you don't do the carpet," Jeanine echoed at his heels.

"Lindsay," I said, trying to read her panic. I looked desperately around the room for something she could wear to obscure the ridiculous dress. "Wait—here." I swiped the kimono-print silk throw off the bed. "Wrap this around your shoulders like a pashmina." I held it out, but she didn't take it. "Lindsay," I prompted.

"Lindsay," he said.

"Lindsay!" Jeanine snapped.

Her hands were still frozen inside her gown, her eyes on the carpet, her voice low and shaky. "I have a lump."

Chapter
Eight

Here's what I learned in the first few weeks following Lindsay's diagnosis: There is a social chain that organically forms in these situations. Each friend or family member finds someone who will grip his or her hand and say, as many times a day as needed, "*It will be okay.*" Because then said person leaves the doctor's office, hospital hallway, or kitchen, and says the same thing just as urgently to someone else involved. Tom convinced Lindsay. Lindsay convinced me. I convinced Michael. Who cheered up Jeanine, who yelled at the campaign staff not to be "fucking maudlin."

"Babe?" Pax's voice would come through in a whisper on my cell, waking me from where I had fallen asleep sitting up in the Davis's den.

"Yeah?" I'd answer, checking the clock in the dark.

"Just wanted to see how you're holding up."

He called every night from DC, as if determined not to let me go an hour where I could be wondering if this was all too much for him—how we collided from estrangement to cancer in a single day.

"I'm the same," I'd whisper back. "It's the same."

I'd stumble out to find Tom by himself on the living room

couch staring at the wall, his expression inscrutable, and think, *Who can he express his fear to? Who does he have? His dad? Belle?* That was laughable. He had to be the strongest of all of us.

While we waited to find out if the cancer had spread, everything at the office came to a standstill, except a string of fundraising meetings that had been months in the making. After much agonizing, Tom decided it would be in poor taste for him to attend and that Brian should go to keep things moving, with me along to assist. Brian, ever the New England gentleman, had been reasonably gracious about our break-up. With mortality hanging over all of us we were forced to have capital P Perspective on everything.

"You want the radio?" he'd ask, with a glance at the rental's dashboard.

"No. Do you?"

"No."

The circumstances having rendered us emotionally incapable of the chitchat necessary to mitigate the awkwardness, we travelled in silence to the hulking residences of those who could line the Davis war chest in silence. One eye on my phone, waiting for the call about Lindsay's test results, and struggling to focus, I sat beside Brian with what I hoped was an enthusiastic smile as time moved in increments the size of tea sandwiches. To his credit, Brian pitched each yacht-tanned face like Tom's candidacy was just occurring to him, the prospect of losing Lindsay hovering over us like a seagull fixed on our poached salmon.

I was in the middle of touring one zillionaire's unimaginably expansive cannonball collection when my phone finally buzzed with Tom's number. I ducked out to the car to take it. "Amanda," his voice was raspy. He was struggling to speak. Bracing myself, I got in and slammed the door.

"Okay," I heard myself say faintly as I trained my eyes on the algae-glazed lips of the spouting dolphin at the drive's center.

"She wanted me to call you. We just got confirmation—it hasn't metastasized."

I dropped my forehead to the steering wheel. "Thank God," I kept saying. "Thank God, thank God."

"Is that Mandy?" I heard her grab the phone.

"Lindsay, I'm so relieved."

"Listen. I need you to let Brian finish the fundraising and get back here today. I'm going to have a double mastectomy—" I heard Tom say something in the background that sounded like, "Now hey, Linds."

"It's aggressive," she continued. "And there's a difference of opinion."

"I just don't see why you have to do anything that radical yet." Tom's voice was muffled. "Right as the campaign is gearing up—"

"And the boys aren't even in first grade yet," she said to me like that ended the matter.

"I understand," I said, although I couldn't imagine my mother making that kind of drastic decision with us at the forefront of her mind.

"Now, *here's* the fuck of it. I can't recuperate at this construction site. My oncologist says it's a dusty, toxic, off-gassing hellhole—too much strain on my immune system. There's no time to rent something so . . ." I heard her gird herself to ask for something. What was it? "Can you help move us back to Riverside?" In all the talk of radiation, of chemo, it was the first time she sounded defeated.

"Of course," I rushed to reassure her. Because I knew what she was being forced to do: recuperate in a bed just on the other side of the wall from Ashleigh's.

She went through with the surgery and, to cope with the stress, Tom took up running. He announced he wanted to do a marathon in the fall to raise money and awareness for breast cancer research. While I sat with the nurse in the kitchen, waiting for Lindsay to text us a request, he'd take off and come back hours later, drenched in sweat like he was trying to outrun the specter of another loss.

One such afternoon, Lindsay called me up to her room. Their king-sized bed had been replaced with an adjustable hospital model and from beneath the bedclothes the clear plastic drain snaked like a stick of candy striped red and yellow. She was pale, had lost a lot of weight, and her hair had grown out to reveal a good inch of gray. "What can I get you?" I asked as she pressed down with her knuckles to sit up.

"I want him to go back to the campaign before he gets a bone spur," she said, her voice still raspy from the tube they'd put down her throat during the surgery.

"Oh, Lindsay, I think he wants to be here. I'm sure he couldn't concentrate if he tried to put his mind on anything else."

"Well," she said, eyes closed, "Let's find out."

The next day Tom and I returned to campaign headquarters at the Davis Center and Jeanine and Michael rounded us up to discuss Tom's official announcement, only a few weeks away, and what they brashly termed the "Lindsay Factor." While she had thankfully slipped from the memories of talk show comedians, everyone was anxious about introducing her to the public after the first attempt had inarguably failed. Half the staff thought it imperative that she be there. Jeanine, speaking for the others, adamantly disagreed, worrying Lindsay's presence would be "a fucking downer."

"She lost all this weight." Jeanine's highest compliment. "But now her skin just looks—deflated." Jeanine's faith in the power of weight loss was visibly shaken. "Spotlighting Lindsay's ordeal will just plant doubt in the public's head about Tom's ability to focus on them. We have to face it—she could be a fatal liability."

After all those nights of finding him catatonic in his den, I thought for sure Tom would leap in to reprimand her—point out the inappropriateness of such hyperbole given the actual fatality Lindsay had just escaped. Instead he simply asked, "What do I do?"

"Well, I think, like it or not, we need her. A politician runs with his wife, that's just the fact of it. And no one more than the president," Michael said, and that was somehow the final word.

When the day arrived Lindsay appeared backstage exactly five minutes before go time, having been subjected to Jeanine's ministrations. Newly blond, freshly bronzed, and perched atop thin heels she looked anxiously to Tom. But he seemed too nervous to notice—or perhaps he had already pumped her confidence at home.

Fighting the Percocet enabling her to endure fabric against her fresh scars, she reached out for his hand to keep steady and, with a final powder of their noses, the two walked out on the courthouse steps as if the last three months were just a bad movie they'd seen on a plane. She smiled adoringly as he spoke, waved emphatically as the crowd cheered—and collapsed into the car as soon as it was over.

I ran over to her, my heart still pounding in time to everyone chanting Tom's name.

"Do you want me to get him?" I asked as I got in beside her.

"We did it," Lindsay breathed, a sheen of sweat on her forehead.

"You did," I corrected her. It was hard to hear each other over the screaming. She lolled her head to me on the seat. "No, he did." She closed her eyes, giving into the adrenal crash. "Despite me."

Online chatter was enthusiastic—the resounding public response seemed to pick up right where Merrick's concession speech had left off. The private funders started to throw their weight behind Tom. Our super PAC's website went live and those critical grassroots donations started to trickle in—what we would depend on to keep ad buys going through the primaries.

Jeanine ordered the crepe dress in four colors and planned to rotate Lindsay through them for Tom's upcoming appearances. The Lindsay Factor now had a protocol: hand her a Percocet and keep it brief. It seemed we finally had momentum on our side when, just weeks after Tom's announcement, the former secretary of state made her own.

Meredith Lanier's arrival to the primary race posed a formidable threat to Tom. He polled well with the elderly and minorities, but women made up his strongest voter block. For the first time since Lindsay's diagnosis, Michael invited her to join the team in full crisis-management mode. She sat beside me quietly on her old living room couch as Jeanine explained to a packed room that, moving forward, Lindsay would need to shift center stage.

"What?" Tom balked.

"You know what the secretary has?" Jeanine asked.

"Both her breasts," Lindsay answered, wearing one of the old oxford shirts of Tom's she'd come to favor with her drawstring pants.

"Exactly. *And* a vagina. Tom, your only shot here is to reintroduce Lindsay into the narrative and make the secretary run against both of you."

"*Both* of us?" Tom balked from where he sat on the other side of her. "What is Lindsay running for?" She shifted beside me.

"We've marginalized her for obvious reasons, but now we need to rebrand you as a package deal."

Tom and Lindsay both took this in as I tried to read them. "I don't know." Tom shook his head. Everyone watched him, waiting for him to continue. "She's still tired from the radiation. I don't know that I'm okay with asking that."

"*She's* right here," Lindsay said.

"Linds." Tom took her hand and looked at Jeanine. "No," he said firmly. "Right now she needs to rest."

"The twins are starting kindergarten. You're never here. What I *need* is a project." Lindsay squeezed his hand and released it to wipe her hair from her face. "And badly."

"Well, I'm not letting you travel. Unless you guys have some magical way of her doing it from bed—"

"That's it." Jeanine extended a Bordeaux-colored nail at him. "She'll do a book. Tell your story through hers."

"A book?" Lindsay repeated, sitting up. I could immediately see it.

"Absolutely not. You don't have the energy for a book." Tom said.

"To tell my story? Our story? To get you to the White House? I can do that. I would love to do that, actually."

"The truth of the modern wife, the modern marriage—you've been a working mom, a stay-at-home mom, and you know Tom better than anyone," Jeanine decreed. "Done and done."

The journalist Karen Fousard, who penned the bestselling "as told to" memoir of a female astronaut, was selected as Lindsay's writer. In addition to approving everyone Karen wanted to interview, the campaign had to sign off on every question Karen planned to ask. The only veto I ever saw was a name Tom crossed off Karen's list— Shannon Burkheart. Whoever she was her side of things would not be making it to Karen's ears.

Each Monday Karen submitted a chapter for Jeanine and Michael to mark with red pens, followed by conference calls, which I only ever heard their end of. I wondered how Karen fared writing at breakneck speed while being screamed at on a daily basis to make the "truth" Jeanine was so excited for "more fucking flattering for fuck's sake!" When the last word was vetted the manuscript was rushed to the press and a fresh prescription for Xanax was rushed to Jeanine.

Tom's copy arrived via FedEx to the Wyoming ranch where he, Brian, and I, had flown at the behest of a billionaire wanting to kick his tires. After a day of shooting, riding, and roping, Tom was icing his shoulder when I found him in the guest wing. He slipped on his glasses to gaze at the handsome picture of Lindsay sitting on their front porch that adorned the book's cover.

"Tom, he's waiting," Brian called from the doorway. "Drinks in the study."

Tom quickly flipped the pages until he came to a stop, his eyes darting back and forth to read. "Mm," he murmured and then handed it hastily back to me. As he walked away, rebuttoning his shirt beneath a canopy of antlers, he called over his shoulder. "Have at it, Amanda. I know you're dying to." I flipped open to the page that had gotten crushed down.

It was the details of Ashleigh's passing, limited to a succinct paragraph. I reread it as if the few sentences would magically expand with details. Neither Tom nor Lindsay had been home the night Ashleigh took her dad's car out, despite the restrictions of her learner's permit. Her best friend—Shannon Burkheart—had been buckled into the passenger seat so she hadn't gone through the windshield as Ashleigh had. I flipped to the middle of the book to find a photograph of Ashleigh and Shannon holding triple ice cream scoops with their arms around each other. I imagined them getting the news—two sets of parents cleaving on opposite journeys of indescribable gratitude and grief. What had they done to get through the minutes, hours, and days that followed? Lindsay concluded by saying that she didn't share anything more because there was nothing more to share.

We have found it in our hearts to forgive the driver who ran that red light. He is God's responsibility and only God can judge him. We'll never know why Ashleigh decided to go out without our permission—or chose not to buckle her seat belt. Our journey has been one of making peace with that.

Going back to the beginning, I sat by the fire and read every word. Even though Karen had written the book, it captured what I loved about Lindsay. Simply told, but with Lindsay's dry wit and unflinching gaze, she shared about how it had been to manage her illness for her family, equating her terror that it might deprive her children of a mother to the prospect that her honesty about the experience might deprive her country of Tom's leadership.

The sky was star strewn beyond the windows when Tom returned from dinner and a moonlight cigar. "It's so good." I held it to my chest. "You're going to love it."

"I don't need to love it, Amanda," he muttered as Brian indicated with a head shake to me that our trip had been a fool's errand. "I lived it." Tom closed his door, leaving a trail of dusty footprints in his wake.

Chapter
Nine

LINDSAY'S MEMOIR WAS TO BE RELEASED the Monday after Thanksgiving and Jeanine landed her a spot on *Good Morning America* to promote the launch. It was to be an intimate one-on-one with Robin Roberts. Final confirmation from ABC didn't come through until we were parting for the holiday. Jeanine was so elated I thought she was going to break me with her bony hug.

Desperate to finally have four whole days to spend with Billy and Ray Lynne, I had assumed Pax was going to be joining his family for their annual trip to his aunt's in London. But when he started asking about Luker "Thanksgiving traditions," I realized he thought he was coming home with me. Having no idea how to casually tell him *over my dead body*, I found myself riding shotgun on the four-hour drive to Tallyville.

I was feeling disoriented, as always, by our relationship. In the books I read as a teenager, intimacy builds in clear steps. Date one: come check out my mill. Date two: let's run through the moors. Date three: I discover you have a wife locked in the attic. Somehow, ultimately, happiness prevails. But Pax and I kept skipping around on the time line. We'd seen each other naked years before we kissed. Our first six-week run had been all sleepovers and no dinners. Now we essentially lived together on our weekend visits, cooking meals, folding laundry, but then subsisting for weeks in between on texts. And here I was bringing him home for Thanksgiving, which felt simultaneously premature and long overdue. The very phrase, "Thanksgiving traditions," conjured parents waiting to greet us in matching sweaters, a graying childhood pet running out to the car as we arrived. That would not be the scene at Grammy's, that much I knew for sure.

Not that the Lukers didn't have traditions. You could set your watch to Thanksgiving growing up. Refusing to go to Grammy's, Mom waited until the last minute to start cleaning up the trailer for her mother's visit. Having been cooking since dawn, Grammy stoically drove the meal over in her red cooler. Greeted with harried annoyance, she then made no secret of her desire to leave, further compounding the insult to Delilah.

One year Mom stepped out for a smoke and Grammy asked me where the mess was hidden. I admitted it was wedged under Mom's bed tighter than the Stouffer's stuffing in the turkey. Mom returned and asked why we were laughing, and Billy, too young to know any better, told her. The holiday ended in tears 100 percent of the time. Still, we persisted in attempting it as if the government had assigned us the ritual. Which it kind of had.

Since Tom had made a televised appearance at the Riverside food drive on Wednesday night, Pax and I drove down from my apartment late Thursday morning and were standing on Grammy's porch by midafternoon. "Enjoy this last moment of silence," I whispered to Pax as he squeezed my hand. "You're about to experience the Miss America pageant as scripted by Tennessee Williams."

"Well, look at y'all." Grammy came to greet us in her fanciest apron. "You didn't have to do all that." She took the bouquet Pax brought for her, obviously tickled.

"Thank you so much for having me, Mrs. Luker." He held the door for me.

"Please, now. It's Grammy."

Ray Lynne leaned out from the kitchen doorway with that shy smile of hers, and I rushed to hug her; a first grader now, she was too big to scoop up.

"You two must be tuckered. Amanda, show Pax to the living room so he can relax." Ray Lynne and I automatically stopped in the doorway, but he went directly to the family photos on the side table.

"Grammy says we can't play in here, Mandy."

"I know," I said, overcoming my own childish trepidation. "But we're not going to play. We're going to visit."

"I don't want to visit. I want to take my Barbies to the dream castle."

"Yes, totally do that." Not wanting to miss a minute of her, I reluctantly gave permission and she darted off. Pax bent to study a yellowing picture of me on a neighbor's Slip 'N Slide.

"So, Mandy had a thing for Princess Jasmine," he observed.

I felt like I'd left my clothes in the car. I'd never brought anyone here. "Me and every other seven-year-old."

"I was more of a Genie guy, myself." He smiled. "I always try to imagine you little and the best I can do is your head, but on a little body. But you really were little," he said tenderly.

"I sprouted up in eighth grade. That suit was too big but Mom knotted the straps with a twist tie. I'm sure you'll hear all about it."

"I'm counting on it." I realized he was actually excited to be doing this thing that I was siphoning breath to get through.

"Mandy?" Mom came clomping down the stairs in her white patent heels. She hugged me tightly and I dropped my head to her shoulder to keep from coming away with a cheek full of her foundation. She smelled like Wild Turkey. "The nerds are winning the war, huh," she said, summing up my outfit. Despite anticipating that she was going to comment on my navy shirtdress's high neckline, I had no rejoinder.

Pax kissed Delilah on the cheek. "Great to see you again, Delilah. Happy Thanksgiving."

"What are we doing in here?" she asked, as confused as Ray Lynne.

"We're having a cocktail before we sit down for dinner," Grammy instructed as she brushed past us with a tray of them. "These two have been driving all day."

"And we're using the good glasses?"

"Yes, Delilah," Grammy said, her smile straining as she set it on the coffee table.

I heard Billy jogging down the stairs and turned to see his hair had been shaved on the sides. Tossing a "what up" in our direction, he collapsed into the couch, arms crossed. Grammy smoothed her skirt and sat down, indicating we should follow. She handed Pax a little embroidered napkin and gave the plate of pimento cheese and crackers to Delilah to offer him. Mom looked at me and then at Pax and her turquoise-rimmed eyes narrowed. None of her boyfriends had been invited into this room, let alone this house. The plate stalled on her lap. "Someone's getting the VIP treatment," she said before taking a swig of her drink. Grammy cleared her throat and slid a coaster under Mom's glass before she returned it to the table.

"So did Mandy have a pet rabbit?" Pax generously prompted her, pointing at a photo. "How old was she there?"

If we'd been at the trailer I knew what would've come next. Mom would have launched into stories of her carousing, intending to embarrass Grammy. But we were not on Mom's turf and to my alarm she did the one thing she never had: she went silent. Immune to the potency of her sullen expression, Pax chatted with Grammy, who was an expert at ignoring Delilah's gathering storms. Billy and I exchanged looks the way I imagine hostages might.

When we sat down to eat Mom drank steadily, fidgeting with her napkin ring as if waiting to be excused. I was so grateful that Grammy's receptionist skills kept the conversation moving, almost as grateful as I was that Pax's grooming left him immune to the swaying head of an inebriated dining companion. Every cell in my body on edge, I didn't taste a bite of the canned cranberry or green bean casserole. By the time Grammy pushed back her chair to get the Sara Lee pie from the oven, I thought we might be in the clear. I was wrong.

As soon as the door to the kitchen closed, Mom asked, "What's Jacksonville like?"

"It's nice."

"That's what I imagine," she said to the flower print on the wall. "Nice."

I stood up to clear the plates.

"We should come to Jacksonville." She swung her smile past Billy and Ray Lynne. "Wouldn't that be nice, guys?"

"Yes, definitely," I answered automatically.

"Right? It'll be fun. What's her place like, Pax?"

"It's cute." He squeezed my knee as I cleared his plate.

"Aw, he's sweet, Mandy." She stared at me, her eyes watery from the wine. "We could use some cute."

I clustered all the silverware in my left hand. "Great. After dinner just let me look at Tom's schedule and we'll pick a weekend I'm not flying."

"No, no, no, honey." She dropped her fists on the table, rattling the china. "We're gonna come stay with you. How 'bout it?"

Nervously I glanced sideways at Pax. "How about drinking some water?"

"And let's all finally take that trip down to Disney World." She looked at Ray Lynne. "Wouldn't you like that, baby? Meet a real princess?"

Ray Lynne nodded eagerly.

"Okay, Mom." Fed up Billy pushed back his chair.

"Your guy, Davis, can hook us up with some of those passes that let you cut the lines."

"Really, Mandy?" Ray Lynne asked.

Trying to ignore her until she could pass out, sleep it off, and come to her senses in the morning I stacked the last plate and Pax stood to gather the serving bowls.

"January," Delilah continued. "That'll give me time over the break to get them registered at their new schools." She didn't mean stay, she meant live—which I had really known as soon as she said it.

"Mom, my place isn't really big enough for—"

"Is it bigger than the trailer?" Her voice was suddenly sharp.

"Y-yes." I lifted the stack of plates into my arms. "But I'm sorry. I just don't know that this is the time for travelling when you need to focus on figuring out a job—"

"I'll have much better luck in a city—look at you. It's settled!"

"What's settled?" Grammy asked, backing through the door with her oven mitts on as Billy and I went to help Mom from her chair.

"We're moving to Jacksonville," Mom announced, the pendulum of her head starting to pull her body dangerously off balance.

"Oh, goodness gracious, Delilah, there you go again," Grammy said, like Mom was four.

"Stop condescending me!" Mom flailed out her arm, narrowly missing Billy as she upended the pie onto the carpet. Grammy turned red. Ray Lynne burst into tears. Mom pointed an accusing finger at me before she slid to the floor, her dress riding up to her waist as she passed out.

~

Having been unable to sleep all night in the twin bed beside Ray Lynne's I was awake when Pax's knock came just before dawn. I tiptoed to the door, half-impressed he had the courage to say it to my face. "Bob called—a pipe's burst at the office. I've gotta fly back. Can you call me a cab?" As excuses went it was inventive, I could at least give him that.

When we heard the honk in the driveway I tugged on a cardigan and walked him silently to the car. "Okay. See you soon," he said, his kiss landing on my cheek. I turned to follow his gaze to where mom sat smoking on the far side of the porch, her knees pulled up under her Marlins T-shirt.

"Will you?"

"Will I what?" he asked, opening the car door.

"Nothing. Yes. Fly safe. Good luck with the flood."

"I just hope we didn't lose all our computers," he muttered, his brow furrowed.

I told myself to let go of his hand, not to run after the car as he pulled out. I could feel Delilah's eyes on me as I walked back up to the porch. I'd make a big breakfast for the kids, take them bowling and then to the mall where I could really talk to Billy—get us out of here for as much of the day as I could. Suddenly, I heard the taxi backing up and spun around. "Hey!" Pax rolled his window all the way down. "I love you, Mandy Luker."

I grinned. "You, too."

"You, too, what?"

"I love you, too. Now get out of here!" I happily waved him away.

"I guess things just work out for some people," Delilah said coolly as my fingers wrapped around the screen door latch.

"I'm not some people." I turned to where she sat with the

turquoise fabric stretching over her legs, her eyes shinning in the darkness. Coiled up. "I'm your daughter."

"That and a dollar." She flicked her cigarette into the roses, waiting for me to take the bait, but I went back inside, damned if I'd give her the satisfaction.

It turned out that since moving into the Victorian Billy had developed his own strategies for avoiding Mom, meaning he didn't want to hang out that weekend beyond my giving him rides to his friends' houses and fronting him pizza money. So I dropped him off and wandered the half-shuttered mall behind Ray Lynne, who stood still only to change her earrings from the rainbow pack of studs she laboriously selected at Spencer's. Watching her amble around the fountain in repetitive circles, her elbow sliding along the stone, she suddenly looked like one of the puppies I used to see sometimes with the guys hanging out behind the gas station. They were so cute, but the guys were already taunting them, already pushing and prodding them to become fight dogs. *What way would you bet?* I wondered. *Which forces would be strongest?* Third child of a single mother who lost her trailer. A grandmother twenty years more worn out than when I got rides to the library—back when there was one. A town twenty years worse off. But she had me. The money I sent and the world I was building a bridge to. For all of us.

Leaving that Sunday I had the hardest time letting her go.

Returning to my apartment Sunday night, I dumped my clothes with their tenacious smell of Delilah's cigarettes directly into the laundry and promptly passed out.

"Amanda?"

I answered my cell in the dark. "Lindsay?" It was a little after midnight. I was supposed to get on a flight to San Diego with Tom in just a few hours.

"Where are you? DC?"

"Jacksonville," I said.

"Shit."

"Are you okay? What happened? Is it Tom?"

"Oh my God, Amanda, *Good Morning America*, live, in front of five million people." Her words were a rush of panic. "When Tom said he had this San Diego trip I said fine, but I should have said not fucking fine and now my phone won't stop buzzing with texts from Jeanine about the fucking speaking points. That loud stylist is going to be there with those claustrophobic dresses and I just—what was I thinking doing any of this alone?"

"Oh, Lindsay, you're going to be great! And this time you won't even have Nancy "Stick-Up-Her-Ass" Merrick to contend with."

She let out a laugh, but I knew her eyes were staring wide. "Amanda."

"Yes. I'm right here," I said softly, wishing I were.

"Can you come?" her voice was small. "Please?"

Rousing Tom's pilot from a dead sleep to meet me at the hangar and giving the order for takeoff in an otherwise empty jet felt like confirmation of every wish I'd had standing in front of the stagnant mall fountain, just a few days ago, throwing change in alongside Ray Lynne. As the plane climbed so did my certainty that I was securing our future. We leveled in the indigo sky and I set the temperature of the cabin to my preferred degree, putting my feet up on the empty seat across from me. En route to the number one morning show in the country, I tried to memorize every deluxe detail around me as evidence that this, *not* the weekend that preceded it, was my reality, would be *our* reality—Billy and Ray Lynne and mine—as soon as Tom won the election.

What started with a light dusting of snow over Baltimore thickened into a blizzard as we bumped down. The five o'clock drive from the airport to the studio was nail-biting, and I was grateful it was only just past six when I ran across the salted pavement of Rockefeller Center. I was shown to a dressing room where I squeezed past the handlers for the other guests, a bevy of hair and makeup women, before finally coming to a stop at Jeanine—reading off her iPad to the closed bathroom door.

"Tom's a pillar of *strength*. His *strength* saw me through it. The *strength* of our love keeps me going. Amanda's here." She stepped aside and I shrugged off my coat. "Seven minutes with Robin Roberts, Lindsay." The door cracked open and Jeanine jammed her head through. "I want to hear that word in four of them."

Lindsay tugged me inside and yanked the door shut like we were eighth graders stealing a smoke. I looked pointlessly for a place to put my coat down as I caught my breath. Lindsay was sitting on the closed toilet lid, her prosthesis bra lying across her lap like it'd been spanked. The sight of the two scars across her bare chest conjured the eyebrows of a macabre clown. My hand went to my mouth. "Don't," she warned. I blinked back tears. "Not with *that* out there."

"Did you tell her to pepper in the *unflinchings*?" Michael joined Jeanine on the other side of the door.

"Yes," Jeanine said. "Three *strongs* and one *unflinching*. Got it?" she called through the door.

"Does it hurt?" I asked Lindsay.

"My surgeon says the scars are angry. Strong, strong, strong. Unflinching. And angry." She exhaled, laying a palm gingerly over each ragged red line. "I get phantom twinges from the nerves regenerating. It's worse to feel things against them. For example, two silicone water balloons." The bra cups dented her skirt. "The pain is distracting—I don't know how I'm going to keep smiling, keep saying what they want me to. If I take a pain killer I'll come off like Farrah Fawcett."

I reached out and took the bra from her. The silicone bags were unimaginably heavy.

"And Linds," Michael called in. "We're definitely going with the story of Tom carrying you down the mountain after your sprained ankle on that hike, how he's always been there for you and now this is your turn to be there for him."

"Well . . . uh . . . we were in our garden," she muttered to the floor. "And I leaned on him as I hobbled to the porch."

"Karen's version," Michael called pointedly.

Our eyes met in the mirror. This was untenable. I deliberately placed the bra in the duffle at our feet, zipped it closed, then handed her blouse to her.

She looked at me questioningly.

I nodded—forget the bra. "The book is beautiful, Lindsay. I loved your story," I said.

"Me, too," she replied with a touch of sadness as she buttoned up.

"The guy's here with your mike," Jeanine called.

"Okay, here goes," she said, standing up and opening the door.

It took a second for me to compose myself and then I followed her out into a three-way standoff.

"You forgot your bra," Jeanine said.

Lindsay glanced at me. "No, I didn't."

"Lindsay," Michael tried gamely, as if she was joking. "You're not going out there like that."

"Like what, Michael?"

"Without your tits on." Jeanine exclaimed. "We're already letting you do this blah Eileen Fisher thing. Now go in there and put it on."

"I'm a grown woman, Jeanine." Lindsay said to her. "And *those* are not my tits. My tits are sitting in a landfill. If that makes you uncomfortable then I'm sorry." She waved the hovering crew guy over to mike her.

"Fuck *me*, it'll make *America* uncomfortable, Lindsay," Jeanine spat.

"Jeanine's right," Michael added. "It's way too high risk."

"It's not like I'm going topless!" Lindsay cried as she took the tiny microphone from the crew guy and attached it to her collar. "So there's a little extra fabric. I'm going out there to talk about a double mastectomy for God's sake."

"You're going out there to talk about your strong husband so he can be the president! It's seven in the morning! People are standing in their kitchens. They don't want to be depressed, Lindsay! You have to serve this with a spoonful of fucking sugar!"

"I disagree." They turned on me and I swallowed but kept speaking as I mentally flashed to Delilah murmuring about Disney World with her dress up over her thong. "People don't want her trying to look twenty years younger than she is. Or like she hasn't been through what she's been through. *That's* depressing. They want her to act her age with elegance and dignity. No more bullshit, that's the campaign, right? Lanier's government-as-usual and we're the real people—authentic. What's more authentic than this?"

Lindsay gave me a look of such unmitigated gratitude endorphins burst through my body like soda erupting from a shaken can.

"We have to go *right now*." The producer called from the door. "You're live in two."

Despite Jeanine and Michael's terror, they had no choice but to let her walk to the set just as she was.

As we hurried to watch in the greenroom Jeanine muttered that this was it, she quit. She didn't need *this*.

But it turned out other women did. Hundreds of thousands of them.

As terrified as Lindsay looked in the first few seconds, Robin, no stranger to illness herself, immediately put her at ease. "As mothers and wives with cancer," Lindsay confided to Robin, "we do so much to make our families feel comfortable when we're not. That's necessary work. But to wear something that makes you more uncomfortable just so the strangers who we see while grocery shopping can feel comfortable seems, to put it in political terms, like a misuse of our resources." Michael was riveted as Lindsay talked about Tom, telling an unexpected and endearing story of how he'd made her laugh during her radiation treatment by pretending her jar of Aquaphor was talking to them like an old tub of Parkay margarine. Jeanine's cell rang and she silenced it. Then it lit up, and lit up again. Robin embraced Lindsay at the segment's end.

When Lindsay was handed back to us like a child at school pickup, Jeanine leapt from the couch. "The View, CNN, the *New York Times*—they all want you. Do you understand? I don't think you understand. This is pre-Christmas media. You're bumping heavy hitters hocking A-list holiday movies and electronics. This. Is. Huge."

Unable to stop smiling, Lindsay put her hands to her cheeks. "My face is out of practice," she said happily to me as we went to grab our coats. Michael took us to the St. Regis for breakfast where, high from this turn in public opinion, we studied our phones as the hollandaise sauce congealed. Karen kept refreshing Amazon to see the memoir inch up to the top ten. A pair of older women came over and bashfully asked for Lindsay's autograph, confessing that they couldn't have agreed with her more.

"It's Lanier's sweet spot," Michael said like he still couldn't quite believe it. "And we just pissed all over it."

"I wear what I want." Lindsay pointed at Jeanine, who'd have consented to her going naked at that point. "Say what I want. And Amanda is with me for all of it."

Having served as Tom's body man for the VP run, I thought of myself as seasoned when it came to the relentless pace. But I

quickly realized the twins had never factored into his schedule—
and they dictated ours. We would leave after their bedtime, arrive
at our destination around midnight, get up at five to do the regional
morning shows, head to the local bookstore or cancer center for
a book signing event, then board the plane to Jacksonville to be
home in time to do dinner with the kids. It was punishing, but
Lindsay was thriving.

Empowered and appreciated, she was in constant commu-
nication with a reporter or reader. I used the skills I'd learned
analyzing geriatric data for the Davis center to immerse myself
in breast cancer research, leveraging academic and philanthropic
contacts to reach experts at the forefront of the field and keep
Lindsay briefed. When not on her phone Lindsay met with various women's organizations courting her as a spokesperson,
thrilled just to have her mention them in a tweet. Followers
flocked to Tom and Lindsay's social media sites, but Lindsay was
most proud of the sudden influx of donations supporting Tom's
candidacy. Contributions from individual women were up ten-
fold and while their hefty checks were cause for celebration, it
was the few dollars donated by women who had little to give that
meant the most to her.

Tom and Lindsay's schedules finally aligned in Chicago the
Wednesday before Christmas so we brought the twins with us.
Now that Jeanine finally saw Lindsay as integral to the campaign,
she wanted Lindsay to stay up late with her brainstorming over
a room service dinner, as if the linen-draped cart were a camp-
fire. The next morning, Tom's text that he had landed safely was
eclipsed by the editor's call to inform us that Lindsay's memoir,
Mother, First, was going to number one on the *New York Times*
Best Sellers list.

Following a round of champagne, Lindsay dashed at her newly
energetic pace to meet Tom at her lunch-hour reading where she

was going to be signing books for a few hundred fans. That was to be followed by lunch with the team and then, at last, a break—meeting up with the boys so Tom and Lindsay could take them to see Santa. Then Lindsay had another media op.

As I entered the hotel lobby the twins and their nanny, Flora, were just emerging from the elevator bank "Chip needs to pee," she said. "Collin just spilled water all over himself on the way down."

"Lindsay's outside in the car. Tom just went up to change his shoes." This was a typical conversation for us—logistical updates lobbed at each other like military coordinates.

"Any chance you can run up and grab me Collin's other jacket?" she asked.

"On it." She handed me the key card and I jogged to the elevator as they beelined for the lobby bathroom.

I let myself into the kids' room only to be startled by the bleating electronic siren of Chip's new Hess truck that none of us could figure out how to silence. It took me a second to realize it was coming through the open door to Lindsay's adjoining room.

"Tom." I heard Jeanine landing hard on the last letter of his name. "Put the toy down." I went over to the closet to snag Collin's jacket.

"I just don't—why do *I* have to go tonight?" Tom snapped in a way that made me freeze.

"Because *People* magazine is sending a reporter," Jeanine explained. Judging from her tone, it was not for the first time. "Because *Entertainment Tonight* will be there."

The Hess siren bleated.

"Tom!"

Something clattered to the floor. "No! We're not canceling a campaign fundraiser for this for fuck's sake."

"I've already spoken with the Lake Shore Drive organizer. Your fundraiser's being rescheduled."

"What? When? I never approved—"

"Tonight Lindsay will be giving out Christmas presents to children who've lost their mothers to cancer." Jeanine's voice strained for calm. "Foster children. Children caught up in the 'bullshit,' as you say on the trail."

"But why do *I* need to hang on her side there?"

"Because being photographed on the arm of America's most popular mother as she ministers to grieving families is worth infinitely more than not being photographed in a room of execs who'll probably write you a check regardless."

"Probably? What the fuck?" Tom exploded. "I'm goddammed arm candy now? This is supposed to be my campaign. *I'm* running for president—not her. And tell her to stop fucking saying 'our' message. It's mine. My message."

I grabbed the jacket and hurried for the door.

"Tom, you've landed Santa Claus as your fucking running mate! She is beloved—and as long as her Q rating rivals Kim Kardashian's, you'll be her lollipop ring if that's what's required. Or do you not want this anymore?"

I quickly closed the door behind me, trying to steady my breath.

"Just the girl I'm looking for."

I spun to see Lindsay stepping out of the elevator.

"I have Collin's jacket. Did you need something else?" I walked toward her, heading her off from whatever was going down in the suite behind me.

"Oh, just my husband, who is apparently getting pretty for his elf photo," she said with mock annoyance. Her cheeks were flushed from her day. "Actually, Flora told me you were up here and I wanted to catch you in case I don't see you later. I couldn't let such a big day go by unnoticed. Here, I'll trade you." She put out her hand for the jacket and then placed a slim rectangular navy box in mine. Smythson of Bond Street.

"Oh, Lindsay, you didn't need to—"

"Just open it."

I slid off the thin ribbon, lifting the lid to find a robin's-egg blue leather wallet with my initials discreetly embossed in gold at its corner. It was, by far, the most elegant object the Luker *L* had ever come in contact with.

"I noticed yours was on its last legs." She studied me with an eager smile. "Do you like it?"

"I don't even know what to say. I love it." I blushed at the thought of the fraying corners of the black pleather one in my bag.

Suddenly she hugged me, her cheek warm against mine. She smelled like the cold and her hair was soft on my face. *I should say something*, I thought. Warn her. But of what?

Chapter
Ten

THE NEXT MORNING OUR TAKEOFF OUT of O'Hare was delayed due to snow piling up on the runways faster than the plows could clear it. While Lindsay, Michael, and I steeped ourselves in the stats on out-of-pocket costs for treating the five most common cancers, I stole glances across the aisle to where Tom was scouring the web for press coverage of his trip to Chicago. *Tap, swipe. Tap, swipe.* "Hey, Jeanine," he called even though she was all of five feet away. "How come People.com didn't run the pictures of me *with* Lindsay?"

"I'll ask, Tom."

Lindsay's jaw flexed. She'd been tense since I met up with them at the hotel during checkout. It was a tenseness I recognized, had grown up learning how to navigate when—despite Delilah's avid intensions—some relationship she had started to count on was going south. She would push herself to move through the day—stripping the sheets for the laundromat, scraping out the mayonnaise jar—but her muscles would be flexed rigid.

I imagined that Lindsay had been looking forward to Tom joining her in Chicago as an opportunity to show him Team Davis in action. While I don't know if he'd expressed any of what

I overheard in the suite, it seemed clear that his agitation had bled over into their evening.

I couldn't understand it—with Lindsay's popularity driving Tom's donor base—how could he feel so resentful? On the other hand I had been privy to how unrelentingly charming and gracious Tom had to be to every single person who thrust a hand in his face. It wasn't unreasonable that, given the exhaustion and nerves, he'd had a tantrum. *Maybe that's all it was*—I told myself, *a tantrum.* No different than Chip and Collin getting overtired and kicking on the floor while we waited to be airborne.

We all just needed a break.

Instead I was headed to West Palm for Christmas.

When Pax had asked me if I had plans for the holidays I told him in Tallyville we didn't have "holidays," plural, no ski gear drying by a stone fireplace or steel-drummed carols played by a tiki bar. We had Christmas, December 25—which, depending on seniority, you may or may not have off. The question, from the time you were old enough to scoop or sling, was simply, "You workin' Christmas?"

"How much time do you have till your next flight?" Lindsay asked me as we unbuckled the kids and helped them find all their little plastic toy pieces. Tom was already jogging down the stairs to the tarmac.

"Forty minutes."

"Leave this—I can handle it."

I found a Lego helmet the size of a grape under my seat and handed it back to Chip.

"Oh, God." Lindsay adjusted her watch. "Our parents will already be at the house. I was hoping Tom and I could finally have a few quiet hours by ourselves."

"You both have so much going on," I sympathized, carrying the poster of her book cover signed by the Chicago Bulls, along with my binder on social security by district. "You guys are seriously due a vacation together."

"I'd settle for a date," she answered, shepherding the boys down the steps.

"I hope you guys get that over the holiday—maybe a night away?"

She watched the boys run across the tarmac to where Tom was waiting in the private terminal. She sighed, then forced one of those Lindsay smiles. "You haven't had kids yet, but you'll see— that first year—well, my friend Ally once said, 'just take divorce off the table.'" Lindsay let out a punch of laughter. "You don't know what end is up, you're bone tired, you don't have time to connect, and when you do you can't form a sentence." She turned to me. "This last push to next November—that's all this is. Just like it was with the kids. A tough year. But we'll get through it. We've done it before. And then one day you just suddenly find you have your lipstick back on, and the candles are lit." She slid her sunglasses on as Tom picked Chip up and swung him around. "So maybe we'll get that date—maybe we won't. But I'm not looking for big romance right now—and neither is he. We're just getting through."

As I raced to catch my flight I felt comforted by Lindsay's assessment of intimacy. I didn't know the first thing about marriage. Theirs was the first one I had witnessed close up. And I wanted—and needed—Lindsay to be right.

In the plane bathroom I changed out of my wool work clothes and into one of the outfits Becky and I had packed—a short white dress with an appliqué anchor. She and I had ransacked the J. Crew outlet, snatching up every nautical-themed T-shirt, and cable-knit sweater we could find.

"What should I expect?" I asked as Pax drove me from the airport to the house.

"Taggart's whole family is down from Connecticut. Pym has brought some guy named—I shit you not—Freemont who is the male version of her. He has his own hedge fund and do not—I repeat do *not*—get sucked into playing a game with him. He has zero sense of humor and he plays Boggle like he will cut a bitch. If they ever have children I will sleep with my door locked and one eye open."

Laughing, I leaned over and kissed his cheek. "I'm glad I'm here. I'm bummed I won't see Ray Lynne open the doll house, but pretty much everything else I'm glad to be missing."

"Delilah gotten a job yet?" he asked.

"Believe it or not she has a second interview after New Year's. Doing admin on the citrus farm my grandpa used to work—seated and with health insurance—it's like Jesus was listening. I want this so badly for her I'm ready to ask Tom to wear a Hanover Orchards T-shirt to his next televised stop."

"Amanda, that's awesome—you were so annoyed that she wasn't going for clerical stuff."

"Well, she's started seeing someone and apparently he put her up to it."

"He?"

"Daryl. In keeping with her type, Daryl is currently 'between gigs,' but apparently superinvested in *her* job search."

Pax winced.

"I know," I said as we pulled into the Westerbrook drive. "I kind of wish I was there this weekend just to look him in the eye and get a read. He did just finish a stint on one of the deepwater rigs, which means he has a skill, so that's new. Wow."

The gate, the trees, the stone banisters were all festooned with tiny white lights. It looked like a fairy village designed by Cher.

"Yeah, Mom's decorators go a little crazy at Christmas—she's kind of cool with it as long as they don't use red."

"So Rudolph can go fuck himself?"

"Darling." There Cricket was in a black velvet sleeveless dress, swanning down the entry steps to greet him like he hadn't just run to the airport.

"Mother, you remember Amanda," Pax said as he hopped out.

"I don't, apologies."

The corners of Pax's mouth turned down.

She took my hand as I stood and gave me a smile as warm as the diamond snowflake pinned to her dress. "Dear." She addressed him, still holding my hand. "We're just starting Christmas Eve champagne on the veranda. Min made those little rice balls I just adore. You're not going to be believe this." She placed her other palm conspiratorially on his forearm. "Richard's wife asked to put on carols. Aak!" She mimed clawing at her own skin.

I reached into the backseat and withdrew a shopping bag of gifts for his family. I loved the wrapping paper I'd found at Target—ice-skating penguins and polar bears. "Where should I put these?"

"Oh." She peered into the bag, grimacing. "Not in the living room. Here, I'll take them and find a spot. But do join us once you've changed. I've put her in the room next to yours, darling—no point being puritanical." It should have been friendly, warm, welcoming, honest—it was none of those things.

I followed Pax up the white poinsettia-lined staircase to the second floor and felt less like an adult and more like an anxious teenager with every step. He led me under the birch wreaths to the "children's" wing, where I quickly changed into my next ensemble—a floor-length silk skirt and cashmere sweater. Page 78 of the catalogue. Fall of last year.

In one corner of the double-height living room was a fresh tree trucked down from Kentucky, bathed in white lights and clear glass ornaments. Below were stacked white-on-white plaid boxes tied with white velvet ribbon. Along the mantle twenty white nutcrackers lined up to salute. It was beautiful, but like a sea anemone is beautiful.

"Amanda," Pax beckoned me outside with a glass of champagne. One of his cousins across the patio was unmistakably wearing the same skirt. I couldn't tell whether I was supposed to feel validated or embarrassed so I settled on both.

"Merry Christmas." I kissed his cheek. "So when do you do presents?"

"You sound excited."

"I am. I love that part."

"Really?"

"Yes. Believe it or not Delilah really excels at the gift exchange. She'd have me make a list for Santa early—like October before prices went up. Then she'd ask me which one was the thing I really *really* wanted. And it would be there Christmas morning."

"Now it's my turn to say wow."

"I know. Somehow with all the things she has just never gotten—the importance of one disappointment-free day was crystal clear for her. What about you guys?"

"Oh, Cricket does not do toys. My Santa list was filled by the house manager, who she sent to Toys"R"Us with her credit card. Once James is old enough to appreciate a good broadcloth she'll hit Worth Avenue for him like she does for me now."

"Are you Amanda?" another cousin asked—a teenage girl who would be breathtaking once her braces came off. And her mother stopped trying to stuff her into puffed-sleeve dresses on holidays.

"Yes."

"You're the one who works for Davis. I *love* him. My friends—we make cupcakes and sell them in front of our building to raise money."

"Thank you. Where do you live?"

"Park Avenue. Can I get his autograph?"

"You give me your address and I'll see it gets to you."

She squealed and ran away.

"Wow," I said to Pax. "Fourteen-year-old girls in Tallyville are not baking cupcakes to raise money for politicians."

"Welcome to the rarified air we breathe." He meant it as a joke, but it tempered my smile because I didn't understand any of this—why red was bad or why a string of rooms occupied by adults was still called the children's wing. It felt like every surface was covered in invisible rules and I had neglected to pack the necessary black light.

"Where are the chestnuts?" Cricket asked. "There're supposed to be chestnuts." She left the room.

"I want to give you your present," I said to Pax.

"Me, too," he answered.

I went to the wide hallway that ran the length of the house, where Cricket had dropped my bag of gifts as I went up to change, but it wasn't there anymore. I walked down, peeking in each room as I had the day I came to fetch the luncheon program.

"Cricket, you have *got* to lay off him." It was Pym's voice behind the door to Cricket's sitting room. "Pax likes her—he isn't marrying her."

"But what if she gets pregnant? He'll be saddled for life."

I felt one foot pull me to the staircase, to my suitcase, to a flight home. The other continued right in. "Sorry to interrupt, I was just looking for the presents I brought."

Pym had the good taste to make a choking sound, but her stepmother only slowly pivoted. "Oh, Amanda," Cricket said languorously, no sign of embarrassment in her soft smile. She raised one of her strands of pearls from her tan sternum. "You're not offended. You're a smart girl. You know how unsuitable you are for each other. But I'd be doing exactly the same thing in your shoes."

"I don't want his money." It was all I could think to say.

"That's good, because he doesn't have any. Didn't you know that?" she said.

"We don't discuss it," I stammered.

"My father didn't acknowledge Pax. Pax's father should have set a trust up for him, but who the fuck knows? He may have forgotten he has a kid. Taggart was looking kindly on Pax for a while when he was working for the firm, but now that he's doing this lobbying thing Taggart has washed his hands." It was like she was talking about a dog no one wanted. "So you see?" she said.

"Yes, I do. Thank you." Then I turned and left. I knew my response sounded weird, but it made sense in my head as the first part of an unfinished answer. Thank you for being blunt about your dislike for me. All I've ever needed is to know where I stand. Tell me when the gas is going to run out. Tell me when we're out of food. I just didn't like to be surprised by a cold stove or an empty fridge.

I found the gifts in the coat closet and ceremoniously placed them under the tree while Taggart put on choral music and a tray of hot chestnuts was set on the coffee table. "Here," I said to Pax, who sat in a club chair in the corner while the other Westerbrooks milled around drinking. "I'm sorry, this isn't broadcloth, whatever that is. And the paper is red because I think that's cheerful and I love carols and someday I'd like to have Christmas somewhere cold."

"Are you okay?" he asked as I sat on the ottoman.

"Your mother just tried to scare me off by telling me you don't have a trust fund."

"How do you feel about that?" He avoided my eyes by untying the ribbon.

"Well, it's pretty frickin' funny."

"Why is that funny?"

"Because growing up I set my bar at no criminal record so I don't care if you have a stock portfolio. I'm actually kind of relieved you don't."

He pulled out a pair of cuff links. He looked disappointed for a second until he saw that they said "Dodd" on one and "Frank" on the other. He laughed, then suddenly he took my hand and pulled me outside, tugging harder and harder until we were running down to the beach where a damp wind snapped off the water in sheets.

"See, cold. I'll do anything for you, Amanda."

"Um . . . thanks, but I meant, like, cold outside and we'd be inside. Wearing fleece."

"Okay, in the future be more specific." He pulled me down to the sand where we'd had our first fight. Smiling, he ran his hand through his hair and took a nervous breath. "I love you."

"I love you, too."

"So will you marry me?" It was then that I realized he was kneeling. *Kneeling* kneeling.

I felt everything on my face go round with surprise. "Really?" I did not believe him. I did not believe this.

"Sorry, a ring. Right. Um . . . there is a ring. I'll just need to ask Cricket for it. I will tonight. Shit—sorry—this is all a little unplanned, a lot unplanned, but I looked at you and you don't belong in that room."

"Right."

"I don't either. I want a snowy, fleecy, bright fucking red, Bing Crosby Christmas. You meant Bing Crosby, right—not One Direction?"

I squeezed his hand. "You're being impetuous."

"So?"

"So I don't want to be an impulse purchase." I was only a few words away from really ruining this. I made myself smile.

"I want to be a package deal, Luker."

I realized I wasn't breathing.

"Don't make me beg. Or do. I can beg."

My ribs flared, breath still held. Oh my God, I wanted him, wanted to believe him, wanted to believe *in* him. Despite all fucking evidence men had given me to the contrary over the years. Was Lindsay right? Were some guys just in—no matter what? Supporting you and waiting, knowing the lipstick and the candles would always come back?

I looked into his eyes, wanting to find out. "Yes."

"So, when are you going to do it?" was Lindsay's first question as I accompanied her across the tarmac to her first appearance of the New Year.

"Sometime after the election," I answered, looking down again at Pax's grandmother's ring, which found its way onto my finger after a shouting match with Cricket so vitriolic it was audible on the lawn. The solitaire bracketed with sapphires still looked so strange on my hand, like the plastic ones I used to try on at the drug store checkout. I was glad the election was naturally forcing a long engagement so I'd have time to get used to the idea of all this. And maybe living in the same state as my fiancé at some point would help, too.

"That's a good ide—" Suddenly she stopped walking and put her hand out.

"You okay?" I asked.

"Just dizzy for a second." She saw the look on my face. "I need to eat, that's all. Let's hurry—we don't want to delay wheels-up— Jeanine'll have a fit."

But, uncharacteristically, she slept the whole way to Scottsdale—and the whole trip back.

The next afternoon she called while I was at the Davis Center. "Collin pitched a fit last night about me missing one more breakfast. I think I'm gonna call Jeanine—see what we can do via satellite, limit my in-person stuff to the shorter flights, maybe every other week."

"Lindsay, are you okay?"

"I'm fine, Amanda," she said starchily. "Just a fifty-something mother of two highly energetic boys, post-Christmas, and I need a little break."

"Of course." Kittens would come spewing out of Jeanine's mouth that would be set on fire by the laser beams she shot from her eyes. "I'll e-mail you the most updated schedule and then the three of us can get on the phone and winnow it down."

"Thanks, Amanda. I don't know what I'd do without you."

"You will never have to find out."

"Oh, and Amanda?"

"Yes."

"Tom is under so much stress. I'm not asking you to lie, just not to bring this directly to his attention right now. I don't want him to think I'm letting him down."

"He could never."

With the election only nine months away and Lanier still fighting hard to take the nomination, I was reassigned to Tom and the grueling pace of four or five nights a week on the road. I didn't even see Lindsay again until early February when I was bringing Tom's bags into the house one night. We were just passing through the front door when we heard a crash and rushed into the living room to find Lindsay on her knees.

"Oh, stupid," she said.

"Linds?" Tom asked, running to her side.

"I promise, I haven't been drinking!" She tried to smile. "Help me up."

We lifted her to her feet.

"Tom, you're home. To what do we owe the honor?"

"What happened?" he asked, swiping up a shard of vase from the side table she must have tried to grab for on the way down.

"Floor just wasn't where I thought it was." She sank down on the couch and closed her eyes for a second. "You know, I've been thinking," Lindsay said, taking my hand. "You should have the wedding at the new house—christen it. And give us the impetus to finally finish it and move back in."

"I'd love that," I said, standing over her helplessly, adding, "You know, after the election." Tom smiled. "After the election" was his favorite phrase. "Would you like a damp paper towel?"

"It'll be gorgeous. We'll set up tents. I have a wonderful florist who'll give me a deal."

"Oh, I think we're just going to do something small," I replied. "Maybe just you guys and our families. Mine hasn't really budgeted to 'give me away.'"

"Nonsense," Lindsay said, eyes still closed. "Cricket and I will figure that out—don't give it another thought. What about late May?"

"What?" I asked.

"Late May." She licked her dry lips. "Ahead of the season— could be a little chilly, but there's nothing I hate more than a sweaty bride standing next to a groom patting his forehead."

"Linds, are you sure you want to be taking something like this on, right now?" Tom asked. "We only have four weeks until Super Tuesday."

"You're very busy, Tom. I'm going to scale back on my travel— for the boys—and this will give me something to focus on here at home that's—fun. Okay?"

"Okay," we both said in unison. And just like that, because I didn't know how else to help her with what she didn't want brought to anyone else's attention, I was going to get married to Pax Westerbrook in late May under a tent on the Davis's lawn.

A few weeks later I was surprised to get a call at the Davis Center from Tom's new body man, Gerry. "Miss Luker, you used to be Tom's body man, right?"

"Yes. When he was the VP nominee."

"So what'd you do about the 'holes' in Tom's schedule?"

"Holes?" I asked. "You mean his breaks?"

"Oh, I'm not sure what they are. It's time slots Tom's blocked out where he tells me not to bother him, where he takes off, but then I'm not sure what to tell everyone else. Last time Jeanine wasn't happy with me."

"What did you tell her?"

"That he went for a run without his phone. I'm stressed she or Michael is going to mention it to him and tell him to bring his phone with him and he'll get mad at me. What did you do about the holes?"

"I told them he was sleeping," I lied quickly, trying to make sense of it. "Catching up. A power nap. Does he have a break scheduled today?"

"This afternoon from two thirty to three thirty."

"Okay, well try the power nap thing," I suggested, my mind unsettled. Holes?

"Oh, great, thank you."

A few hours later I was in my car, hands stuck to the wheel with my anxious, angry sweat—tailing a man. I could *not* believe my life had led me here. It was something I had vowed as an eleven-year-old, glowering in the passenger seat, waiting for us to pull over for the stakeout, that I would *never* do. The last few months between Lindsay and Tom kept flashing into my brain like PowerPoint slides that couldn't be shut off. *Please don't be an asshole,* I thought as I stayed two cars behind Tom's, just like Delilah had taught me. *Please, please, please.* It was only a few blocks before he pulled in to the shops on Riverside. There was no hotel here. No titty bar. No massage parlor.

I parked across the street and watched through my rearview mirror. He jogged into the frozen yogurt shop and just as I was about to exhale a petite brunette came into view. She stretched on her tiptoes as he embraced her in a bear hug. When she pulled back he was beaming like the bachelor who got the last rose.

In the course of the next week, as Lindsay locked down wedding vendors with shocking speed, while keeping up with her blog interviews and Ted Talk prep, I decided I was going to tell this girl of Tom's to go away.

I vividly recalled when the wife of the dealership guy knocked on our trailer door and pointed at her three kids, clad in their pajamas, sitting in the backseat of her car. They looked as stunned and scared as I felt, the youngest inconsolable. "Look me in the eye and tell me you're going to take food out of their mouths," she said to Delilah. When she left, her dealer plates shining in the streetlamp, Mom slid to the floor and began keening.

As I glazed over at the three hundred shades of blush-colored linens Lindsay e-mailed me, I planned my speech for this girl. Did she understand what she was putting at risk—for his campaign and his marriage? Did she understand what Lindsay had already lost? Lindsay, who had taken so many chances on me, who was pulling my wedding out of thin air and ensuring that no detail went overlooked, from the bouquet of roses she picked out to the pink-soled shoes she found for me on sale. She was a woman who could make things happen and that was exactly the energy I wanted creating my big day—the Luker women had never gotten what we wanted. But this time I would. I would get this girl to go away and my life, built on their lives, would keep moving forward.

On Thursday, having been given the next "hole" from Gerry, I waited for Tom to leave the yogurt place and then I quickly crossed the street to the door before the brunette could leave. She was still sitting at a Formica table scraping her plastic spoon against the Styrofoam. In a striped sweater and leggings, her legs crossed at the ankle, she looked young.

Her face raised.

"Oh—sh—Shannon?" I sputtered, recognizing her from the photo in Lindsay's book, the name of Ashleigh's best friend surfacing rapidly and awkwardly like a swimmer whose air has failed.

"Yes?" she said tentatively.

I let out a sigh of relief before realizing how she was looking at me. "Sorry, I . . . uh . . . I work for Tom, for the Davises, for the campaign, and we couldn't find him, and—" I stammered, blushing. "Anyway, he was with you, so—" I swallowed. "That's all good."

"You're Amanda, right?" she asked warmly. "Tom talks a lot about you. Do you want to sit down?" It was a sweet request. "Would you like some water?" she asked graciously, accustomed, as she must have become when Ashleigh died, to seeing adults struggle to keep it together.

"No, thank you." The chair was still warm from Tom. "He talks about me?" I asked.

"What a help you've been to Lindsay."

"I'm sorry," I said. "I know what this must look like—there were some . . . holes in his schedule."

Shannon nodded, taking this in. "Is he okay?" she asked.

"I was about to ask you the same thing." Why was he sneaking around to see Ashleigh's best friend? "Lanier refusing to concede the nomination has been hugely stressful—he doesn't want to look like he's bullying a woman, but he's definitely leading in delegates."

She looked down, spinning an engagement ring with her thumb. "I think he just needs someone to talk to. Outside the—the circle, or whatever you call it." She picked up a paper napkin and twisted it, the orange and lime green letters making a chain-link pattern. "After Lindsay's book came out I got some calls, from press and whatnot—because it says how I was the other person in the car—and I wasn't sure what to say, so I called. And he called right back. Isn't that so nice? With the campaign and everything, he could be our next president and he called right back."

"What did he want?" Part of me knew I shouldn't be there, shouldn't be asking these questions, but at the same time I'd become acclimated to talking about Tom and Lindsay when they weren't around. It was the staff's job to discuss where they were headed, what they'd be saying, how we thought they were holding up—so in some ways in felt normal to be asking Shannon these questions.

"Oh, just to talk about dumb stuff. He and Ashleigh—they had a thing—a shorthand—about Lindsay. I think he misses that." I wasn't sure what she meant. But I didn't have a father. I imagine if I did, we would definitely have a shorthand about Delilah. Billy and I did. "I'm getting my master's in education. My fiancé says he wants me to quit teaching after we have kids, but this feels like an awful lot of school to just give it up later." I nodded. "Tom is so kind," she added. "He's offered to pay for my certification, you know, since they didn't end up having to send Ash to college."

"Oh, that's so nice."

"Isn't it?" she asked, looking up. And I realized she was really asking.

"If someone had offered to pay for my school, oh my God . . ." I shook my head, unable to even finish the sentence.

"Right. Yes, no definitely."

"Well, if you ever need anything." I pulled my card out of my wallet, having no idea what I even meant by that. As odd as Tom meeting Shannon in secret like this was, unnecessarily turning something innocent into something suspicious, my being there felt like it was just making the whole thing fishier. "I should get back," I said, standing.

Shannon tugged on the chain around her neck and a small enamel locket emerged from her T-shirt. "I miss her every day," she said touching it. "Every day." From this angle I could see the faded web of scars on her forehead.

"It's a pretty necklace," I said, pushing the chair back in.

"It was Ashleigh's. She loved pink roses."

"She did?" I asked, seeing the tiny flower.

"Did you ever see her room?"

"Not really, no."

Shannon shook her head, a sad smile breaking. "It was so beautiful. It was like being inside a conch shell."

Confirming that Tom was not a cheater should have cemented my enthusiasm about this wedding. I had done the grown-up version of the superstitious habit that got me through my childhood. *If the next car that pulls into the gas station is silver, everything is going to be okay. If I turn on the radio and it's a song, not a commercial, everything is going to be okay.* If I find out that it's just Tom missing his daughter, it's all going to be okay.

But I knew in my gut I still wasn't like the other girls in the stores Lindsay took me to, brides-to-be giddy over gravy boats, place settings, and hoodies bedazzled with Mrs. so-and-so on the back. They all seemed to know, with terrifying certainty, what their lives would look like and that they had the skills to make it all happen.

I didn't know the first thing about being a wife. And I was scared that Pax, sitting on that incongruously freezing stretch of sand, had proposed on the rebound—from Cricket, from his childhood. That I wasn't what he wanted—I was just enough not what he didn't.

He was so focused on work he was just as happy to have all the decisions off his plate—and Cricket's. Pax just kept saying, "Whatever you want," in a way that was intended to be supportive, but just left me more conscious that I didn't know. And over the weeks it occurred to me that this was his way of backing into this. That we were two people, still living in separate cities, backing into commitment when we didn't know what it meant.

So as Lindsay handed me checklists I kept telling myself it wasn't a wedding. It was two hundred rental chairs. Three vegetarian plates. One shellfish allergy. A block of hotel rooms. Transportation. It was any other fundraiser.

The night before the wedding I arrived alone in the lobby of the Amelia Island Ritz-Carlton where the Westerbrooks were staying and hosting the rehearsal dinner—although Cricket insisted on skipping the actual rehearsal. Pax's flight had been massively delayed out of Dulles and Billy texted to say they'd left late so I ended up walking down the aisle with Tom to Lindsay, who—pretending to be Pax—leaned on a chairback for support. She was trailed by Chip, who stood in for Pym, while Becky mimed being Ray Lynne dropping rose petals.

It went great.

After the rehearsal, I found Grammy standing in the middle of the Aubusson-carpeted lobby of the Ritz with Billy and Ray Lynne, looking apprehensive in their luxe surroundings. "Did you guys get checked in all right?" I asked, hugging everyone tightly. They were staying at the Days Inn across the highway. "Mom getting changed?" Everyone avoided my eyes.

"Now don't get upset," Grammy said.

"Where's Mom?" I asked again.

"We didn't want to spoil nothin," Ray Lynne said, twisting away to bury her face in Grammy's waist like a much younger child.

"This place is beautiful!" With a hand pressed against Ray Lynne's back, she glanced around. "My God, look at those flowers."

"Fine, you know what, I don't even want to know right now," I said, finding a smile. "Have you guys ever had lobster?" I put my arm around Billy's shoulder. In my mind I unscrewed a mason jar, stuffed in the disgustingly wriggly feeling of my mother skipping my own wedding, and twisted the lid back on tight. "Cricket wanted lobster. If you hate it just leave it on your plate and we'll hit a drive-through after, okay?" I suddenly wondered if I could do that with the whole wedding—just leave it on the side of my plate and hit a drive-through later.

At three o'clock in the morning, still fuming over Delilah's latest insult, I finally heard Pax's key in the lock. I sat up in bed and turned on the lamp. "Really? You had to fly down the day of the fucking rehearsal? What if it wasn't just weather delays? What if they couldn't get you rebooked? Marrying me wasn't worth taking one extra day off work?"

"Did you take yesterday off?"

"No," I admitted. "Is that what this is about?"

"There is no 'this.'" He waved his arms. "I have been sitting around waiting for takeoff eating peanuts and having a panic attack."

"Wow, I was so *not* sitting around. Pax, do you even know the first thing about what's going down today?"

"You said you had it covered." He tugged off his shoes. "What did I miss at the dinner? Did Taggart welcome you to the family?"

"We skipped the toasts and went straight to your mom finishing off a bottle of Cote de blah-blah-blah and coming after all your male relatives like she was trying to get them into the champagne room. I don't know where she gets off thinking she's better than me—better than Lindsay even."

He held his hands up. "Let's not do this now."

"Do what? Tell each other how we really feel?" I was suddenly completely overwhelmed by everything I'd been avoiding. Like releasing an overstuffed closet door, all my fears came spewing out, hitting me in the head. "Pax, where are we going to live? Do you want kids? A dog? Who *are* you?"

"We can't decide any of that until after the election. I don't know about kids. It's only fair to get a dog if we have the space. See my first answer. And I'm still figuring that out."

I put my face in my hands. "This is so much more than spending Christmas together." I was about to lie in front of two hundred people. Forget richer or poorer, I didn't know if we took each other for anything. Could I love him in sickness? I thought of Lindsay's marred chest. Could I do what Tom had done? Stand by someone through unimaginable loss, unimaginable suffering? Did I love him enough to sustain us the rest of our lives?

"Hey, hey." Pax sat on the bed and lifted my chin. "Look, we're jumping off a cliff together."

I looked in his eyes, the eyes I knew I loved. The way he looked at me, I loved. "I never imagined marriage as a joint suicide pact, but okay."

"So, you clearly just decided that the cliff was over a parking lot. I was picturing water."

I smiled. "See, just one more reason we shouldn't get married."

He laughed. Then I laughed. We were laughing.

Then he wrapped his arms around me and we found that silent place between us and at some point we tipped over onto the bed and fell asleep.

~

That afternoon, as I lifted the shutters of Lindsay's finished sunroom to look out at the guests starting to take their seats in the backyard, I realized I had never seen—or unlike most brides—had never taken the time to *picture* what all these various things I had agreed to would look like together. My eyes grazed the petals and ribbons and I knew I had said yes to each one, just like I had agreed to the dress that now felt like I was wearing a cowbell. Every time I moved the boning at my hips made it sweep into my legs—*ding! Dong!* I had started with tear-outs of long silk columns, and ended up looking like I was welcoming visitors to the Magic Kingdom.

"Mandy? Can I come in?" I turned to see Grammy peering around the door as Pym, Becky, and Ray Lynne passed her to line up.

I put down the glass of champagne that was steadying my nerves. "Yes, please!"

"Oh, you look beautiful. You look like a real princess."

"Yes, I've just realized."

She came in and sat down on one of the parrot-patterned, tufted ottomans. "I brought you something."

"Is it a Mars bar?"

She smiled and opened her crocheted clutch. "Here." It was a hatpin with little sapphire chips, making a flower with blue petals. "This was my mother's. I always thought Delilah was going to wear it." She shook her head. "But if you like it, it could be your something blue."

"Oh, Grammy, thank you, I love it. Can we pin it to my bouquet?" I pointed to the pink roses sitting on the side table. "Where is she?" I asked as I watched her arthritic fingers deftly weave the pin into the ribbon.

"She ran off with that Daryl."

"What?" My mouth went dry. I'd assumed she was so jealous

she'd just decided not to put in for time off or something. She was gone?

"Okay, well, I guess ran off is a bit unfair. He has a job prospect on a new rig on the coast and he asked her to go with him. They don't know about schools and whatnot yet so she decided to leave the kids behind for a bit."

"What's a bit?"

Grammy shrugged, avoiding my eyes.

"Okay, so, in fact, 'ran off' might be completely fair."

"Or she might call tomorrow that she's wiring me their bus fare."

I blew out at the ceiling.

"Don't let this ruin your beautiful day."

"I asked." I put my fingers around my compressed waist, trying to lift my ribs up and out of the boning to breathe. Run off? Abandoned the kids? *Abandoned?* I'd spent so much time fearing the bottomless, endless asks it never even occurred to me she could actually do something worse. I could hear the string quartet start Clare de Lune, the song that was supposed to cue me. Oh God, where was the coordinator person to stick her head in and ask if I was ready so I could say I wasn't? I needed someone to come back with that buttonhook so I could take one real breath. Just one. *You can do this*, I told myself. *You can.*

"Amanda, you okay?" Grammy asked. "I did. I ruined your big day," she said with dismay.

"Oh, no, no." I reflexively rushed to reassure her.

"Amanda, can I talk to you?" Tom knocked on the door.

"Come to get my granddaughter for her walk down the aisle?"

"I was actually hoping to have a quick word."

"Going to spill all your secrets?" I asked, smiling my hostess smile.

He coughed.

"You know, to a successful marriage."

He didn't answer. This couldn't be good. I quickly downed the remainder of my champagne.

"I'll leave you two alone." Grammy smiled. "Mr. Next President," she added as she left.

Tom walked over to the shutters and peered out. "I've just been talking to some Westerbrook cousins about wine collecting. I wanted to say, 'You know the funny thing about you? From across the room you look like people who might want to talk about wine collecting. But, of course, then you'd turn out to be secret crunk dancers or something. But no. You are exactly what you seem to be.'"

"Should we head out?" I asked, suddenly just wanting nothing more than to disappear into being the bride. Music and cake and perfection—I wanted to dive in. ,

"I need to talk to you," he said seriously, the smile that always played around his mouth gone. Maybe he was going to give me a family heirloom. Perhaps he was going to promote me . . . or fire me? Was Lindsay dying?

"Yes," I said.

"This is very important."

"Okay . . . "

"I need to talk to you." He was repeating himself—and scaring me.

"Yes." Were we going to do this all night?

"I've fucked up."

Even as the words tumbled out my mind tried to skid over them. He got me the wrong-sized watch. He didn't check our registry.

"We should get out there—"

He grabbed my bare arms. "I have fucked up and I need your help. I'm sorry to do this now. Today, on your day. But you leave after the reception and by Monday . . ."

I shook my head like a baby trying to avoid a spoon. I did not want whatever was about to get crammed into me.

"You know how hard everything has been since Lindsay's been sick."

He wanted me to nod. But I couldn't. Nodding would mean I was starting to understand whatever it was he was about to tell me.

"And you know how much I love her."

I was blank. His hands felt hotter and hotter against my skin as all the blood shrank away from him.

"It was one night. Just one stupid night."

I wanted to vomit champagne and tiny lobster rolls all over him.

"Back when we went to New York, when we found out about the cancer. The night we went to that awful dinner and I did the PowerPoint Lindsay hated. I went in the hotel lobby. Lindsay went to get God-knows-what."

"Pinkberry."

"What?"

"She went to get yogurt." I was stalling him.

"I went inside and there she was in the lobby. It was like she was waiting for me."

"Shannon?" I didn't understand what was happening.

"Cheyenne."

The way he said the name made me crumple into my dress, the skirt billowing as I pulled Tom down to the carpet with me.

"Lindsay can never know about this," he said.

"Why are you telling me?" Even as I asked, I knew.

"She says it's mine, but it can't be. She's crazy. How could it be mine from that one time? I used protection—"

I turned away; I couldn't look at him anymore.

"She's putting a lot of pressure on me. She's only giving me until Monday to step up or she'll go to the press. Amanda, I need you to take her away somewhere until we can do a paternity test and shut her up. It wouldn't be for long." I stared into the carpet—he still held my elbows. "*Please.* We're so close to winning this thing. Don't let my one stupid hour ruin everything we've been working for. Don't let it ruin everything Lindsay's been working so hard for," he spoke through clenched teeth. "I will die before I hurt her." His grip hurts my arms.

There was a knock and the wedding planner pushed in. "The song has looped three times—everyone's waiting. Are you okay?" she asked.

"I tripped over these stupid crinolines," I said shakily. "I might be a little tipsy. Will you get me some water?"

"I'll wait for you at the top of the aisle," Tom said as she helped me up.

"Ready?" she asked sharply, pulling away the cup before I'd even finished the water. "Don't worry, every bride is like this. It's normal. What you're going through is completely normal."

"Okay." It was the vaguest thing I could say, the thing that would allow me to subsist on sips of air, as if we were about to board a plane, not my future. I took one last peek out the shutters as the ushers peeled away the paper to reveal the pink aisle. And it finally hit me. My "beautiful day" was the dream wedding of a dead sixteen-year-old girl.

Part IV

Chapter
Eleven

I DIDN'T HAVE A DRINK FOR THE ENTIRE reception, the survivalist in me instead focusing on the tactical assessments required for campaign stops. *People look happy. Good. That's good. This is working. This is a success. What's next? Where should I stand? Who should I talk to? What does he need me to do?*

What does he need me to do.

Despite the band and the chatter I heard only a whooshing sound as if an industrial fan had been turned on between my ears. I went through the motions: twirling Ray Lynne on the dance floor, posing for pictures, kissing Pax when glasses were clinked with spoons. Tom spun me around the parquet like he was the Beast to my Belle, sending Lindsay and Grammy's hands to their hearts. But we didn't say another word to each other.

I have no idea what time Lindsay finally ushered Pax and me to her brother's vintage Astin Martin, the three of us ducking through an arc of sparklers held aloft by guests as if we were royalty. She told me she loved me and, as the bursts of light flitted around us, I told her I loved her, too. She reluctantly retreated to Tom's side and he nodded good-bye to us. I suddenly needed to inhale. "Get me out of this dress," I begged Pax when the driver pulled away, but in his champagne-soaked state Pax misunderstood. "No," I gasped as his lips suctioned my neck. "Can't breathe. *I can't breathe.*"

As he ripped at the buttons I realized releasing my ribs did nothing. The space that held my heart had been compressed, squashed, crushed like the cans that littered the bottom of Tom Davis's car—one of his "everyman" touches, as Jeanine called them. But dear God, Tom Davis could *not* be just like every other man, he just couldn't. Even if he was from a town like Tallyville.

Sitting on the floor of our expensive hotel room with my gown down to my hips and my hand around a minibar bottle, I spent the first hour alone with my husband blinded by the reason I never wanted to be married. Was their weakness inevitable?

"Our flight leaves at five?" Pax asked from where he sprawled at my feet. Clutching his bow tie and complimentary bag of gummy bears, he looked like he'd been shot in the back before he could reach me. "Explain to me again why we're going to Sanibel for two nights and not, like, thirty?"

"Work." I reminded him of our decision to put off the real honeymoon until after the election and dropped my head back against the bed, my chest sore from the imprint of Tom's confession, the bruise of Delilah's departure. Oh my God, what was going to happen to the kids? All the kids. Billy, Ray Lynne, Chip, Collin.

"I'm supposed to ravage you now."

"Yes." Another scattered rose petal slipped from the coverlet to my bare shoulder.

"Any minute." He lifted a finger into the air.

"Great."

"My ears are actually ringing." He turned his face to me. "If this is what Davis feels like after one of his shindigs, he's made of better stuff than I am."

"Don't," I said too sharply. "I don't want to talk about them tonight."

"Ah! An opinion!" He lifted onto his elbows. "Now I remember you." He made his way over on his elbows as if crawling under a military obstacle course and raised his face to mine. "Hey, girl I married."

I was unprepared for the simple connection as I gazed down at him. I loved him so much. I did. But I realized I wouldn't know if I loved him enough to make it until I saw if we did.

"Oh, hey," he said with concern, sitting to pull me against him as my tears broke. "It's okay."

I tried to find the words. "I'm just so . . ."

"Me, too," he murmured, stroking my dampening cheek. "So happy."

"Right," I said, grateful that he couldn't know how wrong he was.

The rest of the weekend I impersonated the honeymooners on whom I'd once waited. Thankfully the occasion didn't call for conversation because my head felt like metal trying to stay aloft over a magnetized floor. At least my dazed expression could have been interpreted as a symptom of postnuptial jet lag. Pax and I exchanged knowing nods with the other newlyweds at the hotel, one orgasm ahead of the realization that they could have bought a house with what they just spent on a party.

Monday came and went with no breaking news about Tom so I assumed whatever Tom thought I had agreed to was enough to placate her so far. A hundred times I tried on telling Pax, but it made it all too disgustingly real. Tuesday morning we drove to the airport, Pax bound for D.C., me to Daytona. We clenched hands at the gate until it was time for him to board. He looked back at me. "Really? You're okay?"

I tightened my fingers against his, feeling the foreign pinch of our rings colliding. "I'm bummed that we're back to saying good-bye at an airport, that's all."

"I know. I'd give anything just to get some fucking time together." He let out a stream of breath. "We just have to hang in there until November, right?"

November.

Was saying no to Tom even an option? Would he fire me? Where would I go? My resume had *one* item on it.

But I couldn't let Pax leave like this. "Um . . . don't you mean forever?" I strained for the light intimacy he'd sought since we'd left the sparkler canopy.

He laughed, but it didn't cover the ripple of relief that passed over his face. I'd acknowledged it. We were married.

Tom was scheduled to talk Middle East and Medicare at senior centers along the coast and, steeling myself, I joined the team in Daytona that afternoon. Discovering Lindsay had bowed out to recuperate, I reverted to trailing Jeanine like I had a crush on her. She was juggling a million tasks and happily took advantage of my proximity without questioning its cause. I grabbed one of the interns—me at twenty-one—and offered an exhilarating amount of access, while ensuring that Tom and I were never alone, praying that if I deprived him of the opportunity to follow up he'd be forced to find an alternate solution.

For the whole week I only risked eye contact when he was in front of the crowds being the man I wanted him to be. Standing by a back wall as he listened attentively to some elderly woman, I found it inconceivable that such a compassionate, intelligent person could ask me to do *it*—as I had come to call his request. *Was it really necessary, anyway?* I wondered. *Say this Cheyenne person did make some sort of claim. Couldn't he just tell Lindsay the woman was crazy—some crazy fan?* Women were swooning over Tom wherever we went. Lindsay's decision not to put her energy there pre-dated my arrival—it was one of the first of her strengths to impress me. *Was it such a stretch that a groupie had gotten lost in her own Tom Davis fantasies? And, minus one detail, wasn't that what had happened? I mean, essentially?*

It was my mother's logic and I knew it. But Delilah's was the only other voice in my head.

Friday evening Jeanine sent me to the concierge at the Breakers to check for the tie that hadn't been returned from the cleaners when Tom was suddenly behind me. "Got a sec?"

I'd thought he was already working the fundraiser in the ballroom. "Sure!" I reluctantly followed him behind an urn of pungent flowers. "We're triaging your tie—"

"Oh good—there'll be hell to pay if they don't find that thing." He was serious. "Listen." He stepped closer. The bouquet's cloying scent made me ill. "I can see you're taking this to heart, Amanda. And I feel like shit about it."

"Oh, no, that's okay," I said reflexively, even though it was the farthest thing from the truth. "I'm just glad you see that I—"

"You're the only one I could trust 100 percent." His put his hand on my arm as I realized he wasn't backing down. "The only one who gets the magnitude of what this stupid thing could do to her." He held it in place. "What it could take from her." My stunted exhale was like canal water slamming into a lowered lock.

"Tom."

"Amanda, that Cheyenne keeps trying to get to me," he said furtively, his face contorting to an expression I'd never seen on him: fear. "It's putting everything everyone's worked so fucking hard for at risk. Every day that I don't deal with her—look, you know it's been a shit year for Linds and me. If this were any other time, if we had more solid ground to stand on, if she hadn't just been straight to hell and back, if she wasn't, as I stand here with you . . ." I realized he was blinking back tears. "Then I would talk to her. We would deal with this. Of course we would. But she's not strong like she was. All this BS . . ." He waved his free hand toward the ballroom of men marking time until cigars were lit. "Has taken such a toll on her. You see it. I know you do. Don't make her pay for a burden that should be mine alone. Don't do that to our kids. If you really do love her—"

"Tom." Jeanine rounded the urn. We sprung apart. "They're waiting. Amanda, teach Gerry how to fill out a fucking dry cleaning slip, will you?"

Tom's shoulders lifted and he turned to go in and give his stump speech. I walked quickly past the concierge to get outside. I couldn't argue with a thing Tom had said—not a word of it. However appalled and disappointed I was at the situation his logic paralyzed me like a mouse in a constrictor's coil. My cell rang in my clutch. "Grammy, I'm sorry. I'm in the middle here. Can I call you back?"

"Mandy?"

"Ray Lynne?" I plugged my other ear to hear her little voice.

"Mandy, you have to come right now. Okay?"

"What's wrong?" I clenched the phone. She'd never called me before. "Where are you? Is it Grammy?"

"Grammy's yelling and Billy's yelling and Billy said curses and Grammy says she's going to call the police when he comes back."

"The police? Back from where? Where's Billy? What did he do?"

"Mandy," she took the staggered breath of a child who had held it together as long as she could. "Come." Her *m* sloped into a sob that sent me sprinting past the valet, screaming for my keys.

I took the highway until I ran out of highway and then I drove too fast on the back roads. Unable to extract more information, I calmed Ray Lynne as best I could before she swore she'd go to her bed and stay there.

Neither Billy nor Grammy answered their phones and it was past midnight when I made it to her driveway. The surrounding houses were all dark and I startled when my headlights swept across Billy laid out on the top porch step. The sound of my car door slamming made him sit up as unsteadily as if he were falling down.

"It's Mandy, Billy." At least he was here—alive. "*What* is going on?"

"She's a bitch," he said drowsily before his head dropped forward.

"Who? Grammy? Mom? Is she back? Hey." I stepped forward to grab his shoulders only to turn my face away. It smelled like he'd been getting stoned in a sealed closet. "Answer me."

"Can't have people over . . . can't leave. Not going to play fucking cards with her like everything's—she's bullshit."

The light from her bedroom window suddenly spilled over the porch roof and onto the lawn behind me.

Not letting go of his shoulders, I dropped my voice and crouched before him, locking my elbows to keep him from slumping into me. "Why did she call the cops?" I asked, although the answer was in my nostrils.

"She's fucking miserable . . . like Mom says. Said she'd report me if I stepped off the porch. But she won't let me in. Ha!" His lips curled into a smile that his face was too high to follow through on.

"Did you just smoke or did you take something? Shoot it or snort it or whatever? Fucking tell me the truth or I'll take you to the hospital right now and have them pump your stomach, I swear to God I will." I peered into his dilated pupils and for a disorienting second I saw the kid who once begged me to make him a superman cape out of a bath towel. He dropped his gaze to my chin.

"Just smoked."

"Don't. Move."

Using my key, I took the steps inside two at a time. Ray Lynne was slumped over her stuffed raccoon and a box of Nilla Wafers on her coverlet. I went to Grammy's door. The light beneath it clicked off. "Grammy," I called softly. Silence. I turned the knob and it took a second for my eyes to adjust to the darkness. There in the single bed next to the one my grandfather had slept in, she lay staring up at the ceiling from beneath her quilt. "I can't do it again, Mandy Beth."

"When is Mom coming back?"

"Her phone's turned off. And don't think she and that loser don't know it."

"For how long? You haven't heard from her at all?"

She was silent. I tried to stay with the immediate fire.

"I'm so sorry about Billy. I had no idea that was going on. Not that it *is* going on. This is just all so much change for him. I'm sure with Mom out—"

"She's out, all right."

"Right, okay, well . . ." I walked over to her. "I'm sure it's because of that. I'll talk to Billy. He's got a good head on his shoulders. Let's get some sleep and we can sort this out in the morning." I went to take her hand and she suddenly pounded the bed with her fists.

"No! I can't! I won't! None of you have the right to ask this of me." She was rigid, her breath shallow. "Just get them out. And leave me in peace."

I numbly stuffed a bag for both of them. Weighing practically as much as me, Billy was the harder of the two to move and, for a harrowing moment, I doubted I'd be able to. His head lolled over the seat belt. As the town lights receded, the blackened farms on either side of the road enveloped us, leaving me with nothing to ground my racing thoughts. *Get them to my apartment—take it from there—to where? To what? What are you going to do with them?* I had a 5 a.m. plane to board, an empty refrigerator to fill—a fucking husband to vet this with.

Ray Lynne moaned.

"Hey, bunny." I checked the time, an hour more to Jacksonville. "You're in my car. I'm taking you and Billy to my house for a sleepover so just rest your eyes, okay? We'll be there soon."

"My stomach feels bad."

"Bad how?" I peered at her in the rearview.

"Bad," she repeated before vomit spewed from her mouth.

I swerved to a stop. Trucks whizzed by as I triaged the mess with Billy's T-shirts and the dregs of my water bottle. It was bright Nilla Wafer yellow. I helped Ray Lynne change into a fresh pair of pajamas and climb back into the car. Then, as I swept hair from her sweaty forehead, she threw up on both of us. For a second I was too stunned to move. She began to sob for our mother. My phone rang. Mentally coming back to the scene, I leaned down to hug her against me, the sick gluing us together. I reached into the front seat for the phone. "Grammy?"

"No, it's Lindsay."

Billy sputtered awake, his face contorting from the stench. He groaned.

"I was just going to leave you a voicemail. You could have just let it go. I didn't mean to bother you."

"No—I'm—how can I help you?" We were out of water, pajamas, and Billy's T-shirts. Everything reeked. Squatting like a duck next to the open side door, I rubbed Ray Lynne's shuddering back.

"Well, it's stupid, but—I hadn't heard from Tom tonight and I was going to ask you to have him call me. You're still at the Breakers, aren't you?"

"No. I mean, yes. I mean, he is. Should be. Sorry, I might need to call you back—

"Are you okay?" she asked with the taut alarm of a mother.

"No." My voice broke as Billy fumbled to push his door open to retch. "No, I'm not."

Pulling to a stop at my apartment complex, I left the kids asleep in the car and ran in to get a makeshift bed set up for them. Punching in my key code, I was stunned to find Lindsay in my living room, making up my couch with flowered sheets. She didn't so much as blink at what I must have looked or smelled like.

"I set our air mattress in there for Ray Lynne." She pointed to my bedroom. "And I brought a few of the twins' stuffed animals to make it more homey for her, although she might be too old for all that now." She gave a small smile. "I figured Billy could take your bed so you could have a little space out here to collect yourself. I stopped at the gas station for milk and cereal, the basics. That should get you though the morning."

For a second I couldn't take it. The contrast between discovering that Grammy's love was—as Delilah had always claimed—finite, and that Lindsay's generosity was not, made me feel like I was disintegrating. Lindsay Davis, still in her pajama top, stepped forward to take me in her arms. She stood firmly without comment, judgment, or need, like it should have been with my own mother but never, ever was. And there was nothing, not one fucking thing that I would not have done to repay her.

Between my siblings, our MIA mother, and the woman I'd committed to "taking off the grid," getting Pax onboard for what happened next required serious selling. I pitched him that a trip with Tom's groupie could provide a practical solution to my suddenly overcrowded apartment and lack of childcare, offer us the honeymoon we had put off, and provide a fully funded, five-star, four-week break from the campaign—time together.

Pax was convinced enough to meet up, but as the five of us were shown to the Kiawah Island Golf Resort reception desk, his jury remained understandably out. Especially when I asked for his Amex. "I had to give them back my corporate card, obviously," I added, as if my assignment was standard campaign protocol. By "them" I meant Jeanine, who'd arrived at my apartment that morning to download logistics. As she explained it, the resort was on the shore of a gated island community off the coast of South Carolina that was best known for its golf course, which meant the media was only allowed in for the PGA. Cheyenne was due to deliver in four weeks, but could go earlier if I "offered her spicy food" and "encouraged her to do aerobics." Above all I was not to "rock the boat" or "shake the cage" in any way. "She wants a perineum massage you get out the lotion, just keep her off the six o'clock news, are we clear?" When I asked Jeanine her opinion of the situation she said it was an "irrelevant question" and the less we discussed it the better. "We're sending them receipts and they'll reimburse me when this is over," I reassured Pax as he reached for his wallet.

By "this" I meant the tiny pregnant woman who we'd chauffeured from the Charleston airport. Cheyenne sashayed around the lobby, an oversized straw hat flattening her blond bangs to her eyelash extensions. Her Pucci caftan read like graffiti against the muted seersucker attire of the milling guests and about a hundred bangle bracelets on her stick-like arm served as an unintentional wind chime as she bent to take in the sterling lemonade service. "Love," she stated to the concierge like a queen who'd stopped her hunting party to offer compliments to a peasant. He managed a humoring smile.

"Just had to get her here," I murmured to Pax. "She'll do her thing. We'll do ours." It was clear this was the cruise Cheyenne had been saving a lifetime for. From the private plane to the mini ketchup bottles, everything delighted her at a voluble ten.

"I don't want some stranger carrying in my jewelry." She pointed at the brass dolly ferrying in her things. "You can do it." She eyed Pax before turning for the elevators. "See you up there!"

But she didn't. See us, that is. Cheyenne was too busy criss-crossing the three bedrooms of our suite like a coked-up Goldilocks while we stood dumbfounded with the bellboy. "This view of the beach in this room is so glam but the water pressure isn't very strong. . . This one has better pressure, but, oh, no, the bird print in this room would *have* to go—"

"How do you know this chick?" Billy finally spoke after a day of grunted responses.

"I told you. I work with her. And her name is Cheyenne."

"I like Cheyenne's bracelets." Ray Lynne threw in her two cents.

"I'm home!" Cheyenne pronounced from the master bedroom before four pillows flew out the doorway in rapid succession. "No synthetic inserts, thank you!"

I apologetically showed out the bellboy and his armful of rejected hollow fill. Billy had disappeared into one of the other bedrooms while Ray Lynne, dually pooped from a morning of being shuffled through lines, hopped on the couch where I helped her find the Disney Channel.

With the kids squared away, I sought out Pax, who was set-ting himself up at the desk in our room. We were *finally* together. And in a hotel, no less. This was our good familiar territory. I went up behind him and wrapped my arms around his shoulders. "Hey," I said, leaning into his ear. "Can I make an appointment?" He twisted his lips to mine as his cell chirped in his pocket. "Cricket?" I asked.

"I'll call her later," he said between kisses as he walked me backward to the door.

"See?" I reached behind to secure the lock. "We just had to get them settled and—"

"Mandy!" Ray Lynne screeched.

"One sec." I squeezed his hands and sped out to the living room where Cheyenne was aiming the television remote with purpose. She clicked to CNN then dropped it on the couch beside an outraged Ray Lynne. "There." Tom's face appeared and she lit up. She spread her arms in front of the flat screen as if introducing us to God. "*There* he is."

"Yes, we've met, Cheyenne." I stepped between her and the anchor giving polling updates I already had on my phone. "Ray Lynne was just going to chill out for a little while so maybe we could—"

"Oh no. No. No-no-no-no. We must give him energy." She dismissed me fervently.

"I want to give energy to *Dog with a Blog*," Ray Lynne clarified.

Cheyenne picked up her sun hat, the brim of which could shade a helipad. "Off to the pool!"

"Oh, great." I grabbed the remote to change it.

"Don't." She spun back to me. "I need to keep the connection strong."

"But you're going to the pool. Can't you . . . connect from there?"

"I'm pregnant," she said, like that was an answer.

"Yes."

"So I can't carry a phone or be checking my iPad—the radiation isn't good for the baby. This is how we stay connected, Amanda. You're not going to interfere with that are you?"

I couldn't begin to know how to respond, which was just as well because she wasn't seeking confirmation. She blew a kiss to Tom as he talked about health care and then repeated the gesture from her rounded abdomen. "And follow up about the pillows, 'kay?" She headed for the door. "Once we've gotten our vitamin D I'll be back for a nap."

She left. Ray Lynne looked to me. I looked at the TV—there was the tour stop I should have been at, where a thousand penned-in people waved Davis for President signs. I took Ray Lynne's hand and led her to the room she'd be sharing with Billy. "Where did your brother go?" I asked, finding it empty.

"He left." She went over to the bed where he'd set out her stuffed raccoon.

"Left?"

"To check the place out. That's what he said. Did you talk to mommy yet?" She dropped her head on the duvet and held the remote out to me. Grammy had been right, Delilah's phone was turned off. I hadn't even been able to leave a message.

"I'm sure I will in the next day or two. Until then we'll have a nice time here at this fancy place, okay?" I found *Dog with a Blog* and kissed her on top of her head. She nodded as the show resumed, its tranquilizing effects setting in.

I scurried back to Pax only to find him on our balcony, looking down in consternation. He tipped his chin at the pool six stories below where the Lilly Pulitzer set gawked at the woman trying out every deck chair-umbrella combination in search of the perfection she was due. "Do we know if Cheyenne got the off-the-grid memo?"

"I assume so. I mean—I'm sure she did." Honestly, I'd been so busy trying to get us out of the house while keeping my instructions straight that I had no idea *what* she'd been told.

"What, exactly, does she think we're all doing here for the next four weeks?"

"Well, he's married, which she must know. So she has to be hidden away to send him energy or something until she has her baby, at which point he can prove it's not his. I don't know what he's told her—" My eyes landed on Billy surveying the pool in his Beer Me T-shirt. Between his low-rider shorts and scowling expression, he looked like he was about to hold somebody up. "So, she thinks he's taking care of her."

"Until he can unload her."

"Look, Jeanine said the less we all talk about it the better."

"Why not just pay her expenses directly? The Davises are well connected. He could get a friend to give her money."

"Because he doesn't want to make this any more complicated than it needs to be."

"He's asked you and, by proxy *me*, to babysit a grown woman—that's not complicated?"

"It's not like I raised my hand for this assignment, Pax. Look, he trusts me. Me. Mandy Luker—who used to sleep on the floor at campaign headquarters. He's now relying on me to keep this nutcase under control." I took Pax's hands, tipping my face to catch his downcast eyes. "I don't think Lindsay's doing well. I don't know what the stress of finding out about something like this would do to her, but I doubt it'd be good. If I can help spare her that then I have to—I owe her so much." I kissed him as though the conversation had been concluded and grabbed my bag. "I have to get Billy some Bermuda shorts and Cheyenne a golf hat before she takes out someone's eye with that thing. I'm going to sign Ray Lynne up for sand art or something. And we should plan a fun dinner. I think they have a barbecue on the beach. Keep an ear out for Ray Lynne and please don't touch CNN. Sorry, thank you. Love you. Bye."

It was a bust. All of it. A wild goose. A greased pig. Whatever you want to call it. Cheyenne stuffed the visor in a trashcan as if I'd asked her to go Amish. Billy threw his hands up at clothing he deemed "stuck-up bullshit." And Ray Lynne ditched sand art to call a psychic hotline about Delilah.

While Pax commuted back and forth to DC, my days at Kiawah were spent tending Cheyenne's gestational vision, cell stalking our mother, and watching Billy stare off from between his headphones.

My Billy.

His grade-school restlessness was hardening into adolescent anger, which, in our town would rust into middle-aged hopelessness. It was the last thing I wanted for him.

"I don't understand," I said as he marched stubbornly ahead of me on the beach. "You've been asking me to rescue you for years now and I finally have and you barely say three words to me." With Cheyenne occupied at the spa, I'd found Billy playing cards and getting high with the caddies behind the golf club's dumpsters. The sun was now setting as I pursued him past the happy families picking up their monogrammed bags to head in for cocktails. "Or why you won't come into town and let me buy you some books. We could go to the library like Grammy used to take me—"

"Look." He spun around, stopping me short. "I don't like to fucking read. That's you, not me. I don't like school. That's you, not me. And I *never* asked you to rescue me."

"I don't mean literally." I tried to soften my statement. We stared at each other. When did we become the same height?

"I'm just saying, don't get it twisted, that's all."

"Billy, I get that the last few months must have been awful. I know it's a lot to suddenly go from that to this. *Believe me*, I get that. I just want to talk to you so maybe we can—"

"What? What are we doing here, Mandy?"

"Getting a break! Isn't this a break for you? Three and a half weeks that you don't have to deal with Grammy or school. And

I'm trying to take care of Ray Lynne so that's not on you. Tell me what can I do?"

"You left." He swiped at his glistening eyes. "And then you went and got married, okay? To Prince Fuckwad. We were there for the whole show. So just stop acting like you want me and Ray Lynne tagging along." He marched away, sand kicking up behind him.

"Billy!" I went to chase him, but my phone rang—Jeanine.

"I'm so glad you called." I hadn't heard from her or Tom since we'd left Jacksonville. I tried to keep my eye on Billy as he cut back between the yellow umbrellas. "What exactly has Cheyenne been told because she's—"

"Here she is, Lindsay," she cut me off. I froze as Billy jogged up to the boardwalk and out of view. "Amanda, you're on speaker."

"Amanda?" Hearing Lindsay's voice was like seeing a flare go up from shore. "Where are you?" she asked, her voice tight.

Fuck. Fuck-fuck-fuck. My phone buzzed and I whipped it away from my cheek to see Tom's schedule had just been texted to me—from Michael. "With Tom . . . in Toledo."

"He hadn't mentioned you so . . ."

"Oh, because I'm not with him right now, this second. I've been out working with Donner on the—" I glanced down. "Spaghetti social for tonight, so . . ."

My phone buzzed with a second text from Michael.
Tom fired Donner.

"On my own. I mean, I wish Donner were helping me. It's so much work. Even Donner would have been a help."

"Are your brother and sister with you?"

"With me? No. No, they're with Pax. In DC for the week . . . a few weeks, actually. I'm going to see them when we break on—" I yanked my phone away to check the schedule. "Saturday. So, yes. What can I do for you?"

Lindsay was silent for a moment. "I just hadn't heard from you since you brought them home."

"I'm so sorry." God, I missed her. I wanted to tell her everything so badly, as if none of this pertained to her, as if this was just my fucked-up life I needed advice about. "I had to get them up to Pax's and find them a sitter." My mind raced through the logistics that would have been necessary without this "solution." "I haven't had a moment to—"

"You'll tell me if there's anything I should know," she said pointedly.

"Of course." There was a silence on the line. Did she know? Could she know?

Finally, Lindsay said, "If I can help you, you know I want to."

"Yes." I felt wretched. "No, of course. Thank you. You've been amazing. Really."

"Have Tom call me."

"I will."

"Bye."

"Bye, Lindsay."

I sat down right where I was in the sand. For the first time since the fundraising dinner I shakily called Tom's phone, but got his voicemail. "Tom, Lindsay just called—I told her I was with you and that my brother and sister are with Pax. You need to call her. I told her I would tell you to. So . . ." I squinted against the glare of the sun lowering behind the hotel. It stung to look directly at it. "Just please call her."

"Ah-man-duh." That night Cheyenne's singsong intruded just as I drifted off. I startled to see her leaning over me.

"What's wrong?" I blinked awake.

"I need your bed."

"What?" I groped the nightstand for my phone. "It's three o'clock in the morning."

Pax opened one eye. "What's happening?"

Ray Lynne, who'd been having nightmares since we arrived, shifted in the surprising amount of space she commanded between us.

"I dreamt Tom and I were making love and suddenly there was a python where his penis should be and I just—" Cheyenne patted my leg to move over and sat on the edge of the duvet as if at a sleepover. "When we're together it's pure. We've found that adventure in each other. There's lightness to us. It's been that way from the beginning. In cars, planes—"

"Cheyenne?" Pax interrupted, his eyes still closed, as Ray Lynne sleepily stretched a knee into his groin and he winced.

"Yes, Pax."

"What do you need right now?"

"Our bed," I sighed.

"I knew you'd understand." She hopped off.

"Seriously?" Pax asked.

"Yes. The energy in my room is bad—I didn't see it at first—but my dreams are dark."

"Doesn't that happen when you're pregnant—crazy dreams?" Pax asked, trying to stay asleep.

At the word crazy Cheyenne whipped her face to him, her eyes catlike in their unsettling focus. "What did you say?"

"We're going, Cheyenne," I said as Pax begrudgingly stood and lifted Ray Lynne into his arms.

"But I can't sleep on your bedding."

"Then call housekeeping," Pax muttered as we shuffled to the door.

"I can't wait for that! I have to get back to sleep right now, Pax."

And so my husband and I walked back and forth like zombies

past a muted CNN to switch out our sheets, settle Ray Lynne back in her own bed, and then fall onto Cheyenne's. "He can't possibly have fucked her," I said into the synthetic pillow she'd thrown out after us. "Nobody could stand her long enough."

"You mean when they *made love*?" he said to the ceiling.

"Did you see the look on her face when you said 'crazy'—that was crazy."

"So crazy." He rolled on his side to look at me. "This is a lot of trouble to go through for someone you fucked once."

"Pax."

"It just doesn't sound like a one-time thing to me."

"According to Madwoman of Chaillot in there! Because she's delusional. If she'd say all that to us, with a kid laying there, can you *imagine* what she'd say to the press?"

He reached for my hand to shut me up, his grip loosening minutes later as his breathing deepened. I was growing so envious of his ability to return to sleep in a finger snap. Staring at the moon's shadow on the shutters made me think of Lindsay's sunroom. And it occurred to me that aside from what Cheyenne could say to the press about Tom at this point—what could she say to Lindsay about me?

With Cheyenne's due date in sight, the perpetually buzzing campaign coverage intently reminded me of what I was missing—*protecting*, I'd remind myself. Of what I was *protecting*.

I couldn't believe there'd been a time when my only desire was to be a hotel guest, a woman of leisure with nowhere to be and nothing to mark time between room service deliveries except the shifting sun and tide. Because two weeks into the honeymoon-that-wasn't, my only desire was to check out.

When not in DC, Pax worked from the resort's business

center while I tried to cheer Ray Lynne on through every sporting activity on offer so she didn't spend her days watching CNN with Cheyenne. Billy slept forever and then met up with the caddies. To contextualize my feelings about Billy's pot smoking, let me just say that by eighth grade I was one of the few kids in my class who hadn't tried meth. From that lens at least the caddies were keeping an eye on him. Eyes bloodshot, Billy would return begrudgingly for dinner, where we each attempted to move through the menu as if trying the almond tilapia might be the thing that would make this all fun. Cheyenne initially dined at the resort's restaurants, but after a week on her own she interjected herself into our meals and said she needed to talk. God, did she. Her favorite topics veered between graphic reminiscences of Tom that even the kids lost interest in and a ludicrous vision of herself as first lady that turned the warm rolls in my mouth to paste. Then, every few days, she'd seem shattered by a new dream and insist that the "vibes" had shifted in our suite and we needed to move to a fresh one. The next day she would try to "shake it off" with numerous spa treatments and purchases at the boutique. All the while Pax and I signed for everything all over the resort.

I couldn't wrap my head around what this was going to cost Tom once that paternity test could be taken.

Early Monday morning of our last week before Cheyenne's due date, I walked Ray Lynne to the pool, where she looked hopefully around for another kid to play with. She was becoming skilled at sizing up new guests for their toys. And, as crazy as this all had been, I was savoring the chance to get to know her. I didn't want that to end. But I needed to get back to the campaign, to Lindsay, and Ray Lynne needed her mother, even if that mother was Delilah. I sat on a deck chair to make my first call to Delilah of the day.

"Hey." Our mother's voice was suddenly in my ear.

"Mom?" I stood up. Ray Lynne's face flew to mine.

"Leave a message. Bye now." It was her voicemail.

"Is it Mommy? Is it?" Ray Lynne ran over to tug at my elbow. "Mommy?" she called, her lower lip starting to quiver.

"One second. I'm just leaving a message. Mom, you've *got* to call me. I don't know what in the hell—" Suddenly the phone was taken from my hand and I spun to see Cheyenne.

"Please," she said, her voice panicked. She'd lost all color. "He's not moving. Please help me."

Pax was away that day, so I texted Billy, grabbed Ray Lynne, and rushed a weeping Cheyenne off the island into Charleston toward the address of the doctor the concierge had e-mailed to me. Even though I hadn't heard a word from Lindsay again, Michael was texting me Tom's schedule daily as a precaution. I knew Tom was in New Orleans and still asleep, but I left him a voicemail anyway.

"I'm calling his hotel," Cheyenne said when I told her I hadn't heard back from him.

"How do you know where he's staying?"

"Because, I'm carrying his child," she said, so simply that the road became a momentary blur. "Yes." Her voice became forceful. "I'd like to leave a message for Tom Davis . . . Yes, I'm sure he is . . . Because I know he is—you tell him Coco Saunders called and it's an emergency."

Cheyenne used the same name when the nurse called her in for the checkup, which made Ray Lynne want to know what game she was playing. When the doctor told Coco that her baby was perfectly healthy and doing exactly how he should be *with two more months to go*—so did I.

Chapter
Twelve

"Two months?" I grabbed the OB's arm as he went to drop his gloves in the trash. "You mean two days."

"It's because her frame's so tiny, makes her look like she's ready to pop—she isn't." He winked, indicating that he was picking up what I was laying down. He wasn't. "Small meals throughout the day, okay, Coco?"

Ray Lynne opened her mouth and I shook my head to shut it.

"You should probably look again, though. Just to make sure." I knew I sounded ridiculous. Tallyville wasn't exactly a mecca for birth control—most women in the park were trailed by a stream of dirty kids. But none of those women were vegan. It hadn't even occurred to me that Cheyenne could be grossly overestimating her gestation.

"I don't like that he just stopped moving," Cheyenne complained as she pulled her attention from her dark phone. No one had called. "We've been totally in synch until today."

"Your baby boy was just taking a catnap." The doctor picked up her paperwork.

"But I was doing my meditation walk and he always kicks when we meditate. I say my mantra to his kick." She laid her free palm on her belly. "We do it together."

"He's bigger now. Your motion rocks him to sleep, same as it will when you carry him after he's born."

"In two months," I repeated like an idiot.

"Give or take a few days. Now where y'all travelling back to?" He scribbled on his report.

"Minnesota—"

"New York—" Cheyenne and I answered at the same time. Her eyes flashed to mine.

"Well, we're happy to have you down for a girls' weekend." He signed the chart with a flourish before patting Ray Lynne's head. "A little fun before your cousin arrives, huh?"

"What do you mean?" Ray Lynne furrowed her brow. "Why are you saying that?"

"We'll go out with you," I said quickly as Cheyenne sat up. "So you can make us a copy of the report while my sister gets dressed." I grabbed Ray Lynne's hand. "To give to his daddy."

To avoid giving Cheyenne's ID, I charged the visit on Pax's Amex. Back in the car Cheyenne secured her seat belt without taking her eyes from her Galaxy as if her concentration could make the device morph into Tom. We rode silently, me squeezing the wheel, Cheyenne squeezing the phone, Ray Lynne asking us what was wrong. "We'll talk about it later," I repeated, which was as effective as not answering at all.

Two more months? September would be the *earliest* Tom could get that paternity test—wait—seven months ago would mean the baby was conceived last . . . January. When I'd started travelling with Tom again. I was the last person he saw every night and the first person he saw every morning. We were never separated by more than one very flimsy Hyatt wall. I had to hum to avoid eavesdropping on his phone conversations. So he was either having silent motionless sex between midnight and five in the morning or he had Cheyenne stashed in his garage because that was the only place I lost sight of him before Lindsay caught it.

Spinning to call her out, I saw Ray Lynne from the corner of my eye and bit my tongue. The doctor's report was folded on what remained of Cheyenne's lap. As soon as we pulled up to the resort I was going to snatch it and fax it to Michael. I almost felt sorry for the boot kick coming her way.

As we crossed the bridge to Kiawah Cheyenne lowered her window to take a deep breath of the marsh air—then flicked the paper out. My head spun to see it flitter to the guardrail then get sucked beneath the wheels of the car behind us. It was gone.

"You're not allowed to do that," Ray Lynne, knowing this much, informed her.

"It's biodegradable." Cheyenne turned over her shoulder. "And you're not in charge of me."

Returning to the suite, Cheyenne slammed the door to her room and I steered Ray Lynne to hers. "Billy," I called to the lump under his duvet. "Watch her for a few." He didn't budge.

"I don't need to be watched!" Ray Lynne slapped her arms at her sides.

I tugged open the curtains, circling back to shake our brother's sun-peeled shoulder. "Billy."

"Sleeping," he groaned.

"Mandy talked to Mommy," Ray Lynne said furtively. That woke him.

"You found her?" He sat up.

"Almost." I paused at the end of his bed, my hands on my hips, my mind on the woman across the hall.

"Almost. Like, a piece of Mom? Her arm?"

Ray Lynne's eyes widened.

"No! Jesus, Billy! Just that her phone is back on. Look, it's been a hectic morning. Could you please just—"

"Is Mommy coming to get us?" We both looked to Ray Lynne, who'd grabbed her ragged raccoon. She seemed afraid of my answer. She was too young to be afraid of an answer.

"I'm sorry." I sat down on the bed so we could be eye level. "I'm sorry this morning has been so weird. Please don't worry. I'm going to talk to Mommy and it will all be awesome, I promise."

"I'm starting to think that word doesn't mean what you think it means," Billy said to his sheets. Ray Lynne looked equally unconvinced.

"Guys, please." I took her hand and led her to his bed. "We're moments from unloading Crazy. Take yourselves to the beach or the driving range. Anything. I just need an hour to get her packed up and we'll finally be done with her."

He reached for Ray Lynne and she climbed up to snuggle into him. "I used to hold you like that," I said softly. Billy nodded his chin against her hair. Then something clunked loudly in the other room, followed by a clatter. "Change of plans. Don't come out until I say."

I found Cheyenne half-undressed in the middle of her room and closed her door behind me. The dress she'd been wearing was on the floor where I stood, along with her wrap. Her bra flew toward me and I ducked. "Hey!" I cried as it hit the door.

"Where is he?" She hurled her phone and I leapt out of the way as its rubber case bounced off the mirror.

"You're scaring the kids." The flat screen across from her bed was on CNN, but the story was about Lanier. It was an hour earlier in New Orleans. Tom would have just finished the local morning shows and would be en route to the rally. "Can you please keep your clothes on for a minute while we talk?" I picked up the bra and tossed it back at her.

She glared at me, making no motion to catch it. For a moment I thought I should wait for Pax to do this, but he wasn't due in

Charleston for a few hours. Standing there in her underwear, devoid of her usual costume, Cheyenne looked momentarily like a normal, albeit distraught, woman.

"Look." I took a step closer, dropping my voice. "Don't you think you should start making a realistic plan for your baby?"

"Excuse me?"

"You're seven months along, which puts conception in January. You and Tom weren't even in the same country last October. You told us yourself you were in Paris. And I know where he was."

"It's you." Her eyes narrowed. "*You're* the one in his ear. *You're* the reason he's not calling me. What are you telling him? I want to know right now."

"I'm not in his—look, *when* I talk to him I will tell him what I saw with my own eyes on that report. I'll tell him the truth."

"I want to be on that call. I don't trust you."

"*You* don't trust *me*." It bore repeating.

"It's been two hours since I left him that message," she said, her face quivering with desperation. "Did you tell him our baby might have been dead?"

"He was doing press all morning. I just told you, I haven't talked to him yet."

"So he didn't call you back either?" She twisted her lips, wrapping her arms under her protruding belly. "*Why* isn't he calling us?"

"There is no us and oh my God"—I wanted to shake her by her tiny shoulders—"Tom Davis is not going to call you, Cheyenne. He's never going to call you because *that is not his baby!*"

"Stop!" Her hands flew in front of her. "Just stop that," she said as she yanked open a dresser drawer and dug through the mess inside. "I may be a rare spirit," she muttered as she tugged out what looked to be a handful of copper-colored string. "But I am not . . ." She stepped out of her thong and pulled the bikini up around her. "The Virgin Fucking Mary. Your attitude is wearing on me." She flipped her hair down, scrunched her face as if about to plunge under water, and then sprayed a foot around her head with Elnett. Dropping the can, she whipped her hair up, threw open the balcony door, and took a deep breath of aerosol-free air. "I won't have it," she gasped as she marched back. "I won't." She swiped on lip gloss, stepped into towering heels, and picked up her phone. "Not from a drone like you."

So.

Over her.

"Fine."

"Excuse me?" she cocked her head.

"I said fine. I don't give a shit what you will or won't have. Your jig is up. I'm going back to the campaign and I won't ever have to see you again."

"Oh, right, what day of the month do they process checks?" she asked like we were in the middle of putting away groceries.

"Excuse me?"

"The campaign. They owe me for my last invoice."

"Invoice?"

"For my styling services. Or, Miss Immaculate Conception, do you think those Charvet ties Tom wears just sprouted out of the ground in *Florida*," she sneered.

"You're styling Tom's ties." I almost laughed.

"His ties, socks, pocket squares. They sure as hell aren't from *her*. That woman couldn't appeal to a younger demographic if—"

"That woman," I snapped, "had *three* children with Tom, who is *her husband*. I will endure hearing about every blow job you gave him in your fucked-up mind, but I will not listen to you trash talk Lindsay Davis. Her name doesn't even belong in your mouth. Are we clear?" My heart was pounding.

We stared at each other. She pulled the triangles of her bikini top forward and shimmied her bulging breasts into place. "He'll call. And he'll come. And I promise you'll be sorry you ever took that tone with me."

I watched her march out of the suite, for all intents and purposes, naked.

Pax was in a meeting. Jeanine was in a meeting. Michael was in a meeting. The whole fucking world was in a meeting. I texted them all a coded SOS and then stood in Cheyenne's room. Just stood there, among half-drunk bottles of Fiji, scarf-draped lamps, and spilled-over candles. Fluorescent, animal-print, and fluorescent animal-print fabrics overflowed from opened drawers—Delilah's mess, only bankrolled. My phone rang. "Michael."

"Hey, Amanda."

"She's *working* for the campaign?"

"Well, that's overstating it." I could hear the whistles and shouts of the rally behind him and turned to the TV. Tom was about to take the podium.

"But she's his *stylist*?"

"I don't know about that. She sent him a few things. Look, did you calm her down?"

"How long have you known about this? About them?" CNN's camera panned the huge crowd. I studied the screen as if I could spot Michael.

"Same as you. Where is she now?"

"Swimming at the pool. Stripping in the bar. I don't know."

"Is she still worked up?"

There was Tom taking the stage, his shirtsleeves and solid blue tie revealing nothing of their origin. "She wants to talk to him. But they did an ultrasound—there's no question that this baby was conceived in January and we all know where Tom was then. There weren't any holes in his schedule, that's for sure."

"Holes?"

"Michael." I waved my hand. "The point is she knows she's

caught. She threw the doctor's report out the car window, but I'm sure if you call the office and say you're her husband—"

"Amanda!" He was angry with me. It was the last thing I expected. "We cannot afford to antagonize the woman right now. You get that, right?"

"But she's lying!"

"She's left some very upsetting messages for him this morning," he accused as if I was her ventriloquist.

"Well, she was scared," I balked. "Look, can't you get the police to talk to her? She has nothing on him." Billy came to the doorway. I gave him a one-minute finger, but he didn't budge.

"I hear you. And that's a huge relief. But a transgression occurred at some point. That's a fact. We can't know who might have seen something and put it together. We can't have her out there making any kind of a scene."

I went to the balcony. "What makes you think she's going to let anyone test this baby after it's born?"

"First we deal with the knowns." He invoked his favorite saying as Billy followed me out to the balcony. There was nowhere else to go but down. "How're you set for cash? Can you front a few more months?"

"A few more months!" I spun to the waves crashing below. "Michael, I have my whole family here! I can't—we have to get home already. I need to get back to the campaign—"

"Yes, right. Of course."

Billy came to stand at my side. "So you'll send someone out to relieve me?"

"Yes," he said emphatically. "We will."

"When?"

"Soon."

"Tonight?" I sounded like Ray Lynne.

"It's going to take a day or two to find the right person to let into this circle, Amanda. I don't have to tell you we have our hands full. You're doing an incredible job, okay? Your loyalty and discretion have not gone unnoticed over here."

I closed my eyes against Billy's stare. "What do you want me to say to her? She knows I know."

"*Whatever. She needs. To hear.* We're going to take care of you, Amanda. Sit tight and we'll talk shortly." He hung up.

"You okay?" Billy studied me.

"Yeah," I managed.

"You got Ray Lynne all worked up," he chastised.

I slid down the railing to a crouch. "I'm sorry."

He nodded, sitting on the edge of the nearest chaise.

"But it's a good sign Mom's phone's back on," I tried. "Maybe her boyfriend's job started and she's making plans for you guys."

"Maybe you've been with Crazy too long."

"Billy." I reached my hand to his knee. "They just told me that in two days we'll be leaving. We have to get back to real life, right? What do you want me to do?"

He jerked up to stand. "Whatever you have to. Call Mom. Don't call her. Just keep it to your damn self. Ray Lynne doesn't need your bullshit on top of Mom's."

"I'm not bullshitting."

"Really? 'Cause you're there for Ray or you're not. Just rip the fucking Band-Aid off already. I'll take care of her. It's not like I don't know how."

I squinted up at him, backlit by the midday sun. He was tall and certain and dead set on taking charge. For a sickening moment I recognized the temptation Delilah had been unable to resist when I was the one looming and she'd been the one crouched—the terrifying ease of letting a child's desperation for order seem like an ability to restore it. I dropped my head to my hands to get my bearings and when I looked back up, he'd left for the pool and had taken Ray Lynne with him.

I was coming out of my skin. I wanted to drive to the Gulf Coast and start going door to door with Delilah's picture, but instead I had to somehow shake off the last few hours so I could convincingly kiss Cheyenne's ass whenever she deigned to return. Desperate for clarity, I left Delilah a succinct get-your-shit-together message, threw shorts over my suit, tied on my sneakers, and took off running down the road that circled the island.

The sun was high in the cloudless sky as I pushed past whir-ring sprinklers and shaded verandas, thinking of the times Tom had gone to run out his frustrations and returned refreshed. I stopped still—almost felling myself with my own momentum. Was *that* how he'd done it? Had he stashed Cheyenne down the road? No, it was a crazy thought. Cheyenne was delusional.

I picked up my pace again and, with burning lungs, I repeated Michael's recognition of my work. Tom Davis was leading strongly in the polls. I was so close to working for the president of the United States, for fuck's sake. I just needed to get through this and get back to the campaign. And before that, I'd get Ray Lynne and Billy settled with Mom wherever she was and someday, when Billy was free to leave her, he'd understand that I did the best I could as a sibling without parental rights. Darting between the mansions, I tugged off my sneakers and ran into the waves.

Back at the suite, I dropped my wet shorts and went directly to Cheyenne's doorway to find her flipping through a *Vogue* on her bed. Housekeeping had come in the interim to contain her chaos. Focusing on the orderly splendor, I channeled Carson addressing Lord Grantham. "I'm sorry about earlier," I said with downcast eyes. "I shouldn't have made assumptions. It's really none of my business. We want you to be comfortable—I hope you know that."

She continued to turn her pages. "I'm sure."

"Mandy, your phone keeps buzzing." Billy came into the entryway.

"Who? Michael?" I turned to him. "That's good."

The suite's phones rang. Cheyenne didn't so much as look up. My feet slapped against the stone as I ran to the living room to answer it.

"Amanda?"

"Michael, sorry about that." I leaned to move Ray Lynne's water glass from the edge of the coffee table where she was making a lanyard.

"Where the hell have you been?"

"I went for a—"

"Look at your e-mail." I waved at Billy to pass me my cell and clicked the link Michael sent me: *The Daily Mail's* home page with the headline, "New MILF." A paparazzi shot—caramel skin, copper Lycra, the forest-green beach chair—"Former stylist to presidential candidate Tom Davis."

"Shit," Billy breathed as he peered over my shoulder.

"Is she there right now?" Michael asked.

There was a distinct click on the line. She'd been listening.

He hung up and seconds later his text came through.

GET HER TO THE HANGAR. NOW.

The times we'd changed suites were just fire drills. "Who have you been talking to, Cheyenne?" I asked as I threw our clothes into suitcases. "Your facialist? Someone at the spa? Who did you tell about Tom?"

She just shrugged while Billy and I ran in manic zigzags. "Why are you so panicked?"

"Someone at the hotel must have taken that picture and who knows what kind of access he or she has to the room." Cheyenne was in the habit of scrawling lipstick affirmations on mirrors and tearing "inspiration" from magazines, which she'd doodle on like a cheerleader in math class. Her rambling fantasies about what she'd wear with Tom or use to decorate their nursery were scribbled on scraps by the bathtub, on the balcony, and slipped under her bed. I viscerally appreciated the efficiency of a firebomb as we wheeled our belongings to the elevators, each dragging ice-bucket bags bulging with her notes. The whole thing happened so fast that my hair was still damp from the ocean as we raced away.

Pax's flight was due into Charleston any minute, so I texted that we would find him at the main terminal as soon as we had passed off Cheyenne. She was glassy-eyed with excitement. "I wonder where he'll be meeting up with me," she pondered as she did her makeup in the rearview mirror. "I bet it's in Europe."

Yes, that's exactly where a presidential candidate goes before the election. I gave her an encouraging smile. I could give her anything now. Someone else was shipping her off and Jeanine would leverage her media contacts to nip this in the bud. "Who do you think it was?" I couldn't help but ask as I pulled up to the guard booth. "Who took the picture of you?"

"Does it matter?" She pressed her lips together to spread her gloss. "We're out of that hotel, aren't we?" She was right.

We were directed into the private hangar, where the gate slid back across silently behind us as I parked. To my surprise, Pax was waiting near the jet with his raincoat over one arm and his suitcase beside him. "Hey," I called as I got out of the car. "I'm so happy to see you!"

"There was a guy with a sign waiting for me when I got off my flight from DC—he drove me here." Pax followed me to the back of the car as Cheyenne emerged to fluff herself. "What's going on?"

"It's over." I opened the trunk to heave out her luggage. "Didn't you get my messages?"

"Sorry, the donor we pitched was on the flight." He helped me with her largest bag. "So the meeting rolled into lunch and then right onto the plane." He dropped his voice. "So, what happened?"

Billy passed his phone out the opened backseat window to show Pax the *The Daily Mail* home page.

"Jesus. What are they going to do?"

Before I could answer we were interrupted by a squeal and looked to see Cheyenne clattering up the steps of the plane—into Tom's open arms.

"I just don't understand why *they're* here," Cheyenne pouted, her bare feet in Tom's lap. She pointed at the four of us. Tom had been so insistent, inviting us all up like it was the next thing on the agenda, and all at once the cabin door closed and we were barreling down the runway.

"Because I want my queen to be taken care of," Tom said with steady warmth as we were jostled through the clouds. He was massaging her toes. She closed her eyes and dropped her head back seductively. I didn't know what to make of the obvious heat between them. I'd seen it once before, years ago, the way Lindsay looked at Tom on the Westerbrooks' lawn. Was this real? Was that?

"I missed your hands," Cheyenne murmured.

"Well." Tom took the moment, unobserved by her, to look at Pax and I intently, his expression disconnecting from the deep circles his thumbs were making on her swollen instep. "I appreciate your patience."

"Where are we going, Tom?" Pax asked from the seat beside me. Sitting straight up, he was the tensest I'd ever seen him. Behind us Billy and Ray Lynne ate M&Ms and watched their satellite TVs.

"Oh, a friend's place. He's lending me his house while we get this sorted. Pax, I know we need to get y'all covered for everything you've put out."

"Yes, thank you," I said, daring to look at Pax for the first time since we boarded the plain. "Michael said—"

Tom's eyes went round. Cheyenne's drifted open. Tom resumed the look of delighting in her.

I proceeded carefully. "That someone else was coming to . . . care for Cheyenne. Will they be meeting us when we land?"

"I only want you, Tommy." Cheyenne cupped the knot of his tie and slid her fingers down the silk. He tilted his head down to hers. "You're all I need."

"But I have work to do—"

"And where is this friend's house?" Pax interrupted. "I'm assuming we can fly straight home after we make the drop. Correct?"

"Atlanta. This one's a puddle jump and then I have to meet up with the team."

Cheyenne swung abruptly away from him, pulling her feet back and yanking off her seat belt. I'm not sure where she intended to huff off to, although at eighteen thousand feet, I was hoping for the emergency exit. A look we knew all too well darkened Cheyenne's features. Dangling from cloud nine, she was about to start swinging with her free arm.

Tom stood up and reached for her, but she pulled away. He grabbed her again. This time her mouth stretched into a sly smile. Their eyes locked and she let him lead her to the bathroom at the back of the plane.

"What the fuck is happening?" Pax whispered as soon as the door clicked closed.

"Really?" Billy asked him before pulling his headphones back on and lifting his sweatshirt hood atop them.

"He's keeping her quiet. I'm sure they're just talking," I said. At least the whir of the engines made it impossible to know for certain.

"Amanda." Pax turned to me. "The express checkout charge came through from Kiawah while I was waiting for you. It's over *forty thousand dollars*. And it's due in full at the end of the month. That's tomorrow. What's the endgame here?"

"You heard him, someone is meeting us! Boom. Endgame. Let's just keep it together, get her dropped off, and we'll find Michael. They obviously don't want to risk talking business in front of her. Please, Pax. This is the homestretch. Just trust me, okay?" As the words came out of my mouth, I saw Delilah winking at my scowling face while slipping a packet of bologna under her shirt. *Trust me.*

The bathroom door opened a few minutes before landing and the two emerged flushed. Tom had his hand on her right up until we parted at the plane door. He sternly took her chin in his fingers and said, "If I couldn't rely on you it would make me question everything. Everything."

"But you can," she said fervently. "I promise. I love you, Tommy."

"Keep the connection strong." He dropped her chin. "I'm counting on you, Coco."

She reached up and kissed him fully on the lips, right there in front of us, and then trotted down the steps after Billy.

"Tom." Pax stepped forward.

"No." I found my voice. "Pax, just give us a minute—"

"But you won't—"

"I will. Please, Pax."

Clenching his jaw, Pax ducked to go outside. We were finally alone. "What's going on here?" I turned on Tom as he wiped off his mouth with the back of his hand.

"Lindsay's dying, Amanda."

"What?" I managed.

"She's dying. It's back and it's not going away. She has too much fucking pride to let anyone know and I will do whatever it takes to spare her this mess."

"I'm sorry but from where we're sitting you're—" I grimaced. "Making this mess."

"I'm doing what I have to. Do you want her exposed to *that*?" he tossed his hand at the door.

"Of course not—"

"Because you can do it with one call." He shoved his hand in his pocket and thrust his phone at me. "If you're going to be this weak then do it. Break her heart. I'm running for president of the United States. I'm this close. *This close.* Straight ahead of us are wars and terrorists and impossible decisions that make a rock and a hard place look like nirvana. I know I have the guts to do what needs to be done. Do you?"

I stepped back from him, pushing his hand down. "Yes."

"Then get in the car. Drive that girl to the house and do the job that sitting in that shit trailer park you thought you had no right to do. It's time, Amanda. Grow a pair."

The mansion was an hour outside the reach of the city lights, tucked deep into a dense wood that separated it from a stretch of undeveloped highway. At the end of the drive the house was dark. Wasn't someone waiting for us? We kept the headlights on to light our path. Pushing past us, Cheyenne opened the door into a double-height atrium.

"Hello?" Pax called into the darkness.

"For fuck's sake," Cheyenne muttered as she palmed the wall for a panel of switches. An absurdly huge chandelier came on overhead, leaving us blinking to get our bearings. Other than an unopened wardrobe-sized box from some nautilus company, the space—and what was illuminated of the great room beyond—was barren, save a Persian rug.

"They must be meeting us inside," I said, walking in.

"We are inside," Ray Lynne corrected me. "And I'm hungry."

I took her hand. "We'll get you food. Let's just find whoever we're supposed to meet and we'll get dinner on the way back to the airport." I walked her over to the staircase. "We'll check upstairs. Cheyenne, you look down here. Pax and Billy, you check out the gym or pool house or whatever is out back."

"Amanda." I could tell Pax was hitting his limit.

"The sooner we do this, the sooner we get out of here. I'm sure they didn't want lights on that you could see from the front—in case we were followed or whatever. Come on!" Putting on a brave face, I got us up the grand steps to the long hall of bedrooms. But flipped-on light after flipped-on light revealed nothing more than faint dust outlines on miles of beige carpet, raw wires jutting from walls where light fixtures should have been. We arrived in the master suite to find a flat screen as big as a garage door and a king-sized mattress that had yet to be unwrapped.

"Any luck?" I called desperately, my voice echoing as I marched Ray Lynne back downstairs into the kitchen.

Billy came in a patio door with Pax behind him. "Pool's full of leaves," he said, catching his breath.

"We just did a full lap of the property fence." Pax tugged off his tie to unbutton his collar. "There's nobody here."

"There's no way in hell I'm staying here," Cheyenne said. She stepped over a line of ants coming from under the Sub-Zero to get to the sink. "It's filthy." She turned the sink handle to wash her hands but nothing came out.

"Does someone really live here?" Ray Lynne asked.

"I don't think anyone's coming." Billy said it first as he slid down the wall and pulled his phone from his pocket.

"Well, I need to eat now," Cheyenne said testily. "I haven't had anything since we left Charleston."

"I'm hunnnngry." Ray Lynne wilted.

I tugged open the huge cabinets—all empty—until I found a dusty box of PowerBars. "Here." I put one on the granite counter for each of them as Pax lifted Ray Lynne to sit on it.

"I want an omelet." Cheyenne slammed her phone down and pushed the bar away.

"Well, we don't have eggs, Cheyenne," I said, "We have Power-Bars."

"We don't know what's happening here." Pax gripped the counter. "You need to call Tom and demand a wire transfer."

"Pax." I eyed Cheyenne.

"Amanda, we have until midnight tomorrow to make that payment. And she's right, something's really—we need to get out of here."

"I can't eat that." Cheyenne pushed past me to open the empty cabinets. Ray Lynne reached over to play with Cheyenne's phone.

"Can't we just ask your parents to cover it for a few days?" I walked over to press my eyes against the window and peer down the black driveway. Someone had to be coming for us. They had to.

"No, we can't ask them to cover it: (*a*) How the hell am I going to explain it? And (*b*) I gave up being able to ask my mother for favors to marry you, *remember*?"

I spun around. Even Cheyenne, who'd bitten off a huge bite of PowerBar, raised her eyebrows. I blinked back tears.

"Your belly button looks sooo big," Ray Lynne said, staring at something on Cheyenne's phone. "See, Mandy?" She lifted it to me.

"Put that down." Cheyenne spit crumbs everywhere. I looked

at the phone and saw the picture in her photo gallery. The one from *The Daily Mail*. Only whomever she had emailed it to had recropped it before running it.

"Guys." Billy scrambled to his feet and handed me his phone. I looked at the headline: "Davis aide shacking up with husband's pregnant mistress."

Oh. My. God.

I raced to get Pax's iPad from the car, powering it on as I ran back in. There it was on CNN, the headline story. I froze in the atrium.

"Fuck." I heard Pax behind me.

"Pax—"

"They're saying it's mine?"

"I'm sorry. Oh, God, I'm sorry," I kept saying as I frantically called Michael.

"Amanda," he answered.

"Tom?" Pax grabbed the phone from me and I reached to hit speaker.

"Michael, what happened?" I asked.

"It sounds like there were a lot of loose ends at the resort."

"But we didn't talk to anyone! Why would they—she leaked the bikini picture, Michael. I just found it on her phone. She probably concocted this as well—"

We heard a scream from the kitchen and then Cheyenne came stumbling in. "*Whyyy*?" She sank to her knees beneath the chandelier, her face contorting in tears.

Pax shook his head. He was white. "Get off," he mouthed to me.

"Michael, this is too much. You have to make this right."

"I'm afraid we have no choice here, Amanda," Michael said with the casualness of someone who didn't need to be harsh because he was making the rules.

"But we do." Pax found his voice. "I'll drive right to the local news station and tell them—"

"What? That you put over forty thousand dollars of charges on your credit card to frolic with her? Took her to and paid for medical checkups? Cared for her in front of countless witnesses for weeks?"

For the second time in twenty-four hours, I wished for a bomb.

Even Cheyenne was struck silent.

Chapter
Thirteen

Hanging up, Pax looked like the cartoons where the cannonball shoots through a guy's torso and he bends to see clear through himself. It was sickening. I was going to be sick.

Ray Lynne appeared in the kitchen doorway. "Mandy, I'm still hungry."

"Get her your headphones. Get her a video," I implored Billy as I sucked back the salty saliva flooding my mouth. For once, he hustled her away without questioning me.

"I don't understand," Cheyenne gasped between sobs, raising the hem of her oversized T-shirt and wiping her face with it. "How is he going to marry me now?"

"*Marry* you?" Disbelief tipped me toward her at the waist.

"Yes," she shot back.

"He's never going to marry you, you crazy bitch! He has a wife!"

"Okay, fine." Cheyenne fussed with her phone. "Here." She tapped the video page, swiped and swiped until she found what she was looking for, then thrust the phone up at me. It took me a second to figure out what I was seeing: someone holding his camera over Cheyenne's bobbing head working his erection with her mouth.

"Oh, God!" I dropped the phone on the marble tile like it was scalding, but the audio kept playing. Billy returned even though I waved him back.

"Yeah, baby, like that. You are . . . so . . . fucking . . . good." It was Tom's voice.

"That doesn't prove anything," I protested. "The sound could be spliced—doctored."

Cheyenne, Billy, and Pax all raised their eyebrows at me.

"Mmm, yeah, won't be long now," Tom's voice snaked up from the floor like it was winding around my ankle. "We got Illinois. Lanier . . . *has* to. . . concede." Oh my God, this was really recent—this was the week of my wedding. "*You* . . . are gonna . . . be . . . the first . . . lady . . . of the . . . United States . . . of America."

"How?" I asked, my voice low and rough. "How did he see that happening?" It was the most irrelevant of all the new questions about Tom's inner life, but I needed to know just how fucked up he was.

Cheyenne's arms were crossed. She unwove her right palm and gestured to the sound of grunts coming from the floor, allowing Tom to answer for himself, his voice coming in dreamy, grunting bursts. "We'll let the people grieve"—*grunt, grunt*—"After I leave office I'll adopt this one and we'll tell him the truth"—*Grunt. Grunt. Grunt.*

I dropped my face into my hands. It was inconceivable—intolerable—that I had put my life, my future, my husband's future in jeopardy. For *this*.

The sound of Tom's climax came from the floor, seeping into my ears like some Shakespearean poison. Through my fingers I saw Cheyenne's face on the phone next to Tom's deflating penis, her smile as she said with the intensity of a zealot, "*You* are going to be king." The last thing to fill the frame was her pregnant belly before the video stopped.

I looked up, yanked from stunned to incredulous. "Wow," I said. "So if you want to give the future president a literal and metaphorical blow job you have to tell him he's going to be *king*. Or maybe a *fairy princess*. Or an *astronaut*."

"Amanda—" Pax stood.

"Is this what men want, Pax? You could have a woman like Lindsay—smart, accomplished, substantive—or get your dick sucked by a sycophant. Is this what men want? Really? So badly that they'll risk losing the White House?"

My phone rang and Pax bent to retrieve it. I lunged to take it from him. Someone over there—Michael, Jeanine, or Tom—was coming to his or her senses. "Mandy, hey, sugar, it's Mom!"

"What?" I couldn't even process this.

"It's Mom!" She was exuberant. "Are the kids still up? Can you put them on?"

"No."

"Oh, Mandy, come on, I'm just so excited to talk to them—"

"Today." I finished the sentence for her.

"Yes, today." I could tell by her tone that I was confusing her.

"Not yesterday. Or any of the other yesterdays since you took off—"

"Mandy—"

"No!" I shouted and Billy took a step forward, then back, like he was torn between grabbing the phone and running out of the room. Years of swallowing my words because she couldn't take it, because it only made her mean, because it was pointless, were coming to a hot end. "You don't get to decide what the job is! You don't get to decide it's crackers for dinner some nights because you forgot the fridge was empty. You don't get to decide not to come home because you think nine is old enough. You don't get to pick half the responsibilities and decide you get a pass because you were only sixteen! I don't care! I don't care that you were fucking sixteen. You were the only mom I had and I deserved better. The kids deserve better. And no, you can't have them. You gave up. And I don't forgive you." I threw my phone down in the foyer next to Cheyenne's.

"Whoa, whoa, whoa!" Pax scrambled for it. "Call her back, Amanda."

"No!"

"So, what? We're raising them now?"

"Thanks a lot," Billy said. "Fuck you, too."

"Dude, sorry but you know what I mean." He glared at me. "You have *one* job right now and that's to fix this shitmess—you get that, right?"

"Pax, I will. I will fix this. But she just doesn't get to decide how this goes!"

"She doesn't—or Tom doesn't?"

"Both of them! There are rules! You don't want to be a husband anymore—get a divorce! You don't want to be a mom, use a condom! But you don't get to be a husband or mom on your own half-assed terms. That's not how it works. I have never half-assed a single fucking thing in my entire life."

"Except us." He stared at me with such sadness my breath left me.

It felt like nettles on my cheeks. Across my chest. Because he was right. A thousand reasons burst through my brain: the demands of my fucked-up family, of trying to get a man elected president, of taking care of his wife who was on death's door. But as exhausting, and painful, and relentless as it all had been, it had still been more comfortable than truly letting myself land in *us*. Because cookies get eaten, men disappoint, and even mothers eventually reach the end of their love.

Pax pulled out the car keys. "Where are you going?" I asked, panic raising my voice.

"I need to not be here. You get that, right? I need to be—I don't actually know yet. Do I show up in public saying this story is bullshit? Do I lay low? I seriously wish this wasn't my problem eight weeks before an election when *my* job—if you give a shit and if I even still have one—is supposed to be helping raise money for candidates who are pro-financial reform. But I know I'm not sleeping here tonight."

"Are we over?" I asked, barely able to make the sound.

He ran a hand through his hair. "As we are—as we have been—yes. Can we find a way to be different? I honestly don't know."

"Pax." I was about to beg him to stay, but then I realized I couldn't ask for a single thing. I was the ship slipping below the waves and he had to get off or drown. "I love you." It was the last thing I said before we heard the door shut.

I turned to Cheyenne, whose tears were drying as mine were starting. She looked so different than she had a few hours ago on the plane, all triumph, certainty, and entitlement drained from her. "Cheyenne, you have to help us. You have to help me fix this." I wiped off my face with my hands and went over to help her to her feet. "You have the only proof. On your phone—in your belly."

"I just need to sleep." Her response was frantic. "I'm pregnant—I can't be undergoing this kind of—I just need—to sleep." She wandered up the stairs and I was left alone with Billy, his face blotchy the way boys get when they're trying not to cry. I just wanted to hug him but I knew he wouldn't stand it. He left to find a mattress for himself and I climbed onto the one stool at the kitchen counter with my feet dangling off the floor. I turned on my laptop and stared at it like the answer would pour forth from its screen like a genie.

Eight weeks until the election. Enough time. But barely. I had one chance to do this. I couldn't wound. I had to kill.

Chapter
Fourteen

I NEEDED TO PRESENT ENOUGH EVIDENCE—publically or privately—to force Tom to fully resign the nomination. And with enough time to convene a special election to select Lanier in his place—otherwise I'd be causing just enough scandal to hand the other party the win.

I tried to log in to the campaign's virtual office and was immediately told in red bold letters that there was no user with my e-mail. Fuck. I had to see exactly what they had planned for the next few days in order put things right for us. I took a breath and entered Jeanine's e-mail. She had a handful of passwords she would shout over the heads of everyone when she needed an errand run. I typed in *laboutin*.

Nope.

I wiggled my fingers. *Norman*—Jennifer Aniston's old dog. For some reason the name tickled Jeanine.

Not that either. I blew out. I had one more chance before I was locked out, and I'd never be able to guess Michael's. Tom's, maybe. It was probably *KingDavis*. I concentrated very hard, like I was trying to see Jeanine's brain. I imagined it looked like a smoker's lung. Suddenly it came to me. Praying I was right, I typed *assmunch*.

Access granted.

I went to the calendar and my eyes sprung wide. The next night Tom was scheduled to film a one-hour interview with Diane Sawyer at the Mandarin Oriental. I wondered if he planned to show Diane the seat in the lobby where Cheyenne had first been "waiting for him" as he'd put it.

This was my shot. Now how the hell was I going to get in there?

"Mandy . . . Mandy?"

I startled, my face aching from where I'd fallen asleep on the keyboard. "Mom?" I jumped down from the stool, stumbling on my leg that had fallen asleep tucked under me. A man was standing beside her, holding her hand. He was wearing a plaid flannel shirt and work boots. His hair was thinning. And he looked like a grown-up—that was my first thought about Daryl. Nothing sheepish or shifty. As exhausted and car rumpled as they both were, there was something solid about how he stood there. "What are you doing here?"

"Pax called me," she said, looking more concerned than I could ever remember. "He said you needed help." At the word my eyes instantly dampened. "Daryl and I drove all night."

He dug in his back pocket and produced a folded bandana. "It's clean."

I stared at it in my hands, my vision blurring with tears.

"Oh, baby." Delilah wrapped me in her arms and I let her. She smelled nice. It was a dumb thing to notice, but she had always smelled like a deep fryer—or a bar fight. Always sad. Now she smelled like fabric softener and some kind of perfume. It made me want to curl against her. Crying, I pulled back. "They're sleeping somewhere around here."

"I'll find 'em," Daryl said reassuringly. He squeezed Delilah's hand. We heard his boots squeaking across the marble foyer to the staircase.

Delilah wiped my hair from my face. "You know it's going to be okay," she said and I saw myself at thirteen, holding her shoulders on the couch, rocking her as she cried. Billy's dad already long gone. A few hundred bucks for an abortion sitting in an envelope on the table. *It's going to be okay*, I'd said.

"Pax is done," I sputtered. "I've fucked it up. I've fucked everything up."

"Shush now," she said, taking the damp bandana and refolding it to find a dry corner for me. "You haven't."

I took it from her. "I have, Mom. I have. You don't understand. You never came this close."

She looked at me for a long moment. "I was supposed to marry Freddie after high school."

"I thought you met at the dealership?"

She shook her head. "*I* was supposed to have the split-level ranch with the fenced-in pool. But I got in a raging fight with Daddy one night, had too many beers, and fucked some guy in the parking lot behind the Clover. Suddenly I wasn't marriage material anymore. Freddie was ready to forgive me, but his parents weren't going to see their son supporting some kid that wasn't his."

"Exactly, you fucked up."

She took my chin in her hand. "You're not my fuckup, Amanda Beth. And I've loved you the best I knew how. I'm sorry if it wasn't enough."

"Why couldn't you just work a job, get promoted, get us a house. Why did you have to run around looking for something better in the back of cars?" My lips twisted against the pain as I arrived at the core of it. "Why wasn't I enough?"

"You didn't have a thing to do with it. I just—wanted to be

chosen. I had a right to want that. But look." She held her left hand out to me and there it was—a gold band on her fourth finger. She smiled so softly—I had never seen her smile like that. "We've rented a little house near the rig. Three bedrooms, so they can each have their own. BP's put a lot of money into the area for goodwill and the other wives—they welcomed us with casseroles. Can you imagine?"

I looked at her. I hadn't ever thought of her as a woman, not really, not beyond my defensive posturing to show people I could judge her before they did. I hadn't ever let myself see her as a girl whose parents ran out of love. A girl completely alone who watched other people get what she had every right to—someone to choose her.

"Daryl seems nice."

"He's already painted their rooms. He put Hello Kitty decals on Ray Lynne's wall and Harley-Davidson ones on Billy's. He's a real good guy, Mandy. Better than I deserve."

"Don't say that."

"I want to do it different with Ray Lynne."

I nodded, wanting that so badly, too.

"It feels so good just to be out of Tallyville. It was like women used to just come by the diner or the bar—to watch me grow old. 'Oh, look there's Delilah Luker, used to think she was such hot shit.' And Grammy always standing with her arms crossed every time I turned around—I'd get flustered thinking I wasn't doing anything good enough and then, boom, I'd wash a dark sock with your favorite shirt, or forget milk. And I'd just picture her shaking her head."

"You should be allowed to do this on your own terms," I said, meaning it. It was the flame under the air that had blown me to Tom in the first place.

Daryl walked in with Billy and Ray Lynne. "Found these two on a couch the size of a tar pit."

"Mommy!" Ray Lynne ran and jumped into her arms.

"Oh, baby, baby, baby." She squeezed Ray Lynne tightly.

"Hey, handsome," Mom called over to Billy. She reached out her hand to him. Billy looked at it uncertainly. He looked to me and I gave him a small shrug. He walked to her and shook it. That's all he was up for.

"Okay, then." She nodded. It was a start.

"What is this place?" Daryl asked.

"The end of the road," I answered. "Let me go find Cheyenne and we'll all get out of here."

It took all five of us two hours of opening every door, every closet, pulling back every curtain, walking every inch of every acre before I accepted the truth: Cheyenne was gone. My only proof—on her phone and in her belly—gone too.

Darryl packed up the car and they drove me to the airport. Two parents with a son and a daughter. They looked like the dream nuclear family. Billy even managed to drop his scowl long enough to hug me good-bye.

"Are you okay with this?" I asked him, touching the stubble on his face.

He nodded. He said he was tired. We had both used so much energy keeping the fear at bay that she wasn't coming back for us. I think he wanted someone else to step in and figure things out for a while. God knows I did.

I kissed Ray Lynne and Mom came around the car to me. "I have no proof. No game plan."

"You'll figure this out."

I smiled ruefully. "You've always thought that."

"And I've always been right."

I nodded, not really hearing her, needing to get on that plane to New York and hoping a plan was waiting for me at thirty thousand feet.

It wasn't.

No one had left one in the taxi either.

I checked into a small hotel a few blocks away from Columbus Circle, showered, changed, and then went straight to the Starbucks across from the Mandarin. Here's what I had learned in my years on the trail: no one bothers the crew girl on the coffee run. I ordered a large tray, the most cumbersome-looking thing I could. In the lobby I walked up to the security detail holding the list.

"Delilah Luker." I flashed him Mom's license and he checked me off the list, before pointing me to the elevator filled with lighting equipment being ferried to the penthouse. I rode up with some guys from the ABC crew, gaffer's tape dangling from their belt loops, wondering if this was going to be the last time I ever went so high.

Ducking my head behind the coffee, I tried to walk briskly enough that I looked like I knew where I was going, but not so fast that I couldn't pick up where I should be heading. At the end of the hall was an open door. I prayed I wasn't about to come face to face with Tom or Lindsay. Instead I saw Jeanine and Michael's backs clustered around the suite's breakfast bar, where a monitor was displaying the feed from the other room.

"Now, Tom, we're going to shift gears here a little bit." I heard Diane's signature professional warmth, like sambuca over ice. I took a few silent steps forward and stood on my toes so I could see Tom's face on the screen over Jeanine's shoulder. "Were you surprised when the story surfaced yesterday that your aide, Amanda Luker, has been living on the lam, as it were, with Cheyenne Russell, your stylist? Who is purportedly pregnant by Amanda's husband, a Pax Westerbrook?"

"Frankly, Diane, no I was not." That's true, he was not.

"Amanda grew up in a trailer park outside Tallyville, Florida—an area of our state, like so many, that has faced the scourge of methamphetamine." He shook his head sadly—paternally. "We have tried to give Amanda, and so many people like her, a chance on every campaign since my first run for senator. But sometimes people cannot rise to the opportunity." My toes gripped in my shoes, my calves cramped. *He's implying I'm a meth addict?!* "But that does not mean we should not keep giving people chances. That is my platform. Washington's not creating enough opportunities for people who want to work their way out of poverty."

Oh my God, this was such transparent bullshit—even for a politician. Lindsay had to be going ballistic somewhere. Did he have her sedated? Locked in a closet?

"And what do you say to rumors that have surfaced today that the only factor these people have in common is you? That you must be the father of this baby."

I leaned forward like I was on skis. *Admit it, asshole. Admit you've been cheating on your dying wife. Admit it and pass Lanier the ball.*

"If I may, Diane." The camera pulled back to reveal—Lindsay. My jaw flopped open on its hinge. She took his hand, smiled at him adoringly. "I'd like to answer that. Please tell me how he could possibly be the father of a child, judging from the pictures of this woman, conceived during a time I was so sick Tom never left my side? Tom is a loyal husband." Again the adoring smile. "Pax Westerbrook, however, has not been loyal." Loyal must be Jeanine's word. Lindsay had been instructed to say it three times. "Pax was unfaithful to his wife. Any other suggestion is simply just a story trumped up by some super PAC—you mark my words—to distract everyone from our message of helping to make lives better. We remain loyal to our mission and each other."

So it was "our" message now. Was that the trade-off? She'd

help him pave this over in exchange for what? A spot on the king's dais?

"Cut!" the director called. "Lindsay's getting a little shiny." Shiny was a euphemism. In seconds she'd become drenched in sweat like a hot flash. "Let's break."

I tucked back into the suite's foyer and watched her cross the living area to one of the other bedrooms. "I need a minute alone." She waved off Jeanine. I waited until everyone was engrossed in their BlackBerrys to follow her, praying the door wouldn't be locked.

It wasn't. She was sitting on the bed in a hotel robe, her silk blouse in a heap on the floor. Her eyes swung to me and for a split second she looked relieved, as if I'd dismounted from my steed. But then she visibly caught herself and her guard went up. "What do you want, Mandy?"

"What do I want?" I was unprepared for the directness of the question.

"You always want something. From the beginning you have trailed us like a stray dog looking for scraps and a pat on the head."

"Is that how you see me?"

She shrugged, her face hard. "I just can't believe you'd have the gall to put everything in jeopardy like this and then show up here."

I squared my shoulders. "Is that what you're all saying to each other until you believe it?"

She looked away.

"I want him to resign the nomination. Today. In time for the DNC to get behind Lanier."

"No." Her voice swung like a steel pipe.

"He *has* to."

"Huh." A rueful smile. "This from the girl who went so far as to help him hide his pregnant mistress?"

"You have to know I was trying to protect you." It sounded so flimsy now.

"Me?" she asked, "Or your job prospects?"

My hands flew up. "It's not about that."

"Isn't it? Isn't everything? You have worked your way *up*," she sliced. "You have married *up*. But I know people like you and it will never be enough."

"You mean Tom?"

"You were *always* ganging up on me. The two of you. You *always* took his side. And he let you do whatever you wanted—left me to be the bad guy."

"What do you mean, Lindsay?" I couldn't follow. "That never happened."

"She almost ready?" someone shouted on the other side of the door.

I walked to her, dropping my voice. "Lindsay, you *have* to talk sense into him. The truth will come out. It always does."

"No. It doesn't," she said with cutting conviction. She was crying. "It doesn't."

"He doesn't deserve this. He doesn't deserve you."

"How about what *I* deserve? I have put up with too much, forgiven too much, given up too much not to go all the way."

"What would you tell Ashleigh to do?"

"*Ashleigh left me.*" Her rage plumed like a fireball.

There was a knock. "Lindsay, you ready?"

"Give me two!" she called back. She stood, dropping her robe. She was wearing prostheses in her bra.

"He isn't a good person, Lindsay. He might have started out as one, but you have to see that five years of this has . . . warped him."

"You don't know what you're talking about." It was a whisper.

I bent and picked up her blouse. I smoothed it out and handed it to her. She slipped it on and buttoned it up. Then she looked at me and when she spoke her voice was soft with a sorrowful knowing.

"Forget what you know. Forget what you've seen. Go away. Don't contact us. Try to make something of your life. Start over." She walked past me. But I could sense her hesitating at the door, her back exposed to me. Could I do it?

"What do *you* want, Lindsay?"

There was a moment of silence and I thought she might leave.

"I just don't want to die alone." She didn't turn around. "I want to—I *have* to do right by her. I want there to have been a point to it."

"If I were your daughter . . ." She turned and her eyes caught mine. I fought to keep my voice steady. "I would want you to know that you deserve love, honest love, without agenda. I would hope that your last breath would be with those whose care has not demanded sacrifice, packaging, and lies in return. I can't begin to imagine what you have lost. And with all due respect, nothing is going to give that a point. But doing right? It's on the table here and now. If you can't trust him with your heart, Lindsay, how, in good conscience, can you entrust him with this country?"

She shut the door behind her and I listened to the flurry on the other side as she was repowdered, reconcealed. Cheeks blushed. Flyaways tamed. I heard her ask the makeup artist about his tattoo.

I realized I was trembling. And I was feeling something I had never let myself experience before. Not when I realized somewhere out there was a man who had chosen not to know me, his daughter. Not even when Grammy closed her home to us. Not even when Pax walked out the door in Atlanta.

The pain under my breastplate was acute. My heart was breaking.

I waited until I heard someone call, "Rolling!" before I cracked the door and tiptoed to the exit. Over Jeanine and Michael's backs I heard Diane say, "Lindsay, you have written extensively in your memoir about partnership and sacrifice. How dependent you are on Tom. What are the qualities that Tom possesses as a husband that would make him a great president?"

I knew I should just keep walking. But I had to watch. She looked at Tom. Then back at Diane. Then back to Tom. Then back to Diane. "Fuck if I know."

"Cut!" shouted Jeanine. But it still said recording on the bottom corner of the screen. They'd be insane to stop.

"Excuse me?" Diane asked while Tom coughed until his hair flopped.

"He's a terrible husband, Diane. So if that's the criteria we're basing this on I think the American people should look elsewhere."

Michael and Jeanine were trying to move in multiple directions at once like cartoon cats dropped in water.

"Here's what I know, Diane. Losing a child. Doing IVF at forty-five. Breast cancer. I can speak to any of that. And I hope to continue. So if you're looking to me for insight into Tom Davis I obviously don't have a fucking clue. But if someone can pass me my phone, I have a very interesting video of him getting a blow job I could show you—"

That's when Jeanine tackled the camera.

It was simple to slip out unnoticed in the chaos that ensued, to find myself back in Columbus Circle at dusk.

Starting over. It was familiar.

Just like I did when I found Diego had taken my money. Just like I did when Kurt fired me. Or Mom lost a job. Or I had to drop out of college.

I knew from scratch. And finally, after anticipating it for

so long, I'd arrived at worse-than-scratch. I had a forty-thousand-dollar debt to repay. And I was the woman who had hid Tom Davis's mistress.

I thought back to that day in South Beach, the day I had met both Pax and Tom. The first one I could never completely give myself to, even when I swore I would before God and man and the state of Florida. The other one I gave everything to.

I realized in my own way—hiding in the illusion created by power pumps and hose, BlackBerrys and conference calls—I'd still just been looking to be chosen in the back of cars, too.

I shook my head, done with judging Delilah.

Taking a breath, I pulled out my phone.

"Hello?" he answered tentatively.

"Is this Pax?" I asked.

"Yes."

"This is Amanda. We met at the—"

"I know who you are."

"You remember?"

"It's not like your name's Dave."

"Right." I smiled. He remembered.

"Calling to make sure I'm well-and-truly fired?" he asked. "I am. I'm well-and-truly fired."

"I wanted to see if you were okay."

"Why?"

"I feel super shitty about what happened—I can be a bit of an asshole sometimes."

"When you're not rescuing orphans and feeding the poor?"

"I want to make it up to you," I said hastily, before he could disconnect.

"Make it up to me?"

"Please. I want to. I have to. I'm in Columbus Circle—not far away—I can come get you."

"You want to make it up to me?"

"Yes," I said, "A new dress. Shoes. Whatever you want."

"A do-over?"

"A makeup for the makeup. Forever."

"Get your ass to DC, Luker. I have a threshold I'm supposed to carry you across."

It wasn't how I wanted to leave Florida—hanging from my wedding ring like a gymnast.

No one wants to travel by tornado either. But the important thing, as Dorothy would have probably told me, was to just get where the adventure begins.

Find the starting line.

Then go.

Epilogue

My daughter, waiting patiently at our kitchen table for her toaster waffle, has just asked me why I'm crying.

"Crying is overstating it, honey," I say, switching off the image of Tom on the news and getting the syrup down from the cabinet.

I'm always still surprised when missing Lindsay catches up with me. But on a day like today I shouldn't be.

Once it had been verified that Lindsay learned about Cheyenne at the same time as the rest of the world—and had not spent months stumping for a liar and a cheat—her credibility survived the end of Tom's campaign. Lindsay was even asked to endorse Lanier and did a popular YouTube video for her.

So Lindsay lived long enough to see the first female president of the United States sworn in. I'm sure it was nothing like what standing on the dais herself would have felt like, but she did help make it happen. She mattered.

To me as well, of course.

Once word got out that I had been with Lindsay in the moments before her on-air meltdown, no one involved with the campaign would give me a recommendation. As if I had introduced Tom and Cheyenne, inseminated her personally, all with the goal of sabotaging his candidacy. The one line on my resume was a punch line. I couldn't even get an interview.

Pax's faith in me, however, was unwavering. Even when I abandoned the hunt and threw myself into moving my stuff up to DC, finding us an apartment where we wouldn't trip over each other, acquiring winter clothes, in other words putting one foot in front of the other as Lindsay had taught me to do.

I bought a slow cooker. I stenciled a wall. I got bangs.

And just when I decided going off the pill was my only option to keep busy until an election cycle passed and Tom was just an embarrassing international footnote to our electoral process, I got the call.

The head of Lanier's transition team told me someone had submitted my resume—was I interested? I said yes before even asking in what, simultaneously dialing my pharmacy for the Ortho-Novum refill with my toes.

Now I think back on those three months of seeming free fall and snort. If I had only known that would be my last bit of down time, possibly *ever*, I would have enjoyed it. Now my nanny uses the slow cooker. I put my daughter's crib against the stenciled wall so you would think that only one out of four being done was deliberate.

Pax has been incredibly supportive, leaving work at five-thirty, doing the pediatrician appointments when I can't. I still sit on the edge of the bathtub some mornings, watching him help our daughter with her potty training, amazed that I managed to find a real partner, when that was pretty much a unicorn to me.

And speaking of partners, Delilah and Daryl are still together. Of course my absurdly fertile mother managed to squeeze one more out. But even that couldn't stress them. They watch *Duck Dynasty*. Daryl enters regional gumbo cook-offs and Mom discovered, after Grammy died, that she actually likes to iron. They just get a kick out of each other. I'm happy for her. Everyone deserves to have someone like that, someone who answers the phone laughing and says, "You'll never guess what your mom just did."

Billy goes to UT and loves it, although, true to his word, reading is not his "thing." Ray Lynne has turned out to be a total jock and Mom spends most of her nights getting grass stains out of her uniforms. I hope she can get an athletic scholarship to Georgetown. I'd love to have one of them close by.

"Mommy, will I need my fwog umbwella?" (frog umbrella)

Outside the glass doors of the family room we can see the rain coming down in the garden—a hard, late summer rain. It was just like this the day that Lindsay's sister called to ask me to return to Jacksonville.

I hadn't seen Lindsay in person since I walked out of the Mandarin. I was surprised by the address she gave me, but she said Tom kept the "dream house" in the divorce and she had remained at the old one.

Shannon opened the door, a child on her hip. Her eyes immediately went to my bump, the way a mother's do—sonogram vision. "Congratulations," she said.

"Thank you, but you can hold your applause until it's out of me. How are you?"

"Good. I've been looking in on Lindsay most days."

"How is she doing?"

"Not good." Shannon walked away down the hall and I followed. "She's glad you're coming, though. She's really anxious to see you."

"I've missed her," I said.

Shannon paused at the top of the stairs. "They have her on a lot of pain medication."

I nodded.

"So she asks about Ashleigh a lot, like, in the present tense."

"What should I say?"

"Just go along with it."

"Okay."

Heading toward the wrong door, I was unprepared for Shannon to open the one to Ashleigh's room. "Mrs. Davis, Amanda is here."

"Come in," she called softly. She was sitting propped up in a pink canopy bed, her bald head bandaged in a turban. I sat down next to her.

"Hi."

She smiled weakly at me. "I'm sorry I called you a puppy."

"I'm sorry I hid your husband's mistress."

She smiled.

"Too soon?" I asked.

"He married her, you know."

"I heard that."

"She is, quote, waiting for him."

"She can wait." It turned out, before Jeanine had the brilliant idea to create a paper trail linking Pax and Cheyenne, that Tom had wined and dined Cheyenne on the campaign's dime. Those fabulous neon outfits? Paid for by Davis for America. Her flying saucer hat? Underwritten by some donor who wanted universal health care. The hotel room where he kept her jogging distance from the Riverside house? A line item on an expense report that the prosecutor read out loud on day six. Tom was currently serving six to ten.

"The White House. The Big House. Same diff," Lindsay said.

I wanted to squeeze her hand, but it was bruised from the IV. "I've missed you."

"Me, too. I'm sorry, Amanda. Even after everything I was still irrationally angry at you. It made no sense. I think I was just embarrassed by my own stupidity."

"Millions of people believed in him—he put on a good show."

"I shared his bed—I should have known. It was happening right before my eyes and I didn't want to see it."

"He was clever."

She shook her head. "Not the affair—his transformation." She pushed down on the mattress with her knuckles to prop herself up.

"Can I help?"

She shook her head again. "I'm going to see Ashleigh very soon. I'm in here getting ready to face her."

"She won't hold you responsible for his actions."

Again her head trembled to quiet me. "It was my fault." She held up a hand to keep me from interrupting. "The accident."

"Ashleigh's?"

"They were always a team—from the day she was born. He was the fun one—I was the bedtime enforcer, the broccoli cooker, the homework proofer. He was Chuck E. Cheese, lifting her by her ankles and sneaking ice cream on the way home from a game. Of course you throw that teenage stuff on top of it, the hormones and the hating your mother—well, it got ugly. She wanted to go out that night to a party but I had a brief to write. I didn't want to drive her—she was one of the youngest in her class. Everyone else was already driving after dark—blah blah blah. I gave her the keys. To my old car—a '98 Volvo. Built before cars beeped if you drove without the seat belt buckled. I just wanted to be liked. So you see I can't really fault Tom too much because I understand how much that need can cloud your judgment." She gestured for her water glass and I passed it to her. "I needed you to know the whole story. He forgave me. I have forgiven him."

I leaned over and kissed her cheek. "Thank you."

"For what?"

"Trusting me. Not just with the truth. But from day one—you trusted me."

"How do you like Lanier?" She managed a smile.

"That was you?" I breathed. "Oh my God, of course it was—why didn't I think of that?"

She reached out and took my hand. "You deserved a second chance."

"We all do. Tom wasn't wrong about that." Me and Pax and Delilah and *maybe* even Tom. Someday.

But not today. The parole board has denied his hearing. "You know what, yes, baby, grab your frog umbrella. We're gonna jump in puddles the whole way to camp."

"Okay, Mommy!"

That visit was the last time I saw Lindsay. I sat with her through the night and she passed a little before the sun rose. She wasn't with Tom. But she was with someone who loved her. Still loves her.

I hope she is with Ashleigh and I hope they have forgiven each other.

ACKNOWLEDGMENTS

We would like to thank Crystal and the entire team at BookSparks for their enthusiasm and killer smarts. A pleasure from start to finish.

ABOUT THE AUTHORS

Newsweek declared Emma McLaughlin and Nicola Kraus's *The Nanny Diaries* a "phenomenon." It is a #1 *New York Times* bestseller and the longest-running hardcover bestseller of 2002. In 2007 it was released as a major motion picture starring Scarlett Johansson, Laura Linney, and Alicia Keys. McLaughlin and Kraus are also the authors of three other New York Times bestsellers—*Citizen Girl*, *Dedication* and *Nanny Returns*—as well as the novels *Between You & Me*, *How To Be A Grown-Up and many others*. They have appeared numerous times on CNN, MSNBC, The Today Show, Good Morning America, Entertainment Tonight, and The View. In addition to writing for television and film, McLaughlin and Kraus run a creative consulting firm TheFinishedThought.com which helps aspiring authors of every stripe write their books and build their platforms.

SELECTED TITLES FROM SPARKPRESS

SparkPress is an independent boutique publisher
delivering high-quality, entertaining,
and engaging content that enhances readers' lives.
Visit us at www.gosparkpress.com

25 Sense, by Lisa Henthorn. $17, 978-1-940716-30-5. Claire Malone just wanted to move to New York and live out her dream career of television writing, but by her 25th birthday, she's in love with her married, flirtatious boss. She struggles to hold it together—but can she break away without ruining her barely started career? *25 Sense* is about the time in a young woman's life when the world starts to view her as a responsible adult—but all she feels is lost.

The House of Bradbury, by Nicole Meier. $17, 978-1-940716-38-1. After Mia Gladwell's debut novel bombs and her fiancé jumps ship, she purchases the estate of iconic author Ray Bradbury, hoping it will inspire her best work yet. But between her disapproving sister, mysterious sketches that show up on her door, and taking in a pill-popping starlet as a tenant—a favor to her needy ex—life in the Bradbury house is not what she imagined.

The Undertaking of Tess, by Lesley Kagen. $15, 978-1-94071-665-7. A heartbreaking, funny, nostalgic, and spiritually uplifting story, you'll cheer on two adorable sisters from the first page to the last of this charming novella that sets the stage for the accompanying novel, *The Resurrection of Tess Blessing*.

The Balance Project, by Susie Orman Schnall. $16, 978-1-94071-667-1. With the release of her book on work/life balance, Katherine Whitney has become a media darling and hero to working women everywhere. In reality though, her life is starting to fall apart, and her assistant Lucy is the one holding it all together. When Katherine does something unthinkable to her, Lucy must decide whether to change Katherine's life forever, or continue being her main champion.

ABOUT SPARKPRESS

SparkPress is an independent, hybrid imprint focused on merging the best of the traditional publishing model with new and innovative strategies. We deliver high-quality, entertaining, and engaging content that enhances readers' lives. We are proud to bring to market a list of *New York Times* bestselling, award-winning, and debut authors who represent a wide array of genres, as well as our established, industry-wide reputation for innovative, creative, results-driven success in working with authors. SparkPress, a BookSparks imprint, is a division of SparkPoint Studio, LLC.

Learn more at GoSparkPress.com